The Peeping Tom's Wife

By

Roger D. Ewen

Published by Book Writing Pioneer
Cover design by Book Writing Pioneer
ISBN: Printed in the United States

Table of Content

DEDICATION v

ACKLOWAGEMENT.. vii

PROLOGUE ix

CHAPTER 1 1

CHAPTER 2 11

CHAPTER 3 17

CHAPTER 4 21

CHAPTER 5 29

CHAPTER 6 37

CHAPTER 7 51

CHAPTER 8 59

CHAPTER 9 69

CHAPTER 10 75

CHAPTER 11 81

CHAPTER 12 89

CHAPTER 13 97

CHAPTER 14 104

CHAPTER 15 112

CHAPTER 16 119

CHAPTER 17 125

CHAPTER 18 131

CHAPTER 19 138

CHAPTER 20 145

CHAPTER 21 151

CHAPTER 22 161

CHAPTER 23 167

CHAPTER 24 177

CHAPTER 25 183

CHAPTER 26 192

CHAPTER 27 199

CHAPTER 28 209

CHAPTER 29 215

CHAPTER 30 221

CHAPTER 31 229

CHAPTER 32 237

CHAPTER 33 243

CHAPTER 34 248

CHAPTER 35 255

CHAPTER 36 261

CHAPTER 37 267

CHAPTER 38 275

CHAPTER 39 281

CHAPTER 40 286

CHAPTER 41 293

DEDICATION

This book is lovingly dedicated to my late wife, Susan. She was my greatest supporter, always insisting that I follow my dream to write. She once told me she had always wanted to be married to an author—and so, this is for you, my love. I miss you every day.

ACKLOWAGEMENT

I want to extend my deepest gratitude to my two incredible sons, Dean and Doug, for their unwavering support from the very beginning. Your strength and encouragement, especially in the wake of your mother's passing, have meant the world to me.

A special thank you to Jessica Chain King and Tera J. Paterson for dedicating their time and talent to capturing my profile through photography. Your efforts are truly appreciated.

I am also profoundly grateful to Book Writing Pioneer, Nathan Lurk, and Michael Kerby for their exceptional dedication and hard work. From crafting the book cover to meticulous editing, managing social media, and ultimately bringing this book to publication—your contributions have been invaluable. You are truly outstanding, and I can't thank you enough.

PROLOGUE

The bedroom is in semi-darkness. The window is open, letting in the cool night air. Gisele hears Bill's car pulling into the drive. "Not this time! I will try to control the course of the action. He likes to think I'm asleep. Well, I'll pretend to be." She doesn't hear the downstairs shower running like all the other times. The sound of his footsteps on the stairs makes her lie back on the bed and close her eyes. *I wonder if it will work!* No blanket. Her legs spread slightly. She's wearing only bikini panties. Her breasts are bare, and her nipples are hard from the cool breeze. She feels his presence in the doorway, which heightens her senses. As he moves closer, the rustling of clothes being removed makes her quiver. The feeling of her panties being pulled off brings her fully into the moment, and she instinctively opens her legs wider. All thoughts vanish as she feels his head between her legs. His tongue enters her, making her hips rise as she moans. Then he moves up to lick the swollen, hooded pea hidden there and starts sucking on it. Every nerve ending comes alive! Gisele grabs his head and presses it down as hard as she can, spreading her legs as wide as she can to meet his mouth, loving the sensation it causes. She lets out a small whimper and relaxes her hold as he moves up her body. His tongue leaves a wet trail as it skims over her breasts until he reaches her neck, just below her ear, and stops. Bill's hips push forward as he sucks on her neck.

Feeling his cock enter, she bends her legs and spreads her knees to allow him to go deeper. Gisele shudders each time his balls slap her ass as his thrusting intensifies. Bill starts kissing her hard on the lips, and as she opens her mouth, his tongue slides in to touch hers. His mouth then moves to an aroused breast, sucking on one very erect nipple, his teeth grazing over it before nibbling. That's all it takes to make her climax. The warmth of his sperm on her belly as he pulls out makes her pause. *That's new!* Feeling him roll off to lie beside her, she kisses him and gets up to go to the bathroom.

After cleaning up, Gisele lies back in bed, staring at the ceiling as she starts to plan. *For three years, I've tried to figure out what makes him so aroused after work some nights for him to act like this. There's no pattern to these nights, just spontaneity. He says it's work-related. What the hell could be at work that gets him so worked up? Well, tomorrow is a new dawn. I'm going to get to the bottom of this.* Closing her eyes, she drifts off to sleep.

CHAPTER 1

The morning sun ascends over the vast suburb. The enormous houses stood in rows like mini-castles on each side of the road. The lawns out front are dark green and mowed to resemble lush turf. Paved walkways with statues of animals and human figures of various sizes adorn the sides. Trees line each side of the mansion's property, joined by a fence that extends to the huge backyards to enclose spacious decks that lead to the oval in-ground pool.

Gisele and Bill moved to this luxurious suburban area once their careers took off. Both, not having any interest in having children, let them afford these luxuries. Not to mention, they can focus on their profession.

Bill, a photojournalist, is very passionate about his work, which might be considered extreme. Or maybe it is the filming or taking that elusive, faultless picture. With over 14 different cameras, adding triple the amount of lenses to capture images at any distance also takes up his leisure time.

Standing at six feet one and a half inches, with a muscular physique, he can handle himself in a jostling crowd of reporters. And with that five o'clock shadow giving him rugged good looks, he can talk his way in or out of any situation. That fedora he wears on top of his medium, curly brown tousled hair gives him the significant look he needs for people to take him seriously. Add that to his enthusiasm for taking photos without being detected, and it makes him one of the best in his field. Gisele is just as committed to her career.

Finishing college, not decided on what she wanted to do, her friends suggested selling houses, as she was great at reading people. That got her to start her own real estate business once she got established in the area. Working long hours investigating listings and negotiating with clients, she soon had a thriving career.

Gisele's striking features helped her a lot in achieving that. With long, jet-black hair down past her shoulders, a peek-a-boo bang hanging to the right of those big dark green eyes, pillowy full lips, high cheekbones, and a slender nose, she was hard to ignore, not to mention her hourglass figure with full, firm breasts. And when she walked away, that nice, curved, firm ass would catch anyone's eyes. With features like that, clients were more than eager to go looking at the houses.

Living in this region gave her access to a wide variety of clients, from the very, very rich to more moderate ones. And how fortunate they were to find such an elaborate place so close to the city.

xxx

Gisele wakes with the sun shining over her. Lying there, she slowly pushes the blankets off. Removing her panties, one hand moves up her leg to linger in the pubic hairs while the other continues to her breast to pinch an erect nipple. The warmth flowing through her body started to get her aroused. *Stop it! Your mother is probably right. You are oversexed.* Sitting up, she gets out of bed, puts on a robe, and heads downstairs. *If Bill isn't home, I'm losing the robe. I love walking around bare-assed. I think I could be a nudist if I wasn't so judgmental.* She laughs while walking into the kitchen, robe open to feel the cool air hit her body.

Seeing that Bill has already gone to work, she drops the robe on a chair and heads over to the Nespresso to make a coffee. Gisele starts puttering around the kitchen while waiting, trying to figure out how to get clues to the mystery that presents itself. *I've tried, but not in earnest. I have all week, as there are no showings this week.* Being a successful real estate agent frees up a lot of time when needed. Walking over to take the little black schedule book out of the pocket of her robe, she checks to make sure all the listings are next week. Then she grabs her coffee and heads into Bill's office. Sitting in the chair behind the oak desk, she scans the room as she has done many times before. *No sense checking around, as nothing is ever locked.* To the right is the big walk-in closet where he hangs his work jackets and stores his shoes. *I've checked every pocket over the years. Found nothing of interest. You'd think something could have been forgotten.* The walk-in shower is to the left next to it. *Installed when we bought the house. Bill wanted one so he wouldn't have to use the one upstairs and wake me up on nights he works late.* "Hmmmm," she murmurs, taking a sip from her cup. *Time to get serious!*

First, what could be making him so aroused at work that he has to have sex immediately upon arriving home? Being a reporter, or as he likes to be called at high-profile parties, *photojournalist,* she laughs. *Perhaps in a story, he gets to see women in provocative clothes, some that really turn him on more than others. Naa! That can't be it—he never asks me to wear any seductive clothing. Maybe it's because I wear some without asking. Possibly, it's when he captures the last photo of a big story that excites him. That kind of makes sense. When I negotiate a million-dollar property sale, I get so aroused about the commission that I can't wait to get home to play with myself. Is that all it is? Nope! If that was it, why doesn't he share the hype so we both can get off? I share with him on those occasions. Maybe not the masturbating before he gets home, but the arousal part. There must be something more perplexing. What! What!*

Gisele gets up and starts pacing. *Damn it, it has to come to me!* Then, her thoughts get dark. *He must photograph a lot of gruesome scenes: car accidents, murders, jumpers. Observing a lot of dead women in different exposed positions—half-naked, blouse opened, showing a bare breast or nipple, skirt above the waist, revealing the crotch, or maybe nude altogether. Does Bill have fantasies about touching them? Having sex with them? What the hell is that called? Must google it.* Making another coffee, she takes the cup upstairs to her study. Sitting at the desk, she types into the computer, *sex with a dead body.* Necrophilia pops up. *That's it! God damn it, it's a real thing.* She reads on. *Been around for hundreds of years. Dates back to the Greco-Roman period.* Closing the site, Gisele gets up and starts pacing again.

OK! OK! If it's just a sexual attraction he has to a dead body but no real touching, I might understand. God knows I have a lot of kinky daydreams. One that comes close to what I read is that I'm a nurse in a hospital. Visualizing, I go into a patient's room and see a man sedated. I go over, reach under the covers, and grab his cock. As he's getting hard, I remove the blanket and start to jerk him off. I love making them cum. The shaft throbs in my hand as they shoot their sperm all over themselves. If they wake up, I tell them I have to bathe them, which isn't a lie. That gets me off. Or, lately, I imagine I'm charged with watching over a woman before she goes into the operating room. When no one is around, I reach under the covers, spread her legs a little, and start to finger her. The feel of the wetness as I play with the clit. Listening to her moans as I pinch her hard nipples. That makes me cum! Where these fantasies come from, I don't know! Is it the control I feel knowing that they can't resist me? Could it be that I have no fear of rejection when they're in that state! Will I act on them? No! One, I'm not a nurse. Two, would someone jeopardize a career for a little sexual gratification? It would have to be one hell of an obsession!

With those thoughts still in her head, Gisele goes back downstairs to get another coffee. *Eleven years you're married to someone, surely you get some kind of vibe!* Well, a couple of hours before Bill gets home unless he is on a story. *That's enough thinking. I will go upstairs and enjoy myself. Just feeling a little horny.*

Strolling into the bedroom, Gisele goes to the drawer with all the toys in it and picks out her favorite pink rabbit vibrator. Its silky coral shaft has four gyrating speeds, and the silky clitoral tickler attached to it reaches up from below to ravish her clit—why she has any others is beyond her. Already naked, she stretches out on top of the bed.

Lying there, she enjoys the feeling of the sunshine from the window on her body, turning the vibrator's speed to medium. She rolls it over one breast until the nipple hardens, then moves to the other, slowly tickling it while idly trying to think of a scenario that would suit the occasion. As one forms in her head, she starts to glide the toy over her stomach, past her pubic hairs, until it touches her clit. Her hips push up a little as she moans at the feel of the vibration. Moving it farther down, she slides the pink rabbit in. As the swollen tip spreads her puffed lips apart, Gisele closes her eyes to visualize the fantasy.

Ah, haven't thought of her in years! There is Sara, my mother's attractive friend, who is staying overnight, sitting on the couch watching TV, waiting for Mom to come home. She's wearing nothing but panties and, a bra, and a blanket covers her. Making sure I was dressed the same, I walked over, pretending I got up to get a glass of water. Passing by, I look at the show she's watching. "Oh, I love that show. Can I watch it with you?" Sure, was the response. Jumping on the couch beside her, I pulled part of the blanket over my hips. Concentrating on the show for a while, I finally got brave enough to slide my hand over to touch hers. Afraid that, with me being so young, Sara would push it away. When her fingers slid between mine, I just about gasped out loud with the thrill of it. Sitting there, staring at the TV, too scared to move in case our hands parted, I grew more anxious by the minute.

As these thoughts go through her mind, Gisele shoves the gyrating vibrator farther in so the extended tickler can reach her clit. Moaning, she bends her knees, moving her hips up and down as if that would help get it deeper. With her passion rising higher, she continues with the fantasy.

Sara got up to get us some snacks. Watching her ass sway in those see-through panties as she went, I slid my panties aside so I could insert a finger for a little release. Watching her coming back, I straightened, resting my hand on my leg as she climbed back under the blanket.

With the chips finished and the show about to end, avoiding eye contact, I convinced myself, knowing she liked women, to slide my hand off my leg and onto hers. Holding my breath, waiting for the rejection that never came. Instead, her legs started to open as her hand glided over my leg to rub the inner thigh. Moving my fingers so they were just going under her panties, over her pubic hair, pressing further to touch her swollen lips, a voice broke the silence.

"What are you girls watching?" Mom asked.

Gisele's back arches as she recalls that moment over and over, unable to control the strong urges to climax. Giving in, her body trembles as she come, relaxing back on the bed. Slowly, her breathing returns to normal as she removes the vibrator. *Damn, that was intense! I don't know if the arousal was heightened by the thought of touching Sara's cunt or the fact that Mom just about caught us! Either way, I will use that fantasy again for sure.*

Getting out of bed, noticing the time, she goes down, put the frozen lasagna in the oven, and proceeds upstairs to clean up and dress for dinner. Done, she heads to her study, reminiscing about the nights Sara visited her mom. Sitting at the desk, organizing her schedule for next week, she hears Bill come in and gets up to greet him. Glad that dinner is warming in the oven, she glances at the wall clock—it is almost seven.

Bill hollers from the doorway, "Sorry I'm late. I'll tell you all about it after I wash up."

Gisele replies, "I'll pour you a drink and leave it by your chair while I get supper on the table." She has just finished pouring herself a glass of wine when Bill enters. He starts in on his spiel as Gisele sits at her end of the table, dishing up and passing the dish to Bill.

"What a day! First, a car got t-boned right in front of me. Then, we got invited out for dinner by a high-priced criminal lawyer," Bill says as he chews some food. "Let me start from the beginning. There I was, having a lazy day, thinking about heading back to the office and then home. Spotting some of our newspaper advertisers' stores, I decided to take a few photos of the storefronts that maybe the newspaper could use. I had just crossed the intersection on the other side to get a better shot when *bang*! One car t-boned the other. You know me—I just started snapping pictures. Capturing all the before and aftermath. Then, I had to hang around for the police to take my statement. Then, out of the blue, this lawyer shows up. I'm thinking, *Goddamn ambulance chaser*.

"He hands me his card and says, *I know you think I'm an ambulance chaser, but let me assure you, I am not. The one in the car that got t-boned is my client. I was called because he's up on charges and due in court next Monday. Tell you what—when you're done showing the photos you took to your boss, I'd like to view some. If any will help in this case, I'd like to purchase them. Let's say we meet over dinner on Friday at Étoile Brillante Brasserie, say 8ish. Bring your wife if you like.*

"Then he just walked away. Jeez! As soon as I got to the office, I checked him out. As I said, he's some kind of high-priced criminal lawyer. I don't even know if we could afford him if we ever need one." Bill laughs. "Talking to Ed, he said, *Sure, it seems like a good opportunity for the paper and my career.* Knowing who Mr. Harrington is could help get leads on some great cases. When I say cases, I think he meant the one Harrington is on now. Think about it, hon! I get a front-row seat in the courtroom! This is huge!" Bill stops to catch his breath and collect his thoughts.

Gisele just stares at him, taking everything in. "Bill, do you even know that restaurant? I've only heard my friends mention it. It's one of the items on their bucket list. They say a plate of food runs two to three hundred dollars per plate. And you can't even pronounce what you're eating. That's without drinks and dessert! We are going! Just wait until I tell my friends!"

Bill starts to laugh. "I was thinking more of the opportunities this encounter could open up for me."

Gisele pushes her chair back and stands up, thinking, *I'm glad I decided on this outfit today.* A two-piece crochet high-waist skirt and top. No bra or panties. It made her feel like she was naked. Her nipples harden, pushing against the mesh as if trying to escape as she walks toward Bill. Watching his eyes move down to focus on the outline of her pubic hairs makes her wet.

"That's not the only lucky thing that's going to happen to you today! Or open up!" Chuckling, she starts to raise her skirt above her waist. Bill pushes the chair back as Gisele straddles him.

Ok, handsome, let that one-eyed monster out. Monster, hell—it's a goddamn fence post. What's that saying? It's only four inches, but I'm not telling you how long it is. Feeling the head slide past her ass and between her legs, just below her soaked lips, she lowers herself down, pushing his cock into her. Rising again, then down. Her ass makes slapping sounds as it hit his legs. She bounces faster and harder as Bill pushes her top up to suck one of her nipples. Then he runs his tongue over it as his mouth engulfs as much of her breast as it can. Feeling his cock throbbing and filling her more makes her body shiver! The warm cum shooting into her makes her climax, and she goes weak, resting her head on Bill's shoulders.

"I love you so much," she says.

"Back at you," he replies.

That night, lying in bed, recalling the conversation about the dinner invite, she started to get aroused. Smiling, the last thought before sleep takes over is of her mother and Sara.

CHAPTER 2

The next few days, Gisele tries to keep her mind off the dinner invitation by staying busy, setting up appointments and showing homes to clients. Bill hasn't been home much, as Mr. Harrington and the *New Paper* are pushing to get more on the story, which is taking up all of his time. The client the lawyer mentioned is a prominent person—not to mention very wealthy—and is the top news story in every paper in the country. He's accused of murdering his wife.

Gisele sits at her desk, pondering this while reading the paper. Snooping, she thinks, this is probably the reason. Shaking her head, she goes back to work. She finishes setting an appointment with a young couple interested in a two-million-dollar property, but her thoughts drift back to the dinner date. *Damn, I have nothing to wear,* she thinks. *I'll have to go out and buy something that fits the occasion.* She heads off to the Elysian Collection, a little pricey, but perfect for the event.

As she drives, she wonders what the Harringtons are like. She and Bill don't have many friends since they spend all day dealing with people. They both enjoy solitude. Spotting the store, she pulls in.

Gisele steps into the department store, immediately noticing the spacious layout, the high ceiling, and the grand windows. As she glances around, she sees mannequins placed throughout the store, each dressed in sophisticated attire. No tables of folded clothes—everything is neatly hung apart from each other on the racks. She walks over and checks the prices: $1,000, $1,500, and barely any material on some of these outfits. She smiles to herself. Spying a mannequin in a very sexy pantsuit, she moves closer. After rifling through the options, she picks out a piece she likes—an evening pantsuit with a deep V blazer, fitted lace, and high-waist flared pants. Looking at the price tag, she was trying to decide whether to take it or not. *Eight hundred dollars... hmmm.* Just as she's inspecting it, a woman walks up beside her.

"I was just looking at that same outfit," the woman says, standing next to her. "Trying to get it in red. The salesgirl is checking the back for me."

"I was thinking white for myself," Gisele replies.

"Oh, that would look amazing on you with that long black hair," the woman answers back.

"Thanks. I think I'll take your advice," Gisele says.

The saleswoman returns. "I found what you were looking for. Would you like to try it on?" she asks.

With a nod, the other woman leaves with the saleswoman.

Gisele watches her walk away. *What a striking woman,* she thinks. That blonde hair down to her shoulders, that face with those almond-shaped blue eyes and the hourglass figure that would draw attention wherever she went.   Still looking at how the tight blue jeans accentuated the sway of her round ass. She must be a supermodel! Still daydreaming about how the scent of the woman's perfume, which still lingered, arousing her senses. Startled by the saleswoman's return, Gisele quickly responds, "I'll take that in white, please." *Good enough for a model, good enough for me,* she whispers with a chuckle.

On the drive home, Gisele's thoughts drift back to the woman in the store—the way her white blouse unbuttoned just past her breasts, outlining her erect nipples through the silk. Those tight blue jeans hugged her slim hips and long, attractive legs. *Those big, piercing blue eyes* seem to stir something... Gisele shudders a little at the memory as she pulls into her driveway.

Entering the house, she heads upstairs to put away the things she bought, but her mind can't shake the image of the woman from the store. And that oval face. Those eyes are —a portrait of striking beauty. Gisele hangs up the outfit, undresses, and lies on the bed in just her panties, beginning to fantasize.

She pictures herself back in the store and meets the woman. After all the formalities are over, she invites the woman back to her place. Once there, after a few drinks, she insists they go upstairs to the bedroom. The woman agrees. Opening the door, they find Bill asleep on the bed. Covers half off. Legs apart. Gisele notices the woman's eyes go straight to Bill's cock poking out of the blankets. Walking over Gisele's fingers encircling the shaft, she removes the covers.

Bill's cock stiffens at the touch of her hand. As she slowly strokes it, she looks at the woman, who is now showing shock at how huge it is! With her hand still sliding up over the head and down again, she gestures for her to come closer. The woman hesitantly came over. Gisele responds by reaching for the woman's hand and grasping it to put it on Bill's cock. Now, both are jerking him off. Bill let out a soft moan. The woman does the same. Gisele removing her hand, lets the woman continue stroking Bill while she gets onto the bed, kneeling to get a better position to suck on the head. Picturing her mouth sliding over the tip, with that image in her head, Gisele imagines the woman wetting her jeans, wanting Bill's cock inside her. Then, she envisions the woman's hand still pumping up and down. Her blouse was undone, her tits bouncing. Nipples hard! Then the cock starts to throb the faster she pumps. Imaging the feel of the head pulsing in her mouth as the sperm shoots into it is all it took. , and with that thought, her fingers deep inside her, she cums hard.

Lying there, exhausted, she thinks, *Damn, that was good! Jesus… I am oversexed! I can't even go shopping without talking to one girl and rushing home to masturbate!*

Getting up, she showers and gets dressed, knowing Bill will be home soon.

Downstairs, she starts preparing supper, her thoughts drifting to her sex drive. *It's harmless—I have no desire to act out my fantasies without Bill. He's always in them… well, except for the ones in my childhood!*

With the food ready, she pours herself a glass of wine and sits down. *Does Bill have the same harmless fantasies that only make sense to him? And am I searching for something that's only in his head?* Her thoughts are interrupted by Bill announcing his arrival. Getting up to greet him, her last thought lingers. *I still want to know what it is so I can make it happen more.*

"So glad you're home, hon!" she exclaims.

Roger D. Ewen

CHAPTER 3

Friday morning, Gisele putters around the house, trying to keep busy. *Can't wait until tonight. The girls will be flabbergasted when they find out.* Once again, she finds herself in Bill's study, idly looking around. Her eyes keep coming back to the picture on the wall, even though she has seen it a million times. The name below just says **(Velvet. 5 X 5 Image).** It is of a woman lying back on an oval-shaped loveseat, wearing a long red evening dress with shoulder-length blond hair. Her head rests on one arm, one foot on the floor, the other bent, resting on the other arm. The dress falls away, revealing her long, slender legs. She never paid much attention to it. When she asked Bill about it, he said it came with the house. If you stare at it long enough, it seems you are observing the lady through a window. Going over to inspect it closer, she notices the frame is thicker than usual. Putting her hands on each side, she tries to move it, but it doesn't budge. Hearing the outside door open, her hands slide away but the right finger catches an indent on the frame in doing so, though it doesn't really register to her at the time.

xxx

"Hi, hon." She calls out. "Just headed up to get changed." She knows Bill will likely shower downstairs; if they try to shower together, it will only lead to sex. The thought makes her smile as she wraps herself in a towel and steps out of the shower.

Drying off, she reaches for the newly bought pantsuit, slipping them on, ignoring wearing panties or a bra. *Hmm, I like the feel of the silk on my skin.* Finishing getting ready, she walks downstairs greeting Bill, who was already waiting. Satisfied by his reaction, she sways her hips a little more to help increase his interest.

As Gisele reaches the door, she steps out ahead of Bill. He reaches forward to pat her ass.

"Don't think I didn't see the excitement in your pants," she teases. "I would love to help you with that, but we would be late."

Arriving at the car, Bill opens the door for her. Gisele pauses, reaching back to touch his crotch. "You don't want to make a bad impression, do you?" she says, giggling, and gets into the car. Bill, going to his side, sits behind the wheel, putting the car in motion, tantalizing, "You are going to pay for that!" and then drives off.

Arriving at the restaurant they pull up to the valet parking area. Handing the key to the valet, they walk through enormous glass doors. Walking up to a very attractive hostess, Bill says, "Reservation under Harrington."

"Yes, they are already seated. Let me show you to the table," she replies

While being escorted to the table, Gisele took in the elegance of the dining area.

Soft lighting from the crystal chandeliers cast a warm glow over elegantly set tables. Tasteful artwork hung on the wall to give that classic sophistication. All this just took her breath away.

Eventually reaching the table, Gisele freezes. She presumes sitting beside Mr. Harrington is Mrs. Harrington, a blonde woman dressed in the same outfit as her but in red. Gisele senses her cheeks flush, unsure whether it was due to the matching outfit or the fantasy she had about this woman. Hearing her name, she turns towards Bill and then to Mr. Harrington. Noticing his round gray eyes first, then the smooth, youthful skin of his face that made him seem beautiful. His alluring 6-foot slim body just adds to the sex appeal.

"Nice to meet you. This is my wife, Jennifer," he says, turning to the woman next to him.

"You look gorgeous in that outfit. Glad you chose white." Jennifer mutters, trying to break the ice.

"If I had known we were going to the same dinner, I would have picked something different," replies Gisele. Both women let out a soft laugh.

With food orders and drinks on the way, the guys start talking business. Gisele and Jennifer begin teasing each other about the encounter they had. While talking, Gisele picked up a few words the guys were uttering.

"The car that hit my client. The driver was the brother of the murdered wife." Mr. Harrington was saying. "Can't say much about the court case, but that is in the news. Your photos might prove that the brother tried to kill my client."

Hearing Jennifer's voice, Gisele focuses on her.

"We have to go shopping again. Looks like we have the same taste."

"That sounds great," Gisele answers, trying very hard not to stare at the woman's breast. The moment the food arrives, she sighs, grateful that she could focus on something else. *Compose yourself before Jennifer thinks you are weird.*

The evening ended with Bill and Mr. Harrington planning to meet the next day while Gisele and Jennifer talked about having a lunch date sometime soon.

Driving home, all the while, Bill talked enthusiastically about the prospect of having a freelance client on the side. And how this case will put him in a higher status on the paper.

Gisele grins as if he could get any higher.

CHAPTER 4

As the days went by, Bill got deeply involved in the case of Dan as Mr. Harrington insisted on being called. Jennifer gradually became 'Jen' the more they had dinner together, which was mostly at the Harringtons. Gisele concentrated on selling the property she acquired before obtaining more clients. Days turned to weeks and weeks into months. Finally, she had some free time to herself.

Sitting on a stool in the kitchen, sipping a coffee, her robe opens, letting the morning sunshine warm her body. Deep in thought, enjoying the warmth of the sun that arouses her every time, she heads to Bill's study. Being so caught up in work, she almost forgot about trying to figure out Bill's mystery nights out. Standing in the office, she stares at the painting. Something nudges a thought at the back of her mind. *Shit, that's it. I felt a roughness on the right side of the frame as I was pulling away the other time.* Going over she tries to inspect the right of the frame. Up and down, her hand slides. There, just an inch above the bottom, she feels an indent. Pressing her face tightly against the wall to get a better look, all she can see is that the frame has a small chip missing. Straightening and stepping back, Gisele just stares at it again. It is solid on the wall and has a thick frame. And a chip out of it. No wonder the other owners never took it with them. She sighs. There is something else familiar about it. Then it hits! Hearing Bill come in, she goes to the doorway.

"Hi, hon," she greets.

"Hi, babe."

"Love? You said the painting in your office came with the house". Gisele enquires, trying to find out more about the portrait.

"Hmmm Hmm". Bill replies, heading to the desk to put the briefcase down.

Standing facing her husband and the picture behind him, she continues."Do you think the Harrington could have lived here before us?"

"What?" Looking up at his wife, he asks, "Why would you come up with a notion like that?"

"Well, to be honest. The blond hair, the red dress, and long legs. And the face kind of reminds me of Mrs. Harrington." She answers.

Bill turns to the portrait and hesitates, "Not to mention the V cut in the front to show off her breast almost to the nipples!" He teases.

"Oh, so that is your comparison of Jen's tits to the ones on the painting. Hmmm, got yea!" she teases back.

"Not like she hides them." they both laugh.

"Ok, if you're just going to make light of it, I am leaving!"

Heading to the kitchen, she hears Bill's request.

"Can we order out? Or if you want to cook, how about something quick? Need to catch up on work before Ed gets on my case."

"Sure."

After a while, the supper is done, and the dishes are put away. Bill heads back to the study. Gisele goes up to her office. Sitting there, she knows there is no point in waiting up for him. She riffles a few papers, but her mind is on the puzzle. *Must tear apart that office the next time I get a chance.* Seeing it's getting late, she heads to bed.

However, sleep doesn't come easy as her mind is still on the portrait.

The sounds of Bill's car starting jars her awake. Sitting up, she thinks, *this is my chance.* When he leaves, he is gone for a few hours at the least. Jumping out of bed, she heads downstairs to the office to figure out where to start. *I think with the drawers.* Going over to the desk, she pulls one drawer out and turns it over to examine the bottom. Nothing there. Then the next one. By the time she gets to the third one, she starts to chuckle. *Who the hell do you think you are, Nancy Drew? Or better yet, in a Scooby-Doo mystery.* That is where the idea to look for things taped to the bottom of the drawers came from. Some cartoon show or a one-hour drama series she used to watch as a kid. Putting things back in place, she tip-toes to the closet like in one of the Scooby-Doo mysteries - only to make herself laugh to get rid of the jitters. Feeling silly going through the motions of checking the pockets and finding nothing, she even inspects the shoes for the umpteen time. Being in the office and the closet, she didn't hear Bill pull into the drive. The only thing she heard was the outside door opening. Slinking back to the far wall, holding her breath, she waits.

Hearing the footsteps getting closer, Gisele covers her mouth to muffle a cry. Once the sound subsides, she moves forward. Through parted jackets, she sees Bill standing behind the desk. Removing a film from the camera and writing on it. When done, he starts searching through the paper clips. His hand comes up with what looks like a clip but thicker and straightened on one end. Walking over to the portrait, he inserts the end into the right side of the frame inches from the bottom. Gisele hears a click. The frame swings out from the wall. There is another door that slides to the right. The film is put inside, and closing everything back up, Bill starts to undress.

Gisele goes and presses hard against the back wall again trying to conceal herself more.   Under her breath, she mutters, *No! No! No! Don't come in here!* Then she remembers seeing the dirt on his jacket and pants, not to mention the shoes. She lets out a breath as she knows he will likely throw them into the laundry chute. Gathering up all her courage, she steps back to peer through the opening. Bill steps out from behind the desk and heads toward the shower.

Jesus Christ! I didn't think he could get any larger! She starts to get a little wet, staring at the huge erection. *Pull yourself together! You got to get back to bed before Bill*! Hearing the shower running, Gisele makes her move. Sneaking past the shower taking a quick peek. The silhouette of his huge cock standing straight up just gets her wetter and moving faster.

Once in bed, her mind is racing. *What is he going to think about the light being on in his office? What is in the film that he must have a secret place to keep them? What makes him so hard? Why hide them from me?* Hearing the shower stop, her anticipation heightens. Her thoughts shift to *what is about to happen when Bill gets up here! Should I leave my panties on or off? Lie on my back or side. Get a goddam grip,* she scolds! Finally, she lies facing the wall, panties off, pretending to be asleep waiting.

Sensing Bill in the doorway more than hearing him, the image of him standing there with the biggest hard-on he ever had got the blood flowing. She rolls on her stomach while her eyes are closed and lets out a moan, then spreads her legs apart a little. *Let him get a good view of my wet pussy and that nice smooth ass. It has worked wonders over the years.* Suddenly, she feels his knees between her legs, pushing them farther apart. His cock rests on her ass as he starts pumping between her ass cheeks. She could feel the balls touch her wet lips as he thrust forward. *Looks like it is working again.* Then with the next forward push, she feels the tip spreading her pussy apart. And within seconds, the deep drive makes her gasp. Shivers run up her spine at the sensation of him driving into her. His hand wraps in her hair and pulls her head back. The roughness of his action astonishes her but only heightens her arousal like never before, making her moan, gasping for more. She tries to push her hips up to meet his momentum, but his weight prevents it. Feeling vulnerable, she starts to cum. At the same time, he thrusts forward and then pauses, letting his cock throb deep inside her as he cums. Pulling back and driving into her again like he doesn't want it to end makes her quake. Finally, he rolls off and lies on his back.

Sliding out of bed, "Don't move, hon. I will be right back." Gisele comments.

Coming back from the bathroom naked, she kneels beside the bed. Head resting on Bill's stomach, she says, "Let me clean you up!" Tongue out, sliding down farther, tasting the mixture of sperm and her juices as she licks the tip and gets aroused. Gripping his cock and stroking it, her mouth slide over the head. *I love the feel of my fingers being spread as his cock throbs, getting hard in my hand.*

Head moving up and down, planning on giving a blowjob, her tingling clit gives her other ideas. Rising, she gets on the bed and straddles him. Pushing down so her wet lips spread over the head of his cock as it enters until her ass rests on his balls. Sitting there, another thought emerges. Putting her hands on his chest, leaning forward so that her nipples brush his chest hairs, she starts to slide up his body, allowing her nipple to glide over the hairs, tickling them to an erection. Her body moves forward, causing his cock to slide out, letting the shaft fall on his stomach slowly. Spreading her knees out and legs back a little, she forced the swollen lips to rest on the head of his throbbing cock. The hooded button can feel the skin of his shaft. Slowly moving down cause the hood to move up and allow the clit to rub on the ring that forms the head. Reaching the base, she starts back up, and the moment the clit feels the tip again, she moans. Sitting up, she stops and starts to push down harder and rub her clit faster on the head as the tingling mounts through her body. Groaning loudly, stiffing! Goes weak as her juices start to flow, and the warm sensation of the sperm on her collapses onto Bill's chest. A few minutes go by, and she rolls off onto her back. *God damn it, I am so glad he is circumcised,* was the last thought before falling asleep.

Waking up, Gisele finds Bill already up. Jumping out of bed, she notices the time. *Six in the morning! What the hell!* The thought of finally knowing about the hiding place and what might be in there keeps her moving. Excited, she puts on panties and a tee shirt and heads downstairs. Entering the kitchen, she gets a little disappointed to find Bill sitting at the table. "Morning hon."

"Morning". He acknowledges back. "Why are you getting up so early? Thought you had the day off?"

Pouring a coffee, she gives him a sly look. "Thinking of last night got me a little aroused. Thought I could catch you before you left for work. Would like to thank you."

"Seeing you standing there, I would love to oblige! But can't be late this morning. A lot of catching up to do. Then, have a meeting with Dan. Sorry, love!" Bill replies. Finishing breakfast, he gets up and grabs the briefcase on the chair. Walking over to her, he kisses her and then heads out.

Seeing the bulge in his trousers, she realizes he is not lying. *But sure, glad he had to go. I can't stop thinking of the film. What else am I going to discover?* She was trying hard not to head to his office until she was sure he wasn't coming back.

What seemed like an hour, but in reality, was only five minutes, she laughed nervously, stepping into the study and heading straight to the desk. Ruffling through the paper clips in the dish, she begins panicking not finding it right away. She whispers to herself, "God dam it! Did he take it with him? Ahhhh, there it is." Handshaking a little, all the doubt starts. *Do I really want to know? Will it make me think less of him? Maybe it is just his porn. Likes to hide it in case I am not into that.*

She hesitates when she walks over to the portrait and slides the clip in place. "What's that saying? Once you see it, you can't unsee it!" She pushes, and the frame spring ajar. Grabbing it, she swings it open. In front of her was the sliding door. *Last chance to back out. Could I live without knowing? Doubt it! Just prolonging the inevitable*, she thought, as her hand grabbed the knob and slid the door open. *If it is bad, I am going to miss that seven-inch monster.*

Standing there in amazement, looking at her discovery, she peers closer. There, all in their rows, are hundreds of round film cases. Her mind starts to race. *These can't be for work. One, they wouldn't be here, and two, his work cameras are top-of-the-line.* Doesn't even use film that she knows. Reaching in and going through them, what jumps out at her are the dates. Some are months apart. Others are weeks. No pattern. Then, taking her time, two items catch her eye. One 'The Secretary' written on one. The other four of them stacked together. Pulling the five cases out to examine them, she finds the secretary one has no date. It was close to the front of the opening. The four others are numbered one, two, three, and four. The dates have a pattern. Where farther back, about the middle. Laying them on the desk to study them some more she realizes the cases have 8mm writing on them. Damit! We don't even have a VCR, let alone something to play these! Gisele starts to think. "Slow down, girl. What to do? Can't take a case with me; he might notice." Then it hits her. "I will take out the reel, show it to a camera store employee, and ask them what I need. Think I will keep the first of the four as they were father back. Unlikely, he would want to look at one."

Picking them up, she puts them back in place and locks everything up. Going upstairs, she puts the tape under her stash of dildos.

Back in the kitchen, she starts to think what could be on those tapes! Ju*st old porn. Stop it! Just wait till you get to view one.* Waiting for Bill to come home, she starts preparing the supper.

Just before Bill enters, the last fleeing thought is, *are there any of our college days?*

CHAPTER 5

The rest of the week, Gisele stays busy with open house shows and gets one sold. As she had to finish the paperwork on that sale, she had no time to investigate where to take the film. The case Bill was helping Dan with seems to have gone to shit! Little conflict between what info Bill got from Dan can be published and what info Bill can relay to Dan from the source of the paper. He is caught in the middle of it. All in all a very nerve-racking week.

Gisele curls up on the couch with a glass of wine. "Aaaah, another Friday night! The weekend is free!" *I think I'll try to find out what I need to play that film. Who the hell even uses that kind of camera? Well, Bill, that's who! Pretty sure it's the one he had when we first met. Didn't really pay attention. Why is he still using it? Personal reason, I can only guess. But what for God, dam it.* Just about to dwell on what his secret could be, the door opens.

"In the living room, Hon," She calls out.

"What a day! But finally think I got what Dan needs for his case. Then I will finally get that one great scoop for the paper." Bill answers, walking into the room. "Tomorrow, I think I will work from home. Get everything ready for Monday. Oh, Dan and Jen invited us over for dinner tomorrow night. No shop talk."

"Sounds great. Haven't been over for a while. Kind of miss Jen." she answers while thinking. *Damit! There go my plans. Maybe not.* "Well, if you are going to be busy most of the day, I think I will have brunch with the girls. Brag about dinner that we had at Étoile Brillante Brasserie!"

The rest of the evening went by quickly. Bill talked about how things were coming together with work and the new client, and Gisele idly planned out Saturday. First, find the equipment that will play the film in the morning. Then lunch with the girls in the afternoon, dinner date in the evening. *I really don't like deceiving Bill. Well, I didn't. Just didn't mention going to the camera store. Besides, he is the one who started it!*

Morning finds Gisele getting ready for the day. *Think I'll wear these white leggings with this white blouse. That should give the clerks something to look at.* She heads downstairs and finds Bill deep in thought. "Headed out, hon," she calls, headed to the door.

"Don't forget about dinner," He answered back.

She only half heard him as her mind was already on the mission. Getting into the car, she starts heading to the city. Deep in thought, the GPS sounds. "You have reached your destination." Startle, she pulls into the parking lot.

With the blouse unbuttoned enough to show some cleavage. Tight-fitting white leggings show a little camel toe if standing just right. Smiling, "Bill is not the only one I like to tease." Gisele walks into the store. Opening the door makes the little bell jingle. There are shelves on each side of the walls with cameras covering them. As she steps up to the front counter, a young man appears from out of the back room.

"Can I help you, madam?"

"Yes, I think I am looking for one of these. Heading over to the camcorder section observing the salesclerk eyes checking her out, bends over just enough to give him an eyeshot of a nice tight round ass. Shifting from one foot to the other, she makes the cheeks sway, revealing her pussy lips. Watching men get a hard-on makes her feel that she still has sex appeal. It appears to be working on him. Sure enough, the young man comes over right away. *Ahh still got it.* She stands up, making sure he gets a good look at her cleavage. After flirting long enough to see the young man get an erection, she was a little wet herself when handing him the reel.

"Do you know what I need to get so I can view this?" She asks.

"Let me see. That is a 3" 8mm reel. You will need an 8mm projector." The salesman replies.

"God dam it, how big are those! And what do they cost?" Gisele inquires in despair.

"No worries. They are quite compact now and will run anywhere from five hundred up to a thousand dollars. If you only have one, I can transfer it onto a disk for, say, a hundred dollars."

"No, I found some old home movies, so I should buy the projector," Gisele states.

"Ok, I will order one in. Should be here around Thursday next week." Salesman informs. "If you would like help setting it up, I would be glad to come over to show you," he adds.

"No, that's ok, I'll be fine," she answers back with a big smile as she swings her hips enough to help with the young man's wet dreams. *I still have the charisma,* she thinks as the door shut behind her. A little disappointed, knowing she must wait a week before viewing the film, Gisele heads toward the restaurant to meet the girls.

xxx

Driving down the crowded street, passing the restaurant, she spies a vehicle up ahead, pulling out of a parking spot. "My lucky day." She parks and pays for the meter. Walking back down the street in the afternoon sun, a light breeze tousled her long black hair, tossing her head back, welcoming the fresh air. In doing so, she notices some of the male drivers turn their heads her way as they drive by. A few on the street look back as she walks past. *I love how attractive I feel when they notice me.*

Coming to the waist-high railing, she spots her friends at the back corner table closest to the dining room entrance. The patio had an archway that gave excess from the street. Walking through, she goes over to greet the girls, who all arrived except one.

"Janet can't make it. But said if Greg asks, tell him she was here." the conversation unfolds as she sits. "Well, that girl is playing with fire. Head straight for a divorce!"

Jennette pipes up. "They can be so messy."

Sue speaks up. "That's all; a divorce is an inconvenience to you."

"Well, Jennette, I guess with those size 44 hooters of yours. Jim will likely forgive you for anything." Betty chips in, making all the girls laugh.

Jennette moves side to side a little just to make her breasts shake. The waiter, just approaching the table, looks at the jiggling breast before addressing the rest of the table.

"Point taken," comments Shirley. They start laughing again.

Once they finish ordering, Betty starts the conversation, "You hear about that millionaire who murdered his wife? I guess he didn't want a divorce!"

"I heard he didn't do it. A home invasion gone bad." Sue adds. "Not safe in your own house anymore in this city!"

Shirley picks up on that, "Not what I heard! It's a family thing over the inheritance or something."

"Well, you don't know how true these articles are. Must write something to sell their papers," Jennette speaks up. "Sorry, Gisele!"

"That's ok, hon. Bill just takes the photos; he really doesn't write the stories," she replies.

"On a lighter note, did you hear about the peeper at the university? The female students are frightened." Betty inquires.

"The girls nowadays are so weak! Society is raising them that way! If someone looks at you wrong, you can charge them with sexual harassment." Jennette shakes her head. "Gisele, remember back in college, we had that peeper?"

Gisele smiles while picturing it, nodding her head.

"We didn't hide under our beds until they caught the little shit! What did we do?" Jennette asks, chuckling.

Gisele chuckles with her, "We hunted the little shit down!"

"That's right, and girls you know what we did then?

The others shake their heads.

"I think there were about five or six of us." Jennette looks at Gisele to confirm. "We cornered him in an alleyway, pushing him to the ground. We removed his pants and shorts. There he was lying, bare-ass six girls in a circle around him." Looking at Gisele, "Remember, it was the smallest pecker I had ever laid eyes on."

Both laugh, "I don't recall who, but one of the girls started taking pictures with her phone," Gisele chips in.

"Then one of the girls shouts, 'Let's get him hard, and I will break this shithead virgin in!'" Jennette carries on. "But try as we might, that little pecker wouldn't stand up. We even took out our tits."

"Jesus, how was that going to help? You threatening to smother him to death with those big tits of yours! When you started strolling towards him undoing your bra, seeing those bad boys jump out at him, the only thing he could see was his life flashing before his eyes," Gisele adds, laughing. "Not to mention all of us girls pointing at it laughing."

"I guess, probably still in therapy trying to get rid of the nightmares of big hooters trying to kill him!" Jennette comments.

Betty chips in, "I bet he doesn't eat at Hooters!"

At that, all the girls start to laugh out loud.

"Stop it! I am going to piss my pants," Sue states, laughing so hard she could hardly breathe.

"All I know for sure is the peeping stop in a hurry!" Jennette finishes.

Betty catches her breath, "OK, on a more sober note. Does anyone remember all the panty raids that were going on back then?"

"Yeah, it was kind of a fad back then," Sue adds.

"Fad or not, it was getting expensive to go out and buy underwear every week. What pisses us off more is it was cutting into our drinking money." Betty starts the story. "So, some of us girls decided to find out who was doing it and pay them back. Janet was one of the girls. Any way we concluded it had to be the jocks. More leaning towards the football team rather than the soccer boys."

Betty takes a drink before continuing. "Luck would have it. One of the girls was friendly with the janitor. We didn't know in what capacity and didn't care; we just wanted revenge. So, she got him to let us in the locker room. Having acquired some itching powder we put it in all the jockstraps as we weren't sure which boys were doing it." Betty stops, noticing the serious look on her friends' faces as they remembered that day. "In our defense, we didn't follow football. All we knew was that they had a game that day, and it wasn't the playoffs. We didn't even know about the point system! So, when they lost that day, the whole school blamed whoever did this, causing the football team to miss the playoffs." Betty takes another sip from her glass. "The sad part about this is it wasn't even the football players doing the raids. The goddam boys from the chess club! Probably weren't even sniffing but were wearing them! Bunch of cross-dressers!" She tries to lighten the mood. "They never discovered who was responsible for the prank, but the football players knew it was the boys from the chess club who started all this, and they hounded them for the rest of the season." Feeling picked on as the girls stare at her, Betty tries to shift the blame. "Hell, I would not have told you bunch if I knew how upset you would be. Thought it was less serious than raping someone!" she says, her eye trying not to meet any of her friends.

The girls all start laughing at once.

"We don't give a shit about football now or back then! We are just screwing with you!" Jennette reaches over and hugs her.

The rest of the afternoon went just the same. Everyone teased one another, ending with Sue announcing that she would have to save her story for another time. "Have to get home and get supper ready for Rodger. Oh, don't look at me like that! All this feminist bullshit makes it hard on us stay-at-home wife! A little cleaning here, a little cooking here, a little kissing here, a quick blowjob there, all part of it so I don't have to work. Who are they to say it is wrong?" With that, she gets up and hugs everyone. The rest follow suit, hugging one another and saying their goodbyes.

On the way home Gisele ponders on the conversion of the afternoon coming to the forgiving part. *So, I wonder if the girls think I would let Bill get away with anything just because he has a huge cock! Hmmm. Barring anything to do with kids, they are probably right.* She chuckles. *Shit! Do I really want to watch those films? I have got to know! So much doubt. Ahhhh just a collection of old porn, probably.* As she pulls into the drive, the last thoughts left wondering are what Sue did in college that she would like to share with the rest of us.

CHAPTER 6

Entering the house, she rushes over to the study, planning on giving Bill a big kiss. Reaching the door, she realizes Bill is not there. Her heart skips a beat, noticing the pin that opens the frame lying next to the paper clip tray.

Did he find out she knew about the hiding place? But how? I was so careful! She walks into the kitchen to see if he is there; instead, she finds a note. "Sorry, hon got a call from the office. Have a lead I must follow up on. Be back for the dinner date."

"God, dam it, quit being so paranoid." Upon reading that, she heads up to get ready for the date.

xxx

Coming out of the shower she meets Bill entering the bedroom. She goes over and gives him a big hug.

"You're all wet," he comments.

"Oh, you don't know how wet," she replies.

Bill's hands slowly move down her body, and she shivers.

Pushing him back a little, she teases. "Save that for later. We only have an hour. Planning on more than a quicky."

With that, they finish getting dressed while teasing one another. Gisele laughs as they go out the door and slaps Bill's ass, "Keep those thoughts till we get home!"

They get into the car and proceed to drive to the Harrington.

XXX

Following the direction of the GPS, they drive to the northern end of the city. As the business and streets stretch farther apart, they turn right on Richmond Row. The traffic thins out, and the street is well-paved. As they drive, huge, sophisticated houses stand on each side of the well-lit sidewalks. Hearing ***"Your destination is on the right,"*** an open double-gated drive comes into view. Pulling in, the gates swing close behind them as they continue up the drive. Coming to the center of the semicircle, there is a large fountain on the left with a full-scale statue of the Greek God Poseidon standing in an extra wide shell-shaped bowl. Statue of bare breast woman and cherub naked from the waist up, arms over their heads supporting it. Turning right brings you up to the entrance of the massive two-story mansion. A two-door garage on one side, and on the other, a one-door garage engulfs you as you park. The separate peak roof above suggests massive rooms await you. The scattered lighting gives it that shiny gold look.

As they exit the car, Gisele pipes up, "No, you are not getting one. Every time we come here, you ask. The other residents in our area already hate us for adding that one statue of that stallion rearing up, exposing huge balls and, let's say, a very extended penis! So, imagine if we installed that fountain!"

Getting up the steps, Bill pats her ass, "You enjoy that statue!"

Gisele considers for a moment, then says, "It's not that. They are mad because now they only have seven, and we have eight."

Both laugh as they reach the door.

A huge bronze lion head door knocker with a satin nickel finish, with a ring in its mouth is mounted on the door. Bill strikes the ring on the door three times.

"Every time I use this thing, the sound of booming echoes throughout the Mansion. It feels exactly like in horror movies," Bill grins.

"No, we are not getting one of these either," Gisele chuckles.

"Ah," he says as they hear the door open.

Jen appears in a low-cut red blouse, open right to the belly button, with no bra and a short red skirt, showing off her long tan legs.

Bill's outstretched arms present the wine, and Jen accepts the bottle.

"Ah, you always surprise us. What is it this time?" she asks, raising her eyebrows, "Excellent choice indeed! Chateau D'Yquem 2010 Sauternes will pair very nicely with what is being served tonight. Dan will be pleased indeed." Jen steps aside, "Come in."

Gisele watches the sway of her hips as she escorts them into the living room. Gazing around is overwhelming each time they are invited to see how huge their home is. Entering, you pass between two huge spiral staircases leading upstairs. Straight ahead, you take in a huge hallway that seems to go in a different direction to more open rooms. As they turn right, walking past the kitchen and dining table, you encounter a huge living room - tall bay windows letting the evening light in.

Dan hollers from the kitchen as they pass. "Hello! Dinner will be ready in a few minutes. Have a glass of wine".

"We'll save this for dinner," Jen says, gesturing for them to sit.

Gisele and Bill move to the sofa.

"Let me get us a nice chardonnay while we wait." Coming back with three glasses and the wine, Jen steps in front of the coffee table facing Bill and leans over, setting them down. Pouring the wine, she makes sure Bill gets a good look at her tits. "Oh, you prefer whiskey. Let me get you one," raising and peering into his eyes, she winks before turning away to retrieve the order.

When out of sight, Gisele turns to Bill. Seeing the big grin on his face, she holds back a laugh. She knows he is thinking the same thing as her - the conversation about the painting. As far as the flirting goes it doesn't really bother her; it's kind of arousing, actually. Getting her husband's attention Gisele gets her tongue to push the side of her cheek in and out. Her lips form the word later! Two can play this game. While still grinning, they turn back to face the figure entering the room.

Returning, Jen hands Bill the drink, sliding her fingers over his before walking to sit in the big chair across from them. As she sits, her skirt moves up a little, exposing her crotch. The black transparent lace panties emphasize the shape of her lips, making a small camel toe. Gisele is enjoying the view more than she thinks she should. She can't stop glancing over, sneaking a look at those exposed lips occasionally. In doing so Gisele is certain Jen's legs open a little.

Grinning, she notices Bill glancing over, trying not to get caught. Gisele thinks, *Jen sure is a striking woman. I sure would like to watch her get fucked! Bill's big....* The image is broken.

"I see you are wearing the outfit we picked out. You look tantalizing. I could just eat you right up!" Jen comments.

Did she just say she could eat me out? No! Gisele's thought gets interrupted by Dan walking into the room.

"Dinner is ready."

Getting up, Gisele notices Dan wearing thin white pants, showing off an impressive semi-erection. Raising her eyes to his they seem to be smiling. *Did he catch me looking? Or me being more interested in his wife than Bill is. Hmm wonder if he is thinking I'm into women more than men, and that turns him on. God dam it, girl, get a grip! All this film shit got you thinking about all this craziness.*

Dan leads the three to the dining room. "Tonight, the menu is seafood."

They sit across from each other as Dan explains the different dishes on the table.

"In front of you, we will start with garlic shrimp bacon alfredo. Then I thought you would like to try some lobster tail with garlic lemon butter with a side dish of coconut rice. Finally, to finish the meal a nice dish of poached oysters with pickled cucumber and caviar."

Bill and Gisele just look in amazement.

"Come on, eat up before it gets cold," Dan instructs.

While enjoying the food, Gisele hears Bill's inquiry, "Dan, this is delicious! I always wondered what got you into cooking. Seem a little different than being a lawyer."

"Oh! It is a different skill set, for sure. Came by accidentally. Jen was under the weather one evening when I got home. So, I said let me look after supper. Didn't feel like take-out, so decided to cook. While preparing the food, all the stress from work seemed to drain away. Then, watching Jen enjoy the meal and the appreciation in her eyes. The tension of the day faded away. What is that saying? Just about as good as sex but not quite." Dan finishes and looks at Jen. They both smile. "Experiencing great pleasure from it, I ask the chef who we have come in during the weak to show me some of his secret recipes."

Gisele let out a small laugh.

"What are you smiling at?" asks Jen.

"Nothing. An old saying just popped into my head thinking of Dan cooking," Gisele grins.

"Well, tell us." Dan insists

"Ok. Sex is like gardening. If you are not getting dirty, you are doing it wrong." They all start to laugh. With the meal done, they retire to the living room for a nightcap. Jen continues to flirt, and the conversation stays light.

Then Dan gets up, "What sports or hobbies do you enjoy, Bill?"

"Well, when I am not working and have the time to relax, I go out in the country to capture nature," Bill says.

Or at night, Gisele thinks to herself.

"Come on, Bill, I want to show you the recreation room." He beckons to follow him. "Ladies, would you like to join us? Gisele, you will enjoy this as well."

He ushers them down the hallway, which Gisele was admiring earlier. The walls on either side display elegant artwork, each piece featuring couples in different sexual positions. At the entrance to the rooms, six-foot statues of naked men and women stand guard at every opening.

Upon entering the room, they see a very perky-breasted statue of a woman guarding the passage. Gisele stands in awe while taking in the place. Standing in the middle at one end of the room is an Ascot Walnut professional pool table with a red cloth center. The other end has a walnut foosball table. Along the wall are various pinball and video game machines. Like the rest of the mansion, the rec room was enormous. At one of the end walls, mounted a dart board. A mini bar in the corner and a couple of leather love seats against the wall fill the area. Dan walks them over there.

"Jen and I like to play darts, so we purchased this game called Get to Know Your Guest. Would you like to try your luck?"

Gisele and Bill look at each other, "Sure, we played a little in college."

"Great! Here are the rules. We each take turns at the dart board. The one who gets the highest score is the victor, who, in turn, picks a card from the deck on the table. Then you ask one of the guests, who is not your partner, the question on the card. If he or she does not want to answer the question, then there is a punishment, one of two that the winner chooses. They either drink a shot, or they get turned over the card reader's knees and get spank three times. The game is over when one person asks ten questions. In other words, win ten rounds of darts." Dan pauses and looks at his guest taking a drink.

Gisele, getting excited at the thought of playing, looks at Bill.

"Sounds like fun,"

In the first round, Gisele wins. Dan and others look at her, amazed.

Beaming, Gisele states, "What can I tell you? In college, us girls loved playing drinking games. This is one the boys thought they could play to undress us. They were wrong!" Laughing, she turns towards Dan and looks at the card, "Have you ever used a butt plug?"

"No," Dan answers.

The game continues in this manner. Have you ever had a threesome? Do you like oral sex? Do you like to be hugged after sex and so on? Gisele or Dan wins most of the rounds. No one refuses to answer the questions. Then Dan wins the round, making it the last question of the game.

Gisele sees Dan looking at the card. Slowly lifting his head, he peers into her eyes. His eyes sparkle with excitement.

"Would you ever agree to a foursome?" he reads.

Gisele, breaking from the stare, glances at Jen and declares, "I will take the punishment."

Dan turns towards Bill, "A spanking it will be!" Seeing no objection, he pushes his chair back and motions for Gisele to come over. Walking over, she lies across his knees, feet together flat on the floor, ass in the air, her long black hair hanging to the floor, covering her face.

Stretched out like that, she tries visualizing herself bent over. Wondering how much of her lips between her legs showed and if there were any wet spots showing, knowing how aroused she was. The first slap makes her gasp, her chest heaving as his hand lifts for the second. As it lands, her head tilts back, more in desire than pain. Anticipating the third and final slap, her nipples harden, and she grows wetter, waiting for what feels like an eternity. When the pain hits, a small moan escapes her lips. Finishing, she straightens up, hoping no one heard. Walking back to sit beside Bill, she is captivated by how much pleasure it has brought her.

Dan breaks the silence, "I won! That was fun we should do it again sometime."

"Oh, that is a challenge I accept!" Gisele replies.

Finally, Bill ends the night. "Well, we must get going. I have an early morning tomorrow. A story to get ready for Monday. But would definitely come for dinner again." They all get up and at the door, as they bid farewell and hug.

Gisele notices Jen that while she hugs Bill, she rubs up against him. Her leg touches his crouch as she whispers in his ear. Her view is blocked when Dan steps over to hug her. She feels the bulge in his pants rubbing her leg as he whispers, "Glad you came." Then he moves back and stands beside Jen.

Bill and Gisele turn and walk out the door. Getting into the car, she looks up to see the hosts waving with big smiles. Waving back, they leave.

On the drive home, Gisele turns to Bill. "What the hell was that? Jen was really coming on to you, and Dan sure wasn't trying to hide his hard cock."

"Yea! They flirted a little the other times we were over, but not like this!" Bill says.

"Seem like they wanted a foursome," she says.

"Well, I don't know if I am ready to see you fucking another man yet," Bill replies. "But watching you get spanked was sure a turn-on!" He changes the subject before she can answer. "You sure were eyeing up Jen tonight." He adds.

Gisele just smiles. "Well, she didn't hide much! And that was only until my attention was drawn to watching Dan eat those oysters! Every time he scooped one from the shell with his tongue, he looked right into my eyes! The tip would slide along the shell, then flip it in his mouth! After the fourth one, I was a little wet! That thing must be four inches long! "

"Well, I don't think anyone has one that long." Bill laughs. "Would make it hard for someone in his line of work to speak."

"Don't know about that, but if it was between my legs, it could probably reach my belly button." Gisele teases, reaching over and putting her hand on Bill's crotch.

"I miss all that! Too busy watching Jen eat her oysters!" Bill teases back. "The lips would be in an O shape. Could see the tongue curved in her mouth. The oyster shell pressed against her bottom lip. Didn't even tilt the shell; her tongue slid out to touch the oyster, then just a quick inhale made a little sucking noise, and it was gone! Juice leaves the lips wet. The tongue then slithers over the lips to clean them! After the third one, I was more than hard!"

Gisele's fingers seize the zipper and pull it down. Reaching into Bill's pants to release his erection, stroking slowly, she whispers. "What were you thinking? How it would feel if that stiff cock of yours was sliding between those wet lips. Sitting on the table in front of her, she slowly swallows you! That wet mouth sliding up and down on your cock. You grab the back of her head and push down as you thrust upward. Fucking her face as hard as you can! Faster as your balls hit her chin! That will teach her to get you horny! You are going to shoot that load right down her throat."

Gisele feels the shaft start to throb. Jerking faster, she feels he is ready to cum, "Don't worry, hon, I won't get any on your pants." With that, she bends over and puts him in her mouth just in time to swallow the thick sperm. Sitting up, she licks her lips imitating what Bill described, as she looks at him. They ride the rest of the way in silence. Each in their thoughts. Gisele replays in her mind the punishment, *why was I so stimulated by the spanking? Sure, would like to explore that more!*

Upon reaching home, Gisele is still in the mood for sex. Thinking how she would get Bill hard again so quickly. Then, an idea pops into her head! *I will describe things in the same way as in the car.* With that, she heads upstairs to shower. Lathering up, she starts to think what to say. Her hands go between her legs as she resists fingering herself. *What did he mean by yet?* With that, she steps out of the shower and dries off. With the towel wrapped around her, she steps into the bedroom. Bill is already in bed, eyes closed. But the huge tent his erection is making lets Gisele know that he is not asleep. *I wonder what he is thinking.* She moves over to the deacon bench and sits down. The towel opens. She moves her hands down to her inner thigh and starts to rub. "Come on, hon, you must have thought about having your cock in Jen's cunt just once tonight."

Bill says nothing. *He knows I am past to no return because I only use those words when horny.* "Or having that mouth of hers sliding up and down your cock as you grab the back of her head and push down, all the while watching her tits bounce. The feel of hard nipples hitting your legs. Come on, admit it!!!" *Ah, I am getting to him.* She can see the tent move a little every time she speaks. With that, she sees his head turn towards her, opening his eyes in time to see her slide two fingers into her, letting out a moan!! "Well, if you want any of this, just tell the truth!" Bending her legs and putting her feet on the bench, she spreads her knees farther apart!

Bill, with a grin, answers. "Well, if anything was to happen with Jen. I say if. The only way it would happen is that you would have to be with us!"

"Well, that's the right answer." Gisele gets up, walks over to the bed, and slides the covers down. Bill's huge cock is standing straight up. She barely has to bend before the tip slides into her mouth, her body jerking as she sucks. *He is not going to have all the fun.*

Getting on the bed, she twists her body so that a leg can be placed on each side of his head and cunt lips over his mouth. Soon, Bill's tongue slides deep inside her. She moves her head up and down so the mouth can suck on his shaft as his tongue moves in and out. Then feeling lips around her clit she shivers and lets out a moan. Feeling the throbbing in her mouth quicken, she knew he wouldn't be long in coming! She changes positions so her cunt lips are over Bill's pulsing cock. Her lips part as she starts to push down, and not being able to wait, he thrusts upward hard, making a slapping sound as his body hits her ass. She just lets him, as the sound drives her crazy with desire the faster he drives into her. With that, they both cum. Feeling the tension of the day leave their bodies, she rolls off him, and they both gaze into each other's eyes. He slowly closes his falling asleep.

Gisele lies awake a little longer, reminiscing about the spanking. *How aroused I got at the pain each wallop inflicted. Maybe I can make it happen again. We were never into rough sex! But I like it!*

She closes her eyes as a shiver goes up her spine before giving in to sleep.

Roger D. Ewen

CHAPTER 7

S unday morning finds Gisele in her study, trying to focus on work and having little success as the events of last night keep popping up. *Well, meeting Jen and Dan sure spiced up our sex life! Married 11 years and now into talking dirty. Love it!! Daydreaming about it is fine, but doing it for real is great! And the spanking brings new pleasure.* She laughs a little, dreads the thought of it as a child, but begs for it as an adult. Feeling a little aroused, she removes her robe and heads down to Bill's office.

"Yea, on my way. Be there soon," is all she hears as she gets to the doorway.

"Hey! You didn't wear that birthday suit just for me," he says in a playful banter and hugs her. Bill's hands slide down over her ass and give it a light squeeze. "Can you hold that thought until tonight, hon? Have a scoop that I have to follow up on, so sorry."

With that, he picks up his camera and heads out.

With a sigh of disappointment, she watches him go. *"Must finish this myself. Not the first time and won't be the last."* Then, suddenly, the picture catches her eye. Getting excited, she walks toward it. "I shouldn't, but I need to find out what else is in there." Picking the pin-up, inserting it, swinging the frame aside, and sliding the door back, she peers inside. It's too dark to make anything out, except there are a lot of reels. Reaching as far as she can, she pulls one out. Upon seeing it, she is surprised at the date. *This one was made ten years ago.*

Putting it back, she takes out another. Fifteen years ago. *That was before we met.*

How long has he been doing this? Since he was twelve? Chuckling a little, she puts the reel back when the sound of the phone ring startles her.

"Hello?"

"Hi, Gisele. Janet wants the gang to meet on Wednesday at one. Can you make it?" The voice asks.

"Sure, I can, Betty. Can't wait to hear her excuse why she missed."

"Said she would let us all in on the secrecy," Betty adds. "See you there. Bye."

"Bye." Gisele hangs up.

Going back up to her study she is a little miffed at Bill. *"Shouldn't be. Knew from the very start that his work came first. Hate that saying! As Bill puts it. The scoop comes only once. If you miss it, it is gone. You and I are forever! Not the smoothest one in the gene pool! Thank God, I love him. The seven inches helps.* She laughs. Sitting down, she sets about putting the paperwork together for the house showing on Monday and Tuesday. On Wednesday, the luncheon. *That should keep me busy until the machine comes in for the film.*

xxx

Wednesday afternoon, Gisele heads to meet with the girls. She drives along in deep thought: *"God dam it. I got to see what's on that tape. This is driving me mad. I really can't concentrate on anything else."* Arriving, she notices all the girls sitting in their favorite spot.

The sun seems to shine on that table more frequently, and she loves the feel of the light breeze.

"Ok, Gisele is here. Now spill the beans," commands Shirley.

"All right," Janet shoots back. "As I have told you Greg likes to go fishing with his friends on his vacation. They book at the same camp every year. At first, it was relaxing having the house to myself on those occasions. But soon, that wore off. So, after a lot of nagging and giving head." The girls laugh.

Janet continues, "Which I don't enjoy, but he does. Convinced him I was serious. Well, turns out the camp needed a cook. So, I volunteered to help when I was there. Who knew you had to get up at five-thirty in the morning!" Scowling, she goes on. "Apparently, I had to make breakfast as the guest liked to be on the lake by six!

"So, on this one morning, after everyone was gone and it was time to clean up, Buck and I went out for a break." The girls all look at her, mouth agape. "What!? He is the other cook." Leaning in, Janet whispers, "And he is black."

Sue whispers back, "Why are we whispering?"

"You know it might be politically incorrect to say he is black. Besides, Buck laughs every time people think that he is to be addressed as African American. He says, "I am American.""

The girls all respond at once out loud "You are dating an American!" Then, begin laughing.

Janet huffs. "We are not dating! It's just sex! Let me finish. As I was saying, we were outside on our break. I was wearing tight shorts. You know, the ones that make that valley between the legs men like. Flannel shirt open to the belly button no bra leaning my back against the cabin wall. Buck, standing sideways, was looking at me. He had his shirt off. Those tight jeans he was wearing hid nothing, if you know what I mean! Suddenly, he reached over, and his hand went between my legs! He started rubbing lightly. As my legs spread, he pressed harder! I reached over and started to massage the bulge in his pants! That is all it took. Buck undid my shorts and slid his hand inside my panties. Those thick black fingers were inside me. After that, it was kind of a blur. The next thing I knew, I was bent facing the wall, shorts and panties around my ankles. Buck was standing behind me. Feeling him entering me, I couldn't hold back any longer as I came. Then I felt him pulling out the warm sperm shooting all over my back and ass! That was it! We got dressed, went back inside, and finished cleaning up as if nothing happened."

The girls stare at her with looks of amazement on their faces.

"What?" Janet asks. "Let me explain so you get the whole picture. We chatted while we finished our chores. After that, we went our own ways. Later that day, I saw him on a step stool at the back of a cabin, trying to fix something. I walked over so I was facing his crotch. I unzipped his pants, reached in, and pulled his cock out. Just seeing that black shaft in my hand while stroking it got me soaked. It was hard and throbbing! Then, as I slid my mouth over the head, he started pumping his hips, shoving it farther in my mouth. Grabbing the back of my head, Buck just fucked my face. Those black balls hit my chin. I reached up and cupped them in my hand, squeezing so lightly. That is when I felt him coming into my mouth. There was so much I couldn't swallow it all. Some just ran down inside my shirt and over my tits. I swear I climaxed without being touched. When done, I just looked up at him and smiled. Wiped my mouth and walked away." Janet hesitates. "Ok, does any one of you get the point of the story I just told you?" Janet scans the room and smiles.

Jennette, with a husky voice, is the first to answer, her big breasts heaving. "Not a dam clue! But how would you like to tell us more?"

Sherley, breathing a little deeply, speaks up. "Except to get us aroused by telling us about your great sex life! Nope, nothing here."

Janet interrupts. "Damit! There is no hugging! No kissing! No coming over to one another cabins! It is spontaneous sex! No exchange of words of intimacy. For Christ's sake! Once, I just about burnt my tits on the stove one morning. There we were, cooking breakfast before anyone arrived. Suddenly, down came my shorts. I bent a little so Buck could have better access. When I did, he started fucking me from behind, pushing me forward. My tits just about landed in the eggs we were cooking!" Laughing, she takes a breath. "See! It is just sex when the urge arises!"

Gisele asks. "Then why risk everything? What if Greg finds out? Is losing everything worth it?"

"Well, I thought about that. Here is the thing. Buck is not that handsome. Like in the movies, he doesn't have twelve inches. It is the shiny black skin that does it for me, nothing else. Having him on top of me and those black balls slapping my white ass makes me cum every time. It's the black on white that is my aphrodisiac." Janet pauses and smiles, "Oh, and maybe a little about being caught helps. About the last part, let me explain. We are all friends. Buck comes over at night and plays cards with Greg and his friends. I serve drinks and snacks. There is no awkwardness between us. I treat and talk to him like I do with all of Greg's friends. What I mean by that is I flirt!"

The girls focus on the story, staring at Janet while drinking wine, trying to be quiet so as not to interrupt.

"Wear tight shorts with no panties. The flannel shirt, no bra. Open enough if I bend so that I show some nipple. Greg gets off on that. Knowing that his friends are lusting over me but can't have me. The sex is so great afterward. Besides, one night while we're going at it, Greg asked, *Do you ever think about fucking Buck? He is the only black guy here.* The picture of Buck on top of me while Greg watched made me cum. So, if that happens, I think I would blame it on him for putting it in my head."

Janet starts to laugh, looking at her watch. "Damit, it is getting late. Greg is taking me out tonight, thinking he is going to get lucky. He doesn't know yet how lucky!"

Shirley adds. "I think all our husbands are going to get lucky!" They all start laughing.

"But you never addressed why you were a no-show at the last dinner date." Betty inquires.

"Shit! Thought. you would forget about that." Janet scowls. "OK! OK! Here is the thing. Buck came to the city to apply for a head cook's job at some fancy restaurant. Thought he would call me and ask to meet for dinner. Well, you know the history." The girls nod, smirking.

Janet ignores them and continues, "When I phoned you, Betty, to let you know I couldn't make it, I was thinking about going. Then thought better of it. That wouldn't make it spontaneous sex anymore." She pauses for a minute, then goes on. "So, when I showed up with Greg in toe, Buck got the message, and we all had a great dinner." Sighing, Janet rises.

With that, they hug and say their goodbyes.

Gisele thinks, walking out the door, *don't know about Bill, but I know my vibrator is getting lucky as soon as I get home.*

Driving home, Gisele keeps thinking about what Janet said. *Is that what Bill has?* Something that turns him on so much that he will risk our marriage if he gets caught. She starts to think of some scenario that would cause her to leave, but the phone rings.

"Hello?"

"Hello? This is Bob's camera shop. Your projector is in." the voice announces.

"On my way," Gisele answers.

On the way there, she nearly got into an accident, making a U-turn. "Damn, calm down," she mutters. Pulling into the parking area, she stops and takes a deep breath.

Trying to pull herself together, aroused from the dinner talk and now picking up the machine to watch the films, she gets so excited she can barely think. Entering the store, the salesman comes right over.

"Good afternoon. I have the unit set up to show you how to load the film if you like?"

"That would be great. Thanks." Gisele adds.

Following the clerk to the back of the store, the unit is set up on a small bench in a crowded room. Moving to the unit, the clerk starts to show Gisele how to load the film—first through the projector, then on the take-up reel. Every time the clerk adjusted something, his arm would brush her breast, or their hips would touch.

Is he doing this on purpose? She starts to wonder, but his voice startles her.

"There, now you give it a try. This is just an empty film to let you practice. So don't worry about damaging it." The clerk moves away to let Gisele reach the projector.

After a few attempts, she is finally successful.

The clerk moves in closer, making sure his crotch brushes Gisele's ass as he picks up a cable from the bench. "Now you can show it on your TV using this. Just plug this end into the projector and the other into the TV." Showing her the ends, he adds, "You can't get them mixed up as they have different ends." With that he gathers everything up and brings it to the front of the store.

Gisele thanks the clerk as he seals up the items and hands her the box. Getting into the car, she sits for a minute to collect her thoughts. *Jeez, got to control myself! Had the urge to pull that bulge the clerk was rubbing on my ass out and jerk him off! Dam you, Janet, and your story! I got to compose myself! You have to drive home yet.*

With that, she pulls out of the parking area.

CHAPTER 8

Upon arriving home and noticing Bill's car gone, she sighs in relief. Knowing she would have time to hide the unit, she heads inside the house, thinking. *Where can I put it?* Then it comes to her. She heads upstairs into her study; walking behind the desk, she pulls the left drawer out - the one that the printer should be in. Removing the middle shelf, she set the unit inside.

"Fits perfectly!" She says.

With shaky hands, she starts to get the projector ready for the film. Raising the arms so the reels could fit, she rolls the drawer back in and out to make sure nothing catches. "Great, don't have to take it apart each time."

Straightening up, she walks over to the drawer the film is in. Seeing the black dildo gets her thinking of Janet. *Have to get out of these soaked panties. I am going to get a rash.*

She removes the underwear, picks up the dildo and heads to the bedroom. Lying on the bed, she starts to imagine Janet on her knees, Buck shoving his cock in her mouth.

Gisele bends her legs a little and puts the dildo between her legs while picturing Janet reaching behind and grabbing that black ass to pull the cock farther into her mouth. Her head bobs as she sucks on it, balls hitting her chin. Gisele then slowly pushes the tip so it spreads her puffed lips apart to enjoy the pleasure as the dildo goes all the way in. Moving the toy in and out as fast as she could, she visualizes her walking over to them, reaching down and caressing those big black balls as Janet's mouth moves to the head to lick it. She begins picturing her hand moving up so her finger can encircle the shaft to stroke it in short jerks. Visualizing doing so, Gisele's ass starts to rise to meet the thrusting dildo as she is close to orgasm. Then the image of stroking his cock as it pumps sperm into Janet's mouth makes her cheeks swell as she tries to swallow the load. The cum dripping out of her mouth onto her tits makes Gisele gasp as she comes. Lying still to catch her breath, she hears the car pull into the driveway.

"God dam! Glad I masturbated instead of starting the film." Jumping off the bed, she heads to the shower, dries off, grabs a bath robe and heads downstairs to meet Bill.

xxx

She kisses him and says, "Sorry about supper, hon. Got home late."

"That's ok. Do you want to grab some pizza and wings?"

"Have this scoop to finish; won't be much company tonight." Bill answers.

"Ok," Gisele replies, thinking, *there goes my plans for us tonight. Guess I'll watch a movie and call it a night.* With that, they order the food.

xxx

The next morning finds Gisele fidgeting around the kitchen, trying to contain her excitement until Bill leaves for work. Unable to contain her excitement, she strolls to the study doorway and catches Bill looking at some papers he has. Then, he finally picks them up and puts them in the briefcase, heads over to her and steals a kiss. "I will be late tonight," he says.

Bill is barely out of the house, and Gisele is upstairs. "Can't wait to get a look at the film! Glad you have to work late," she says, smiling. Opening the drawer with the film and dildos, she moves them aside and picks up the film. With hands shaking so bad, just about drop it, she whispers to herself. "Calm down! You won't be able to load the film shaking like this." With that, she puts the reel on the desk and heads downstairs to get a coffee.

Sitting on the stool in the kitchen, she ponders. *Do I really want to look at the film? There will be no turning back. Oh, I know I am going to! Just hope I can handle the consequences.* Getting up she goes back up to the study. She slides the printer drawer out, picks up the film, and starts to thread it through the projector.

Gisele chuckles, "Dam, this is just like foreplay. The closer I get to loading the film, the more excited I get. Not to mention wet." The film is finally on the take-up reel; all that is left is to push play. Sitting down, she moves the lever to start and sits back to watch.

White flashes come on the monitor. Then, an image starts to form. She does not understand what is on the screen. It looks like you are staring through a bay window. The curtains are open a little. You can make out the arm of the couch but not much more, as the light from the dining room just casts shadows. That was all that was on the screen for a while.

When Gisele is just about to give up, she notices through the opening there is some motion. The camera moves to try and get a better view. But no luck! *Looks like people are moving to the couch. Can't make them out, it's too dark.* Then, the figures move beside the couch, and as they do, the man bends the woman over the arm. He hikes the skirt up, as she isn't wearing any panties, and spreads the woman's legs. He raises a little, then thrusts forward, sliding his cock to the hilt. Her body moves as he starts fucking her in slow but steady strokes. The rhythm continues for a while. Then the cock pulls out to slide up and down her ass until he cums all over her back. When done, the woman straightens up. Just then, there is another movement. Gisele strains her eyes. *Are there three people in the room?* With that, the monitor goes blank. Gisele sits there, taken back by what she saw. She looks at the clock, and it is only ten. *I got to look at the other film.* She gets up and starts to go to Bill's study. The doorbell rings, stopping her movements!

"Who the hell is that?" Shutting off the projector, Gisele doesn't bother to get the housecoat. "I am not ashamed of my body." With that, she heads to the door in a tee shirt and panties. Opening it, there stands a very striking young woman.

"Yes?" Gisele asks.

The lady goes into the spiel about some charity she is collecting money for. Only partway listening, Gisele is eyeing the lady up.

Hmm.

She is wearing a low-cut blouse to show off her nice tits, and her long legs are shoved into a very tight pair of blue jeans.

All for the male customers, no doubt. Well, I sure like what I see!

Ready to dismiss the salesgirl, Gisele raises her eyes to meet hers. She notices the woman staring at her crotch and not trying to hide it.

Interesting, let's see where this goes.

"Oooh, I think I have some money lying around somewhere! Come on in."

Gisele leads the woman into the dining room. *What the hell's wrong with me? I was never interested in women before! Oh, yeah, I look at Jennette's size 44D tits at the lunch dates with my friends. But we all do; they are huge, and she likes to show them off! I am getting a little wet just having this girl in the house! It must be the film! Not to mention, Jen got me thinking the other night.*

Bending over to open the bottom drawer, she gives the girl a good look at her ass. Sensing the woman's eyes on her, she spreads her legs a little, trying to get into the drawer, but just to give the prying eyes the advantage of seeing more of her lips through her panties! She stands up and turns toward the girl, who jerks back as she is standing very close to Gisele. *Was she going to touch me?* A shiver runs down her spine. The woman looks startled.

"Do you need a drink, water, wine perhaps!?" Gisele asks.

"No thanks! The other girl I am with is waiting!" The woman's cheeks turn red.

"Ok then, I will get the money." Retrieving the twenty, she returns and walks the person out, all the while watching that attractive ass sway as the door close. She goes to the study to get the other film.

xxx

Back at her study, she starts to rewind the first film. "Well, this makes the foreplay last longer! I am wetter than hell but must do all this shit before I can do anything about it. I love it " She laughs. After finishing the first film, she removes it and carefully threads the second one onto the take-up reel. Switching the lever to sit back on the chair, she rests her hand between her legs, excited about what she is going to see! The scene is about the same as the first film, except the curtains are fully open, and just the sheers are closed. *Still dark! Can't make anything out.* A few minutes go by. Three figures come into view.

"Ahhh, a threesome. Is that the same guy?"

The scene unfolds as with the first. Except now you can see better. One figure lies on the couch putting one leg over the arm and the other on the floor. The other shadow slowly pushes the woman over the arm as he shoves his cock in! Spreading her legs, she gives him easier access and, at the same time, gives herself a better position to slide her mouth down the other man's cock!

Gisele's finger starts to rub in the middle of her crotch as she wishes she could fast forward to the part where the man pulls out and cums all over her! Letting out a moan, knowing there is no such thing, she continues to watch the show. Moving her panties aside, she starts to play with the little hooded button there. Then, as the man on the screen pulls out and starts to stroke himself, Gisele shoves two fingers in. Watching as the sperm starts to shoot out, the fingers push faster, making her cum at the same time. Gisele doesn't move until she hears the end of the film, hitting on the take-up reel. She sits up and shuts the projector off.

"There are two more films. Don't know how many times I can cum, but that never stopped me before." Rewinding the film, she takes the two films back to Bill's study. Once there, she replaces them and gets numbers three and four. Back at her study, she puts film four in the drawer under the dildos and then proceeds to load film three.

When the film starts, it is a lot better! There is light, and both curtains are fully open! You can make out who… Gisele sits straight up in the chair, eyes wide. "What the fuck! Is that Jen's head coming up from under the dining table? " She moves her face close to the monitor in disbelief.

"Who the hell is that beside her?" The film keeps rolling, revealing Dan coming to the table with what looks like dessert. Dan sits down opposite the guest and Jen, who has one hand under the table. The film zooms into the action there. The man's cock is out, and Jen has her hand around it stroking slowly. The other hand is busy putting the cake in her mouth; all the while, the three seem to be talking. With dessert done, the three get up and head toward the couch.

"Aah! This is where film two started."

Leaning back on the chair Gisele gets ready as she knows what is coming next. The film finally gets to where the man is behind Jen and starts to shove. Gisele gasps, "What! Is it in her ass?" Suddenly, she hears a car pull in, gets up and shuts the unit off. "What the hell. You were supposed to work late!" She goes to the doorway in time to hear Bill come in.

Then, his voice comes. "I just came back to grab a lens I forgot. See you tonight," he hollers up the stairs. Hearing Bill leave, her heart slows a little. "That was close. I know I shouldn't, but I can't help myself." Heading back into the room, she switches the unit back on and sits back in the chair, legs spread. The monitor shows the man fucking Jen's ass. Jen's head is bobbing up and down, giving Dan a blow job.

Gisele wished there to be a fast forward. She rubs between her legs as they spread wider waiting for the screen to show what would be eventually, the man with his cock in his hand jerking himself off. As he cums all over Jen's back, Gisele finger herself to orgasm. *Why in the hell didn't I bring a vibrator? Well, I won't forget next time.*

Laughing, she gets up and rewinds the tape. Pushing the drawer back in, she heads to the shower. "Film four will have to wait for another day. Don't want to get caught."

After finishing showering and dressing, she goes downstairs, starts supper and waits for Bill to return. *Why is Bill filming the Harrington? Especially while they are having a threesome!*

Suddenly, the phone rings. "Hello."

"Hi. It's Jen. You want to go for lunch tomorrow?"

Gisele replies, "What time? And where? I just need to finish a few things in the morning, then I will be free around, say, two o'clock?"

"Sounds good to me. How about we try The Crystal Lily? Heard good things about it. The address is 666 Romance Road." Jen answers.

"Ok, see you then." Gisele hangs up the phone.

Once again, alone with her thoughts, she tries to figure out what the films are about! Then her thoughts turn to Jen sucking another cock. That, in turn, gets her thinking of the fantasy about her and Bill having a threesome.

One, I now already know Jen would say yes, as she was caught on film having one! She chuckles to herself, *two, she was flirting with Bill at dinner, who didn't seem to mind. The question is, how do I approach her?* Nothing comes to Gisele as she continues with the supper.

Getting the ingredients ready for the stew, her thoughts go back to the reason why Bill had those films. Trying to understand what she was watching, she ponders. *The first two tapes could be that Bill had uncovered some kind of scandal. Needed it for the paper. But when*

Jen and Dan appeared as stars in the third one, well that was a game-changer. He uses an old eight-millimeter camera. Not really work-related. For blackmail purposes? Naaah, we don't need the money. Putting the portion into the pot, she goes and gets a glass of wine.

She moves to the couch and sits sipping the wine. *What were the dates of the films again? Don't even know if we knew them back then!* Getting up, she moves towards Bill's study but stops herself and turns to the kitchen.

What are you thinking? Are you trying to get caught? Must check the dates some other time. Bill will be home any minute. Standing over the stove, she suddenly stops stirring the stew.

Did he know the Harrington before we met? Why film them having a threesome? Watching the dam films leaves me more confused than ever! There are a lot more of them. Pretty sure they are not all of Jen and Dan. Well, I will be talking to Jen on Friday. See how that pans out. She starts to mix the stew again as she hears the car pull in.

xxx

Gisele greets Bill, who is heading to the study. "Hi, hon. How was your day? Mine was quite interesting." Thinking, only if he knew, she says, "Jen called and asked to have lunch tomorrow. Said they enjoyed the other night and would love to have us over again some time."

"Hmmm," he replies, shuffling through papers.

"What do you think?" she asks.

Walking to the table, Bill sits before replying, "Oh, yeah, sure, but not this weekend. I have to go out of town for a few days. Probably till Tuesday." He answers, mumbling, half asleep. "The story I am on leads to Chicago. The weekend will be the only time I can get what I need to tie up loose ends. The dam thing might involve Dan's case. I'm not saying anything to him until I find out. Newspaper first."

Gisele was half listening, only catching bits and pieces of the conversation.

"The brother and sister may be involved now. They live in a trailer park, and Dan thinks they need the money to pay off their gambling debt. Have to catch them in a casino."

Gisele put in a hmm here and a nod there to show she was listening while lost in her thoughts. *As much as I am disappointed, I can't wait to watch the fourth film and figure out which one I'm going to show Jen and how!*

With supper done, Bill winds up with, "Well, hon, I have to catch my flight at four, so that only gives me a couple of hours of sleep. Have to hit the hay." Bill yawns.

Well, no sex tonight and for a few days, by the looks of it! That's ok; it will make the Skype sex that much more intense.

Tossing and turning sleep doesn't come easy. She is too excited about being able to view the film without fear of being caught and the thought of meeting with Jen. *And do the three know each other? Should I mention the film? No, not until I see the fourth.* Finally, she closes her eyes and drifts off to sleep.

CHAPTER 9

Friday morning, Gisele is lying on the bed in her favorite position - on top of the bed, naked! The window is open to let the sun and warm breeze flow over her body. Loving the warm sensation it gives, she stretches as she starts planning out the day. *Have to meet with Jen around two for dinner! Find something sexy to wear.* She reminds herself that Bill will call tonight but doesn't know what time, so she has to be home early. *So, today is short! I think I will wait until Saturday to view the fourth film. Yeah, it will be my movie night!* Getting out of bed, she doesn't have to wear any clothes as Bill is already gone.

She didn't get up when he left for the airport as he likes to eat at the terminal. So, she slept in, but now she heads downstairs, going over the plan in her head. First things first - walking to the hiding place, she opens it up and, pulls out one of the cases that the reels she is viewing came in, and studies the date.

Dated three years before she was introduced to the Harrington. Also, these are the only ones numbered. The rest there is only a date scribbled on them. *Hmmm, was he stalking them? Christ! Obsessed with Jen; she is one stunning woman. I fantasize about being with her!* With that, she puts the case back and takes out another. *Maybe watch a different film to compare.* She glances at the clock, and her eyes widen, "Dam, I got to get ready to meet Jen. Besides, stick to the plan; don't let yourself get sidetracked. If all goes well, everything will be revealed."

Locking everything back up, she heads to the bedroom to get dressed. Getting ready, she throws on her white semi-sheer shirt and white solid high-waist leggings - no bra. "That should give Jen a good view of my figure."

She heads out, wondering what her new friend has on her mind.

Having a little trouble finding the place as she tries to maneuver in the busy street. *Bill usually drives if we go anywhere, and this is one dam narrow street.* Spotting a parking lot, she pulls in and heads to the restaurant.

Walking into the restaurant, heads turn to watch her. Long black hair flutters as she moves. Breast jiggle a little, making the nipple hard as they press against the material. The leggings hug tight, so when their eyes glance over the crotch, it seems the camel toe is appearing and disappearing, causing a peek-a-boo look. When walking by, the firm tight ass sways, holding their gaze. *I love the feeling I get when all eyes are on me.* Glancing around the place, it gives off a stylish look with spacious booths on each side, close to tall windows covered with sheers, allowing most of the sunlight to enter, letting you enjoy a brighter environment. Spotting Jen, she walks over, giving her a huge hug as Jen stands with stretched-out arms.

Gisele sits down, noticing Jen wearing the same kind of outfit except in black! The shoulder-length blonde hair shone with eyes twinkling in the light. The blouse conceals enough of the breast but lets the nipples form an outline to be noticed. *Wonder if I look as striking as she does.*

The waiter takes their drink order.

Seated, Jen starts the conversation. "Well, Dan and I sure enjoyed the other night."

"Yes, Bill and I did also. Would love to do it again soon!" she replies.

The drinks arrive, and when the waiter leaves, the women review the night before. Gisele gets a little aroused thinking of Jen flirting with Bill. Watching Jen's face, thinking about what's on her mind, she looks a little nervous.

Jen takes a sip of wine, looking at Gisele flirtatiously. "Ok, I will spit it out! I would love to be friends with you. Knowing how I act when I have a little too much to drink, I thought that I might have offended you. You know my flirting!" She stops and takes another sip.

Gisele considers how to respond and takes the high road. "Oh, hon, I did a little flirting myself." *More with you than Dan*, she remembers with a smile, keeping it to herself. "Besides, when we got home, let's just say Bill and I had quite the evening. So, you sure didn't offend me. I would love to be friends." *And more,* but she didn't add that.

Jen starts to chuckle, her face lighting up. "Dan and I had, let's say, the same kind of night." With the air cleared, both women laugh.

Sitting quietly for a few minutes until the food arrives, both are lost in their thoughts.

Gisele, observing Jen, who had a small grin and a gleam in her eyes, asks, "What are you thinking, girl?"

Jen, averting eye contact, takes a bite and swallows, "Don't know if I should say it. It might embarrass you."

Gisele chuckles at that. Reaching across the table, she touches her new friend's hand, feeling a little tingle as she does.

"Look at me! One thing you are going to find out about me as we get close is I am hard to make uncomfortable." Pulling her hand away, she takes a bite of food, not leaving Jen's eyes.

Jen, not diverting the stare, replies, "Well, I was wondering what you thought when my husband picked spanking as a punishment for you during the game?" She waits for an answer, getting a little excited.

"Well, to tell the truth, a little nervous at first, but when no one objected, I got excited at the idea. No one has spanked me, not even Bill, but being bent over your husband's knees, I got a little wet. And when his hand glided across my ass, well, it just heightened the situation." Gisele, trying to arouse her friend with the narrative, stops, waiting for how Jen is going to respond.

"You and me both!" Jen blurts out. Gisele watches as her friend fidgets in her seat, wondering if she is going to take the bait! Sitting quietly, not wanting the conversation to go south, she waits, gazing into her friends' eyes for her to continue.

"Watching Dan's hand strike you and your body response; it was a sight to see." Jen glances away. Gisele sits idle as Jen fiddles with her food and tries to guess what her friend is up to. Or where will all this be leading to? A few minutes go by until Jen looks up, adding, "I would like to add one more idea I focused on that night. Noticing how big your husband is, you know, down there. I got wet picturing myself bent over his knees, that huge cock rubbing against me every time his hand struck my ass!" Jen, picking up a celery stick, gazes at her friend with a challenging stare.

Gisele starts to laugh, getting aroused by the idea and the dare, "Well, maybe we'll have to play that game again to test your luck." Taking a bite from her plate, she grabs the glass of wine and sits back. Watching Jen sitting there eating, knowing they are both getting wet with all this banter. *I was going to reveal something to help with her fantasy and to boast*, she muses. "Jen, I am going to tell you something I haven't told anyone." She hesitates to take another sip to heighten the suspense but waits for the right response, and once she gets it, she continues. "Bill's penis is seven inches long. I made him let me measure it, and it is four inches thick." Hearing an intake of breath, she knew it worked!

Jen lifts her head. Gisele likes the sparkle in her friend's eyes and the raised eyebrows that seem to be sending a message. *Oh, I love this game! I will not be outdone, and not sure how this dinner is going to end, but I want to win.* Leaning forward, Jen seductively whispers, "In foreplay, a cock isn't the only thing to consider! I never thought of measuring Dan's, but that tongue of his, well, that thing will hit places you didn't even know you had down there! And can he ever use it!" Jen stares triumphantly at her friend.

With the secret out, both begin breathing a little heavily. Gisele admires the effect Jen's words had on her. The way her eyes widened during the conversation made Jen realize they were on the same page. The rest of the meal is eaten in silence. Both girls knew how soaked they were from all the teasing that day.

With the dinner ending, Gisele figures she should slow this down. Let Jen win the battle; *I will win the war!* Breaking the tranquility, she says, "Oh, Jen, can I come by sometime? I would like to go over some things with you as I see we have the same interest!"

"I would love that, hon!" Jen replies, pushing Gisele's hands away as she reaches for the bill. "I invited you. It will be your turn next time."

Well, we will see if there will be a next time! After I execute my plan, Gisele thinks as the girls get up.

Hugging each other as they say goodbye sends a tingle down Gisele's body as Jen's breasts press against hers. She takes all her willpower not to moan.

Both girls love the prying eyes on them as they leave.

Driving home, Gisele couldn't get Jen out of her mind. *Dam, is that woman beddable! She just had to bring up her husband's long tongue, how I lay in bed a few nights wondering how it would feel. Thought I should keep that to myself.*

CHAPTER 10

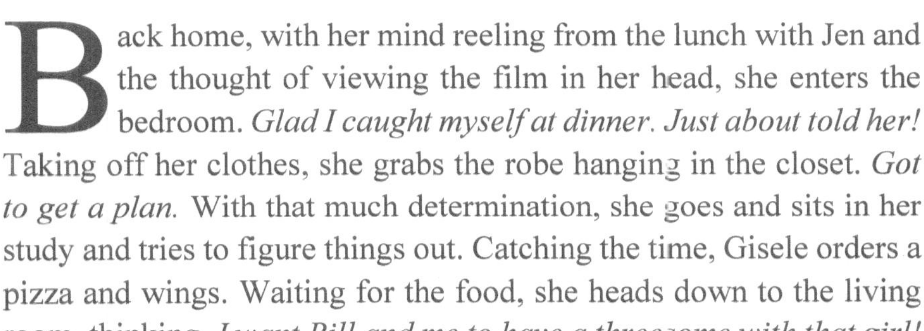

Back home, with her mind reeling from the lunch with Jen and the thought of viewing the film in her head, she enters the bedroom. *Glad I caught myself at dinner. Just about told her!* Taking off her clothes, she grabs the robe hanging in the closet. *Got to get a plan.* With that much determination, she goes and sits in her study and tries to figure things out. Catching the time, Gisele orders a pizza and wings. Waiting for the food, she heads down to the living room, thinking, *I want Bill and me to have a threesome with that girl! Can't include Dan, as Bill will never go for it. How to get Jen to agree? For that matter, Bill! Ok, we are friends now maybe let her realize. No! Show her I know their secret. That is it!*

When the pizza and wings arrive, she sits in the dining room with a glass of wine and starts to eat as she schemes with her newfound courage. *Ok, watch the fourth film to see what it reveals then approach Jen.*

But how to do that? With that rolling around in her head, finishing the pizza and wings, she heads to the kitchen to clean up. Finishing strolls by the study to go upstairs, she stops. A thought enters her head. *This is the only chance I get. Don't know when he will be away again?* Entering Bill's office, she walks to the hiding place, opens it up, and takes out the film with the secretary written on it. *Wanted to view this one from the start. But being that it was at the front, I was too frightened that Bill would miss it. But not now! What is on it? What are you doing, stripping for him or more?*

I don't know if I can handle what I am about to see. If it's more than stripping, I'll scratch her eyes out, the cunt! Picking up the case, she heads to her study, trying not to succumb to the rage building inside her. Removing the one that is there, she threads the other through. She switches to start and braces herself for the worst.

The monitor flickers, and then an image comes on. Showing a square pattern rug floor that goes under an oak desk with a chair in the middle computer case to the left of it. That is all for a few minutes. Then, a pair of shoes bare legs in a dress, come into view. The chair is then pulled back, and the person sits. Seconds later, a hand reaches down and turns on the computer. For a while, the screen is of legs rubbing together moving from one side to the other. Then they spread apart a little, exposing a pair of white lace panties. That starts the tingling within Gisele as she enjoys the sight. Then the thrill of watching a hand holding a pencil sliding it between the legs as they open wider. The pencil presses against the panties, moving idly up and down, making a crease showing an outline of those swollen lips on each side of it as a wet spot becomes evident.

Gisele lets out a moan at the image, and her robe falls open. Next, on the screen the hand is out of sight and the legs close. Then, the hands come into view on each side of the woman's hip, sliding down and removing the panties. The reddest, hairiest pubic hair you will ever see covering a very captivating set of arousing lips comes into sight! So, memorized, Gisele doesn't realize her hand is between her legs. Fingers mingle through her pubic hair.

On the screen, the legs spread as hands move slowly up the inner thighs. Two fingers together start to rub the clit slowly, then faster. After a while, they move down a little so they can enter her. She is not really fingering herself, more like moving them in a circle. The fingers are removed so three can be inserted and then picked up where the others left off. To Gisele, it seems like she is trying to stretch it for something bigger! Eventually finished, the hands disappear above the table. Then the biggest, whitest, most knobbly dildo with balls attached comes into view.

Gisele let out a small moan, watching the head of it spread those swollen lips apart. The red pubic hair slides over the white bumps until they cover the ball. The dildo starts to move in and out slowly, then faster. The ass moves forward to the edge of the chair.

Gisele gasps as she stares at the monitor. Seeing the dildo being removed, a fluid comes out, and her ass rises as it quivers! *Looks like she is pissing..., but in squirts!*

Thrusting the dildo back in for a few seconds, and when she takes it out, the monitor goes blank. The take-up reel makes the film end click as it continues to roll.

Gisele just sits there, trying to figure out what she just witnessed. Her phone vibrates, showing a text from Bill letting her know he will be on Skype in a few minutes. That gets her moving. Shutting off the unit, she pushes the drawer back in. Bringing Skype up on the monitor, she feels the robe is wet, and before they can connect on the monitor, she goes and cleans up and puts on pajamas.

Monitor making a ringtone brings her back to the study. There on the screen is Bill in a towel.

"Hi, hon. Raining and cold here. Had to come back to the room to shower. Just to warm up. Then I have to go back out, dam it. Wanted to hear your voice and make sure that you're all right."

"Ok, here. Went to lunch with Jen. Think she wanted to make sure that we were not offended the other night. I think she has a thing for you, hon."

"No, no, no, you have to rephrase that! I think she likes something about you!" Laughing out loud, he opens the towel, moving closer to the camera.

Gisele whimpers with pleasure as the only thing on her monitor is one huge breathtaking cock growing to reach full capacity.

"You better harness that one-eyed monster if you plan on ending this any time soon! I will be begging for Skype sex! Saying no won't be an option! You know how obsessive I get when aroused beyond no return! I'll drive, fly even take a train, if necessary, but you will put out the fire you started burning inside me!"

Both start roaring with laughter as Bill backs away and sits.

Gisele sighs, "Ah, that is better. Where was I? Oh, I believe the main intention for the call was to find out if I was upset about the spanking." Watching his face, she continues, "I informed her if we were invited to exquisite dining and drinks like that, I would take the spanking every time!"

Bill scowls. "Let's not forget I said; watching that was arousing, but have you spanked at someone else's whim? Well, that is something else!"

Gisele retains a little wickedness. *I am going to try rectifying that!*

"Hon, I was only complementing the dinner, that is all. Plus, I had to let her know that we do not shun friends without talking to them first. Anyway, enough of this, how is the story going?"

Bill relaxes, "I now understand why Dan is such a great lawyer. The intuition ability he possesses is scary! If these two down here are brother and sister, well let's say taboo is the only word that comes to mind but not even closest to describe them!"

"Really, what more do you require before you come home?"

"Well, capture them at their chosen gambling spot! Be it slots, horse racing, or the bookies. Once that done Dan insisted, he could do the rest."

"Love, you're amazing at what you do! I have all the faith that you will accomplish this." She says, all the while shouting in her head, *please, oh please, film them fucking! Add it to your private collection!* She gets excited, picturing him standing there, camera in one hand cock in the other! Her thoughts get interrupted by Bill acknowledging he had to go.

"Ok, love, have to go. Don't want to miss the scoop. My return flight is Tuesday afternoon. Want this story done by then. Don't want to come back here." Bill sighs.

"All right, I will let you go. Then I will put on a movie so I can forget about the second reason I said yes." Gisele replies, laughing wickedly. "Get that story done! I miss you. Love you."

"Love you." They laugh together before the screen goes blank.

Getting up, realizing her pajamas are wet, she steps out of them. Picking up the clothes, she heads to the bedroom. *What the hell is going on with me? Started out wanting a threesome, simple enough! Found a way that I think I could make that happen. Using the film as leverage is great! Played a game where I got spanked, so now I could get into D/S, whatever that is, I don't know yet! Now, moments ago, a mental picture of Bill filming two strangers screwing is getting me off! God dam it, what am I turning into? I don't know, maybe a nymphomaniac! Turning every experience into a sexual challenge! Is that what it means? Must look it up. Not that I mind. So that might be the problem in itself! Well, I don't know about anyone else, but being aroused all day is exhausting.* She crawls into bed, and just before falling asleep, her mind wanders. *What my next erotic adventure will be, and with whom?*

With that thought, she grins, closing her eyes.

CHAPTER 11

Saturday morning, Gisele is naked, stretched out on top of the blankets. As she awakens, she can feel the warm sun and a light breeze flowing over her body from the window. Immediately, her nipples get aroused, sending a slight tingle through her body. Getting up, she mumbles, "Stop that! Save it for movie night. I have a lot of things to take care of first."

She reaches for the robe and then hesitates. *Going to wear my birthday suit all day.* Studying herself in the mirror, she turns sideways, admiring how her breasts are full and firm, making the nipples point straight out. She runs her hands over her body. *Nice flat stomach, body curve in at the waist then out at the hips gives that hourglass figure appearance. Round firm ass, long curvy legs.* Impressed, she walks to the doorway, thinking that going to the gym sure has its merits. *But glad I don't have to leave the house today. No one here but me. Got all the finger food yesterday.* With a big grin, she heads to her study.

"It's going to be a great day!" she says, echoing through the house. She retrieves the file from the cabinet on which she was supposed to work on Friday.

Heading downstairs to put on the coffee, she opens the folder and starts working away. Her mind tries to drift to last night. *Stay focused and complete this; you only have until Tuesday to sort out the other dilemma.* Finishing the work, she puts it back in the folder and heads upstairs. *Love the sensation I get strolling around naked;* she thinks as the light breeze touches her skin.

Standing in the doorway, two things enter her mind. *I have to find a better way to watch the film. The office chair doesn't cut it. And discover why was the girl squirting water out of her pussy.* Getting rid of the folder, she sits at the desk. *This is the easiest of the two. Open Google and type in female squirting.* She realizes there is a lot to read. After a while, she thinks she understands. "It is not urine, has no smell or taste, or doesn't look like pee. Not all women do it. Only about ten to fifty percent can. It can happen during orgasm, but it also can happen before."

Gisele pauses here to try and picture that. *Jeez, that would be embarrassing.* Reading further comes the paragraph, *If you're not a squirter, outline steps explain how to practice so you can.* She whispers to herself, "What! Women want to do this on purpose! I would think it should be the opposite!"

Well, I know I don't, and not planning on becoming one. Glad that I don't; it would probably feel like pee to Bill. Might turn him off. Gisele begins to laugh. *After finding the films and what is on them, how would I know what he likes!* She laughs harder as the thought enters her mind. *So, this is where I draw the line: no squirting!*

Shutting down the monitor, she grabs the cup and heads downstairs. Pouring a coffee while looking at the clock, it is almost noon. She starts making a sandwich. "What is with these films?" Is he making his own porn collection? Does the participant know, and does he get paid?"

If so, the same old question enters her mind: *did he know Dan and Jen previously? All I know for sure is Bill wasn't in the room when the camera captured the secretary's R and R. It looks like it was hidden and never moved once. That one film was done secretly unmanned. No interaction between Bill and the star! Well, get that off my mind. Don't want to confront her anyway.* Finishing her sandwich and coffee, she sits there for a few minutes. Sighing, she murmurs, "Well, on to my next task."

Heading up to the bedroom, standing in the doorway, she tries to imagine the best spot for the projector. The room assembles in her mind. *There, the makeup vanity can be cleared off as the end of the bed is facing it. That's it.* Completing the task, she stands back to admire her work. *Shit, the monitor fits, but adding the projector blocks the screen.*

"Dam!" she curses out loud.

She scans the room to see if a solution comes to mind. There, in the corner by the head of the bed, is a wooden footstool. Resting on top of it is a nude lady table lamp with an elegant black and gold shade. It is used for, as Gisele likes to put it, "adding bedroom atmosphere!" Grinning, she walks over, removes the lamp and sets it on the floor. Picking up the stool, she goes to the vanity table. *Since I will be the only one using this room, I'll make my own atmosphere.*

Setting the stool on the floor, she places the projector on it and stretches the cable out to make sure they reach it. *Perfect*! Plugging the ends in, she goes about arranging the end tables to be ready for the finger food. "Ah, that is done! It is wine time!" she whispers and heads downstairs.

Noticing it's four o'clock, it looks more like a movie afternoon than a movie night. Laughing, she begins gathering the wine and snacks. Being excited at preparing to watch the next film, her mind wanders back to the squirting.

Maybe I should investigate it a little further. Can't be any harm in that. There has got to be something to it if they have instructions on how to do it. Jeez, there is something wrong with me! Dismiss the thought, naaaaah, I just like trying new things, that's all. It is coincidentally that every one of them appears to be sexual.

She smiles at that thought.

Didn't know I liked being spanked, but I do. Could not think how doing that could bring one pleasure, but it does. Well, one way to find out if squirting it is. I will have to study it. Then, if there is no pain involved, ok, maybe a little, I will try it. Finishing putting the snacks and the bottle of wine with glass on the carrying tray, she starts back upstairs.

The last thought going through her mind is *if I am going to try it, no one else will know. We'll see! But now it is movie night!*

xxx

Back in her room, everything is prepared. She double-checks to make sure everything is in its place. *Not want to repeat the mistake made while viewing the film, the secretary!* She checks to make sure the reel is threaded, the snacks and the wine are within reach, favorite vibrator, the Rabbit, is on the bed with a couple of dildos to start slowly. The lights are dim to heighten the mood. Taking one last look around the room, moving the switch to start, knowing there is no pause button, she heads to the bed and props up the pillows. The cool black satin sheets bring a sigh of pleasure when they connect with her body as she lies on the bed stretched out. Another murmur is released as her head and shoulder press against the feel of the silky pillows. A warmth flows through her as an image forms in her head.

Bill was at the shop with her while purchasing them. "Who the hell counts threads, jeez." Laughing, Gisele focuses on the monitor.

Laying there naked, one leg bent, she reaches for the snacks and the glass of wine. The feel of the bed linen gets her more than a little aroused while waiting for the action to start.

The film unfolds about the same as the others. White flickering flashes across the screen before an image emerges, giving the impression of someone looking through a window into a living and dining area—only this time, it appears clearer with the curtains and sheers pulled wide open. Bill either arrived too late or too early, as no one is in the picture! A minute goes by. Moving her raised knee back and forth, a tingle is felt between her legs as she waits.

Then, there is movement at the far end of the room. She sees Jen and a man come from the living room and sit at the dining table facing the window. Dan appears with the drinks and sits at the head of the table closest to them! Jen gets up, goes, and stands between the two men. Picking up the bottle of wine, pouring some in each glass, making sure as doing so, her breasts brush the man's shoulder. The two men chat away. Jen, looking at Dan with a grin on her face, fills his glass. Setting the bottle down on the table beside the two, she proceeds back to her seat, making sure to again press against the guest in doing so.

Gisele, observing the acting, mumbles, "That is a good idea." Taking a sip, she fills the glass again. *How long are they going to talk? Wish I could fast-forward the film. Naaah, this is movie night; let's play it like a movie. Besides, this is foreplay before the grand finale.* She continues watching, propped up on the bed and sipping on the drink as the two men on screen talk.

Elated at the sight of Jen's hand going under the table to rest on the man's thigh piques Gisele's interest! Then, when stroking it, she inches closer to his crotch each time. The man's body jerks a little at the touch, but the two men keep talking.

Under the table, the fingers reach the outline of the hard cock in his jeans. Gliding over it, the hand squeezes a little while she gazes at him, then returns the hand to the top of the table. The guest's eyes widen, but he continues to pay attention to Dan. The talking goes on a while longer. Then Dan gets up and heads into the kitchen, brushing Jen's shoulder as he does. When he is no longer in sight, Jen's hand quickly slides under the table, unzipping the man's pants. Reaching in, she pulls out his cock, which is already hard. Stroking slowly and gently up and down, the hand opens as it reaches the top so the palm can glide over the tip ever so lightly the cock jerks a few times at the touch.

Watching Gisele spread her legs a little, one hand slowly moves down her belly over the pubic hair. Two fingers spread her lips and start gently touching the clit, oh so softly matching Jen's movements on the man's cock. The camera zooms in closer as Jen's hand moves away to seize the man's hand. Pushing it away as it is trying to go between her legs, at the same movement, she grabs his cock again, stroking up and down.

Gisele moans a little as she stares at the action on the screen, then her eyes shift to focus between Jen's legs that are apart, panties shoved aside, exposing a very wet pair of marvelous lips under the skirt. She reaches for one of the dildos and then stops. There was a movement, turning towards what caught her eye in time to see Jen's hand move to the top of the table. Dan re-enters the room with a tray of appetizers! The camera zooms out. Doing so it catches the full view of the table.

Little disappointed, Gisele drops the dildo and grabs some snacks. *I can wait, maybe!* She chuckles at the thought.

CHAPTER 12

Turning back to the screen, Dan sets the tray down and then takes his seat. As more wine is poured, the conversation starts up again. Gisele is not focused on them, but her gaze is peering under the table. Jen's cunt is exposed as the legs close together and then open. She looks at Jen, loving the way her full lips look when she does that.

She moans, viewing that the man's cock is still out and hard. Not to mention big, and the tip has a light glistening at the tip. Gisele fingers are still circling lightly between her legs as she sips on the wine with the other. On the screen, Dan gets up and heads back into the kitchen; his hand grazes Jen's shoulder. Gisele's thought is that it is some kind of cue. As Dan disappears Jen turns and helps to move the man's chair back. Her hand once again grabs his cock.

Holding it straight up, she lowers her head under the table. Her mouth slides over the head and stops. Her hand starts pumping away as if she is trying to get him to cum. Then, her hand moves away, and her lips start to slide further down. Hesitant to open the mouth wider, she glides down more, stopping one final time before sliding down the shaft, engulfing it all.

Without realizing it, Gisele's two fingers slide into her as she stares at the screen. "Man, can she suck cock." On the monitor, Jen's head starts to bob up and down as she sucks him off. *How Jen does that without choking is beyond me.* Gisele can't take it anymore and removes her finger to reach for the vibrator. When suddenly, the phone rings! Gisele jumps, scrawling, and reaches for the phone. "There better be a death involved!"

"Hello!" Gisele tries to be gruff through the heavy breathing, unsure if it worked.

"Hi! Did I call at a bad time?" Jen asks.

Gisele inhales. "Oh no, Jen." Her voice softens as she speaks and tries to slow her breathing. "I thought it was a tell marketer, and I wanted to get rid of him."

Gisele is half listening as her pulse quickens, bringing her to the peek. *Watching Jen sucking off a guy on screen while talking to her on the phone is too much. I am going to cum without touching myself!* Her mind only catches half of what Jen is saying as a wave of sexual passion runs through her body. Pinching the nipples and squeezing her tits, she tries hard to keep from touching her throbbing pussy!

"... so, dinner was canceled. We thought while Bill is away you would like some company. Or you could come over here?"

Gisele can't speak! Her heart is racing so fast it takes her breath away! Still listening to Jen's voice on the phone while watching the action on the screen, which displays Jen who stops sucking, running her tongue up the shaft, and licking the pre-cum off the head of the man's cock! This is too much for Gisele as she starts to cum. She moves the phone's mouthpiece away from her mouth praying Jen can't hear the muffled moans she is trying to hide. She massages her breast until the last shiver leaves her body, then relaxes. Her hand moves to her side; the other puts the phone back in place.

"Gisele, you there?" Jen inquires.

Trying to catch her breath so she can speak, Gisele just stares at the action on the screen. It shows Jen is raising her head back up just before Dan enters the room. *Slowing the action down, thank God that helps!*

"Hello, hello!" Jen probes.

Hearing the voice, she tries to compose herself. "Yea, sorry." comes the reply between breaths. Trying to calm down, she repeats, " Sorry, just got into my PJs and put on a movie. Too bad you didn't call earlier." Her voice is still trembling. *Maybe I could convince you to come over! Would love to have you over to lie on these satin sheets with me! That's another night's fantasy.*

"That must be some movie! Can I borrow it when you're finnish?" Jen purrs, interrupting the train of thought.

"Yes, I'll drop it off sometime," she replies, eyes still focused on the monitor, noticing nothing much happening on the screen.

"Well, I will let you get back to your movie. Talk later," Jen whispers.

Gisele did not want to end the conversation as she would have loved to hear Jen's voice throughout the whole film. She had never felt this sexually high and didn't want it to end. Knowing she wouldn't be able to control herself, they said their goodbyes. Hanging up the phone, she replaces it with a glass of wine. *I can see how Bill is hooked on watching couples when they don't know. But talking to them while they are not aware is something he should try as this is a new high even for me!* Gisele props up the pillows, knees raised and spread apart, her hands idly rubbing between her legs. She stares at the monitor, thankful that the conversation in the film is long. It takes all her willpower not to use one of the dildos. Just thinking about what just transpired makes her want to cum. Trying to hold off the urge until the grand finale, she sips her wine.

The film does not help in that regard as it advances to Dan putting food on the table and heading back to the kitchen to fetch the rest of the prepared dishes. As soon as he leaves, Jen's hand disappears under the table, fingers slowly resting on the swollen lips, with two fingers inching into her up to the first knuckle, getting them wet. Fingering herself, she then pulls them out, sliding over to grab the man's cock and stokes it gently, making it glisten from her juices.

Gisele places a hand in her pubic hair rubbing slowly to try and ease the tingling feeling brought on by this action. But to no avail!

On the monitor it displays a scene above the table of Dan bringing out the last of the food. Walking by the end of the table, he looks down, taking in the full view of Jen jerking the guy off. Sitting down, he glances at Jen with a smile. They start to dish up. Jen keeps jerking the hard shaft until the food is passed to her. She stops, bringing the hand up from under the table to accept the plate.

How that man hasn't cum yet is beyond me! Gisele thinks, staring at the monitor. She finishes her glass of wine and pours another. Watching the three eat, she wonders how Jen's food tastes or, for that matter, smells using that hand to eat. She chuckles—*what a great night, and it's not over yet.* Sipping her wine, she continues watching. The trio continues eating and talking. Jen picks up the bread with the hand that has the juices on it, brings it to her mouth, eats it, and then licks her fingers one at a time, staring right at Dan. When done, she lowers her hand under the table, all the while holding Dan's gaze, grips the man's cock and starts jerking it. This kind of foreplay continues throughout the meal. Her hands move under the table, then up to eat. She licks her fingers, occasionally sliding two into her mouth to suck on—just to get a rise out of Dan. Watching this little performance, Gisele focuses more on what's happening above the table. Turning her attention to the guest, she chuckles at his actions. When Jen's hand is removed and above the table, he would be looking right at Dan and talking. But as soon as he felt her touching him, he would look at his plate. To Gisele, this appears odd. *What game are those two playing when they both know what is happening?* Taking all this in, she watches both men continue talking, ignoring what is going on around them. All she can comprehend is that it gets them off doing so! Dan rises and grabs the plates, taking them to the kitchen.

In doing so, Jen repeats the activity from when the dishes are put on the table. Gisele's eyes are half closed due to all the boring table talk. She alternates between lightly pinching her nipples and massaging between her thighs, trying to maintain the height of arousal. She feels alive, sipping her wine as she anticipates the ending she knows is coming. Still resisting the urge to use one of the dildos, she muses on how intense her climax will be if she can hold out.

Her attention shifts as Jen's head once again disappears under the table, engulfing the tip and sucking while stroking him as if eager to swallow his release. But just like before, her head resurfaces before Dan enters the room, bringing in the dessert.

To Gisele, it seems Dan would like the finger-licking performance being repeated. As standing between them, he bends over, placing the plate of cupcakes, which are shaped a little like breasts with a small ball shape on top to represent the nipple. She chuckles, or maybe that's just her. Dan makes sure the bulge in his pants presses against Jen. Upon accomplishing this, he seats himself.

Jen, picking up on the cue, takes it up a notch. She brings a cupcake to her mouth, slowly sliding her lips over the little ball, imitating the way she would suck on a nipple.

Making sure her lips are pressed against the white icing, she slowly moves her hand away, her mouth coming off the dessert. The mini ball has disappeared, and the icing leaves white traces at each corner and bit on the bottom and top of Jen's lips. The two men just stare as Jen pauses for effect, smacking her lips, making the icing drip, then slide her tongue out and over the lips, licking up all the icing. Gisele's knees are quickly moving back and forth as the tingling between her legs is now turning to a small ache begging for attention seeing that sight! This just almost made her spill the wine. Her eyes catching motion under the table get the juices flowing. The sight of Jen made the man's cock spasm. The wetness on the tip seems a little more than pre-cum.

Dan once again removes the empty plates, leaving the two alone. Jen keeps eating the cupcake, gazing at the guest as her tongue licks at it. The man's cock jerks at each lick. Returning to the dining room, Dan doesn't sit but walks toward the living room. The other two rise, the stranger's cock is still out, and Jen is holding it as they follow. Dan gets to the end of the couch, and hearing Jen say something; he stops and turns. As they approach, Jen looks at Dan, letting the man's cock go. She reaches and undoes his trousers. As they fall to the floor, she bends down to push his shorts down. Her mouth comes close to his erection as it springs out and up. She only breathes on it and stands up.

"This is different!" Gisele moans, reaching for the vibrator and slowly sliding it over her nipples. That makes her back arch and the aching increases. Squeezing her legs together, she turns back to the monitor.

The action resumes on the screen. Jen grabs the stranger's cock and starts stroking slowly, all the while watching Dan's reaction. With her other hand, she reaches for Dan's balls! Holding them, she squeezes gently. Now she stops pumping, moves down and just squeezes both men's genitals. As Dan's cock jerks, the stranger's hips starts to thrust back and forth as Jen's fingers encircle it again. Then, without warning, she lets go. That's the cue for the men to immediately finish undressing.

Moving the rabbit vibrator down to her aching crotch to push all the way to the hilt cease, she thinks, *I would give anything to be able to play with two cocks! That lucky bitch!* Staring at the three very alluring bare asses as they walk to the couch, Gisele watches as the action unfolds.

The scene is being played out just like it was in the other films. Dan lies on the couch, his right leg over the arm and his left leg on the floor. Jen is slowly bent over the arm until her mouth can engulf the waiting cock on that side. The stranger standing behind her spreads Jen's legs apart, hands pulling the ass cheeks apart as the tip of his cock press against the entrance.

Gisele panics for a second, thinking the film is broken, as there is no movement on the screen at that point. Then Jen's head starts to move up and down, which gives the stranger the cue to thrust his hip forward, entering deep and back out at the same pace. The balls slap her ass. *Wish there was sound.* The faster the head moves, the faster the pumping is making the balls slap hard against that ass.

Gisele wraps up on Jen's jerking body as the man slams into her, gives in to her desires, and slowly draws the vibrator back out, then follows their pace. With legs bent and knees wide apart, her ass rises to meet the trust of the vibrator! She forces her eyes to stay focused on the monitor as they try to close as she is near climaxing.

Dan's hips push up, shoving his throbbing cock to meet Jen's open mouth as he cums. As she starts swallowing his sperm, the stranger pulls out and starts pumping his cock between Jen's ass cheeks until he cums all over her back. In the same instant, Jen and Dan turn their heads and look out the window. Gisele's head jerks back, startled. That is enough for Gisele as she climaxes at the same time. Thinking they are looking at her, the camera sways and then the screen goes dark.

She leans back. "I have climaxed twice. That is amazing! Time to rest, and maybe I will break the record and make it three."

Removing the pillows holding her up, she lies flat on the bed, legs stretched out and arms at her side. Her mind reflects on past events. *Well, now I know what gets Bill so aroused. How does he hold out until he gets home is beyond me! I am glad he has that kind of stamina; I sure don't! And the camera doesn't judder once. Love his strong arms.* As she starts to doze off, her last thought is, *Did they catch him? Hmmm...* as she drifts off to sleep.

CHAPTER 13

Sunday morning finds Gisele stretched out in bed naked, a few crumbs, a dildo, and a vibrator spread around her. The gentle breeze and the warmth of the sun flowing over her breast, stirring the nipples to erection, make her stir. She opens her eyes and glances around. Upon seeing the mess, she feels a little disgusted for not cleaning up last night and tries to ease her mind. She whispers, "What is that saying? If you're not getting dirty, you are not doing it right!" Chuckling, she sits up. *Got to have a shower. That was some movie night.*

The warm water running over her sends pins and needles throughout her body. Moving the shower head down between her legs, she lets the warm water ease the soreness she feels. *That dam vibrator sure can work you over!* Waking up a little more, she starts to recall the evening.

Particularly the phone call; *I have never climaxed so hard in all my life.* Lathering herself with body soap, she remembered what Jen's voice sounded like in a whimper, asking to see the movie. *I almost lost it.* Enjoying the thought, rinsing off, and getting out, she dries off and heads downstairs. The cool air on the bare skin sends butterflies through her. *I may never wear clothes again. Well, until Tuesday.* She chuckles.

Making the coffee, she strolls over to the kitchen island and sits. Last night rolls around in her head. The image of Dan and Jen staring right at the camera comes back! *Jeez, did they catch him? If so, did they confront him? That would mean for sure he knew them prior to me being introduced. In that case, why keep it a secret? What the hell is going on?* Hearing the coffee is ready, she walks over and pours a cup. Standing there, tapping her cup, she remembers that there seemed to be quite a few cases before the four films. Not so many afterward. *Ok, that is enough wondering. I am going to check the dates to figure out why. And at the same time, getting to view the before and after might help shed some light on all this.*

The clock chimes ten-thirty. *Shit, I should call Jen, but how the hell to approach her? Seems too soon to be calling her up. It might come across as creepy!* Grabbing another coffee, she goes and sits back down. Pressing the warm cup against her breast sends a shiver down her body. The nipples immediately get erect. *This might be the only opportunity I get for a while. Bill being out of town doesn't happen often. Jesus, look at me. I question Janet's motives! I could lose a friend over this! Well, at least I didn't know her long.* She starts to laugh, reflecting on the pros and cons.

Going over what she saw in the film, she isn't sure how showing it to Jen will convince her to help. *Stop it! You are just trying to chicken out!* Throwing caution to the wind, she ponders. *If she is busy, then it is out of my hands.* With that she picks up the phone and dials.

"Hello," Jen answers on the first ring.

"Hi, this is Gisele. I was wondering what you are doing tomorrow. I would like to drop the movie off from last night."

"Oh, that would be great. Wasn't planning on going anywhere. I was trying to think of something to do. Watching a movie fit right in with my mood." she replies.

"Good. The movie is not, how do I say it? On something that is usually played on, I will have to bring a machine over for you to view it."

"That's ok. Sounds like fun. I like trying new things." Jen whispers.

"Great! I will show you how to hook it up. It's not hard." Gisele replies nervously.

"Or maybe you would like to watch it again with a friend?" Jen whispers. "Once it is already assembled, I mean." Comes a murmur.

Gisele gets a little aroused thinking. *Did I hear right? She invited me to join her. Control yourself; you don't want to spook her.*

Taking a deep breath, Gisele answers. "I would love to. It is, let's say, an unusual film. Would you like me to bring some wine?" She says to herself - *a dildo!* She feels a tingle go through her at that thought.

"No, I have wine. You bring the entertainment. I will supply the appetizer." Jen answers.

"Ok, see you at around, say eleven o'clock if that is, ok?" Gisele asks.

"Ok see you then," they both say their goodbyes.

Hanging up the phone, Gisele lets out a deep sigh. Getting up, she notices the seat of the chair is wet. *Well, one reason to wear clothes or at least panties.* With a big grin, she cleans everything up. *Could you imagine if I squirted like the secretary?* Feeling giddies, she begins laughing.

Walking to the laundry chute, she throws the dirty towel in and heads to Bill's office. Turning the lights on, *why didn't anyone want windows in here? It doesn't make sense. Feels like a dungeon.* Suddenly, she smiles to herself, *I get it, a man cave.* Her eyes move to the painting. *Do I really want to watch more films? I had resisted before as I had alternative motives. The scheme is already in motion; don't screw up now!* Strolling to the hiding place, she catches the silhouette of her body on the wall. She stops and admires it for a minute - the curve of her breasts, flat stomach, round ass, and long legs. *What an attractive shadow. She chuckles at the thought and* continues.

As the portrait swings the frame back and slides the door aside, she pauses, pondering whether to proceed. *Got to know how long Bill has been at it. And if having Jen and Dan staring right at the camera scared him. I will just match the dates and then put them back.* Pushing all doubt aside, she reaches as far as possible to remove one and then get another. With those two on the desk, peering in to locate where the four reels are, she picks a couple in front of them. All four are laid out on the desk she just sits staring at them.

All the old apprehension comes back. *Should I view them? Will this change my mind about tomorrow? Not going to alter anything one way or another.* Gisele hugs herself as a chill runs through her body. *Should have worn my robe. It is a little cold here. Well, I'll fix that,* she scoops up the tapes and returns to her study. Sitting there she writes down the dates on the cases. Little frustrated, she tries to comprehend what good doing all this is going to achieve. *All I want out of this is a threesome! Indifferent to Bill's little secret! Everyone has them. Let him keep his.*

She stares at the paper with the dates, intrigued by the older ones. *These were taken before his college years. Well, it solves the problem if I am going to view them.. For the other two, there seems to be a long gap between the four cases and these. Well, looks like it did scare him some.*

Let's find out what's on them, shall we? Picking up the older of the four, she walks back to the bedroom and stops at the projector. Replacing the films, she stands there and wonders what she is about to witness. Anxiously, she moves the lever to play and sits at the bottom of the bed. The screen comes alive, and a lighted window out of focus can be seen through some branches. The view changes as the branches are gone, bringing the window into focus. Through the dusty panes, two figures can barely be seen standing at the foot of the bed facing each other. A hand moves to the crotch of the other person as the figure crouches. Gisele is completing the action in her mind rather than really seeing it. The dirty windows cloak the inside of the bedroom.

Gisele is leaning forward, elbows on her knees, arms bent, head in her hands, staring at the monitor, wondering why Bill goes on filming. *Well over the years, if nothing else, I found Bill to be one determined individual. If he needs to get their identity, he will.* The figures have moved to the bed. Gisele barely can see the outline of an ass pumping up and down, pair of knees in the air; *well, the blow job was out of the question, I see.* Laughing, frustrated at the quality of the film, she gets up to shut it off. She stops as the window starts to enlarge slowly on the monitor. *What the hell are you up to, Bill? Oh fu... you are not, yep!* It shows a hand cleaning a spot on the window! *Jeez, nothing says who else was here last night like a clean spot on the window does!* Intrigue, she moves the hand away from the lever and sits back on the bed.

A couple of minutes go by and the figures in the film finish. When the man rolls off, the two faces can be seen staring out the window. The screen goes blank. Gisele, visualizing Bill running through the bush, starts laughing out loud. "Run, Bill! Run!" shouting, she lies back on the bed shaking with laughter, trying to remember the TV show she used to watch. Checking the clock, now knowing how long the film will run, she can get one more in before supper.

Gisele gets up, removes the reel, returns to the study, replaces it, picks up another, goes back, and loads that one on the projector. *Well, it is not as arousing as Harrington's, but it still intrigues me.* Switching the lever to play, she sits at the foot of the bed. The monitor flickers as the image appears of a house, with a large picture window set back from the street surrounded by huge, well-kept hedges. The focus is on the figure swaying in the window - a very attractive woman dressed in nothing more than an extremely revealing hollow lace exotic high-side split sheer long black dress. She reveals ample breasts that wave slowly with the movement. Her hands glide down each side of her body over the hips, guiding you to view her attractive long legs. Head swinging back and forth, hair swaying, it appears she is scanning the yard. Subsequently, the dance moves to one side of the window, her head focused on that direction. A hand moves to the slit in the dress and starts to pull it aside, divulging crotchless black panties. The image blurs, materializing two dark figures sitting on the ground at the other end of the hedges. The view on the monitor enlarges the shapes, which seem to be a couple of high school kids spying.

Gisele presumes it's their teacher as it makes it more interesting. She smiles, leaning forward to observe what looks like masturbating.

"Yep, they are jerking off."

Concentrating, she questions, *are they jerking each other off?* Before the thought could grasp the idea the screen blurs again. Focusing back on the window moves to the rhythm, her steps quick and measured, resembling the two-step. Her legs part briefly, revealing an unfiltered glimpse before she spins effortlessly, turning her back to the window. With a teasing sway, she lowers herself, fingers reaching for the floor, every movement deliberate, every reveal intentional. This performance goes on for a while until the woman reaches up and pulls the curtains close. Before the screen goes blank, it centers on the spot where the figures sit, but now they are gone. Gisele gets up and shuts the projector off. *I must make supper because I am starving! I wonder what the other films will reveal!*

Roger D. Ewen

CHAPTER 14

Noticing the mess on the bed, Gisele takes the time to straighten it up before supper, trying very hard not to give in to the desire to view another film. Once done, she walks to the top of the stairs and stops. Not wanting to repeat what happened last time, turning, she heads back to get her robe, laughing as she recalls the incident!

There she was, naked, cooking away when the grease in the pan started spitting as she added the meat. It splashed onto her, leaving small burn marks on her stomach and legs! The saddest part of it all was Bill's response when she told him. "One, I never heard in all my experience of anyone's pubic hairs catching fire from hot grease." Still laughing, he added, "Two, the small burns are for that simple thought; that is why humans invented clothes."

Gisele recollects saying, *well, it could happen!* And remembers storming off to Bill's laughter. She laughs, putting the thought out of her head and goes to the kitchen to start supper. When the supper is done, sitting at the table with the food in front of her, she tries to reason again *why all the films. Making a documentary, but of what? Why should people have their blinds closed so as not to corrupt young minds? Then why the four of the Harrington?* Jen's figure manifests in her mind.

"Yep, that is why," she grins and starts to eat. *What else, what else, ok? Maybe looking at the last two before bed will help. I must finish eating, clean up and head upstairs.*

Going to her room, she starts to rewind the film, and then heads to the study to fetch the next case when suddenly the laptop starts buzzing. She sits down, opens the laptop and sees Bill's name popping on the screen. Clicking on join, she smiles.

"Hi, hon!"

"Oh, babe, do I ever miss you! Another day and a half, I'll be home. Tomorrow should wrap everything up on my end. Then it will be up to Dan." Bill is amused, "Just finished supper, I see. You're wearing your house coat."

"Not going to let me forget, are you? It was not funny! Here, let me help you think of something else!" Gisele grips a side of her robe, slowly opening, uncovering a breast.

"Oh, sweetheart, I must stop you right there! I am stepping out just wanted to say hi before I left. Probably will be out all night. These people are night owls."

Removing the robe from her shoulders, she lets it drop to her waist, "Maybe remembering these will help you hurry home."

Bill lets out a moan, "It will! I must run. See you Tuesday, will tell you everything. Bye!"

"Bye!" Hanging up, her head swirls around another thought with a smile, *or maybe instead of telling me, you could show me. Ok, where was I?* Letting the robe drop to the floor, she picks up the first of the two that are left and goes back to her room. She loads the reel, pushes the lever to play, and sits at the end of the bed, waiting.

Unfolding on the monitor is a well-lit elegant backyard with an oval semi-inground pool. A man and woman frolicking, splashing one another is visible. The pool area now engulfs the screen. The two in the water can be seen clearer.

When the woman rises to shower her playmate, her small bell-shaped breast is exposed, exhibiting two protruding puffy nipples. Gisele moans as a tingle runs through her body. Her fingers lightly touch her nipple, pinching it to see if it would get as erect as the woman's. With no success, she sighs and turns back to the action on the monitor. The two figures are still swimming. Soon a third figure appears at the edge of the pool. Gisele's eyes open wider, thrilled, anticipating a threesome! On the screen stands a young man wearing his birthday suit with a semi-hard-on, talking to the couple in the pool.

"Why no sound, dam it!" she whispers, watching the screen and snickering at what is said about porn stars. The only words they need to memorize are "oh, ah, oh my god and yes, yes, yes at the end," it probably would be the same here. She laughs, leaning back, thinking *I should have brought a chair in.* The man on the screen descending the steps into the pool swims over, joins the others, and starts to tease the woman. This mischievousness continues until the two men swim over to the edge, resting their elbows on it to hold them, backs pressed against the wall, and wait for the woman to join. Obliging, she dives under the water, emerging in front of the two. Facing them, the water around her swirls, giving the impression that she is treading water.

Gisele comes to realize that the water is not that deep, and the woman is standing. She smiles as another image comes to mind. Her musing is interrupted, by seeing the woman take a deep breath and dive under the water. The head of the man on the right slowly goes back only coming forward again when his lady friend's head emerges. This is repeated with the man on the left. Both men look at each other, enjoying how gifted this friend is. As for Gisele, she can only imagine what is going on as she cannot see under the water. *But I sure have the imagination to put it together.* Duplicating the performance a couple more times, the woman then stops and swims to the edge between the two men, resting her elbows on the top of the pool facing the house.

Immediately, the guy on the left swims behind her. With the body's motions, it takes no imagination what is happening. Gisele is caressing her breast softly, loving the pleasure it brings. On the screen, the man finishes and swims away; the guy on the right replaces him. Watching the switch, Gisele's hand starts to stimulate the other breast. "Oh, what I would give to be her right now!" A whisper is let out. The eroticism gets interrupted when the woman in the film rises out of the pool and holds out her arms to help the two men. Turning, the three walk towards the house. The last image before the monitor goes dark is of three very attractive asses swaying as they disappear.

Gisele stands and starts to rewind the film, reviewing what she saw. "How the hell did that girl suck them off underwater?" she murmurs. "Well, one more thing I will have to discover," she mumbles to herself. Retrieving the last one, she loads it, switches to play and sits on the bed. *Don't want to get too comfortable. Just want to watch them without masturbating to them. I wonder what I will have to learn this time.*

A tiny breeze from the open window touches her naked body, making her shiver at the sensation. Sliding her hands softly down her sides, she waits for the image to appear.

The monitor comes to life once again. This film is somewhat like the first one she viewed tonight. Back yard with grass that hasn't been cut in a while leading up to the house's well-lit open bedroom window with curtains semi-open fluttering in the light breeze. Two figures can be seen standing in the screenless frame. The picture on the monitor starts to jerk up and down. Gisele surmises that Bill was trying to get a better position to catch the action. Sure enough, the image stabilizes, and when the cool night air rustles the curtains, you can view the action better. The woman standing close has her finger around the man's shaft, stroking slowly. In return, the man has one arm around the woman's waist, pulling her tight to him as his other hand is between her thighs.

Gisele visualizes the woman getting good fingering, as every time his arm twitches, her head goes back then forward again to rest on his shoulder. The pleasure-making goes on for a while, the figures inching toward the bed. Reaching their goals, the man steps away and turns the woman so she can sit at the end of the bed. Gently, he eases her back so she lays flat knees and feet on the floor. Spreading her legs, his head lowers between her thighs. Gisele lets out a tiny whimper as her hands move to her pubic hair. The image blurs and comes to focus on a car pulling into the drive the lights flickering off.

Gisele's sexual arousal turns to pure laughter as the screen blurs again to focus once again on the bedroom window. Clothes come flying out, followed by the woman pushing on the man who is half out, making him fall on the grass. Laughing so hard, Gisele almost misses the guy bent over, searching through the long grass under the windows for his clothes.

This gets her roaring louder. Then watching him running bare-ass out of the yard has her on the floor howling. Getting back up on the bed, a little under control, she sees on the monitor that the woman is now in bed, covered with a book in her hand. A figure materializes as a shadow in the curtain for a minute, then vanishes. The lady shuts off the light, and the screen goes dark.

Still giving out a little burst of laughter, she gets up slowly as her stomach hurts from laughing. Her fingers push rewind as she stands up, waiting for it to finish. *I got to write down that date!* Shutting off the projector and removing the reel, she enters the study to retrieve the other three. *I better get these back and in the right order, or I will have my own catastrophe!* Still chuckling, she heads to Bill's study. Putting the reels in their place, ensuring everything is as he left it, she heads back to the bedroom. She notices the film for tomorrow lying on the desk. *I think I will thread it here before taking it to Jen's. Not sure I could do it over there as I will be extremely excited. Ok, say it! More like horny.*

With the film all ready for tomorrow, she heads to her study. *Take out Monday's work. I want to get this done as my mind will be centered on something completely different.* Grinning, she finally finishes checking the clock. "Eleven thirty, time for bed." Putting things away, she goes and checks to make sure nothing is missing from the box that the projector needs. *The film will be ok.* Walking by, she glances at the mirror and stretches. "Love my figure."

Rubbing her hands over her body, she strolls over and jumps into bed.

Sleep doesn't come easy. All the anxieties of what could happen tomorrow cloud her mind. Tossing and turning, she finally puts the thought out of her mind. Concentrating on all the cleaning she did, her last thought before sleep takes her is.

Wonder if people hire naked maids. There is really something wrong with me.

CHAPTER 15

Getting up early the next day, as sleep wasn't easy, Gisele goes downstairs for coffee. With her stomach feeling queasy, she decides to skip breakfast. Trying to lighten the anxiety, she recollects the scene from the reel of the man being pushed out the window bare ass. Smiling, she goes to fetch another coffee. Cuddling the cup, she walks to the french doors. Pushing them open, she lets the cool air of the morning rush over her bare skin. Goosebumps form on her arms. "Ah, this is what I need to calm me." Mummering, she tilts her head back slightly as a puff of air washes over her face, and her long hair swirls in the breeze.

"I wonder if that is all the guy required in the film - a little air," she whispers to herself before chuckling.

Sipping the last of the coffee, she starts to muse about what must be accomplished today. Doing so just brings on the uneasiness. Shutting the doors, she remembers a saying - action is stronger than words!

Returning to the kitchen, she puts the cup down and wanders upstairs. Back in the bedroom, she looks around, making sure nothing is left out. She putters around nervously before starting to get dressed and checking herself in the full-length mirror. She likes how the tight blue jeans highlight her curves and how the white blouse accentuates her figure. She examines her face for any cosmetic flaws and, finding everything up to her standards, strolls over to the equipment.

Reexamining, making sure everything is accounted for, she scoops it up and heads downstairs to the car, putting everything into the trunk. Back in the kitchen with a coffee in hand, waiting for ten-thirty to strike, she starts to reconsider her options. *What is the worst that could happen? She says no, and I return with the equipment, or she says yes, and a whole new venture starts!* With newfound confidence, she heads to Jen's.

xxx

The traffic is light, which is a relief as Gisele is not really concentrating on the road, more like talking herself out of not turning around. Taking a few deep breaths, all the negative is gone. Concentrating on driving, she finally reaches Harrington's parking and sits for a few minutes before getting out. With case in hand, she walks up to the door, hesitates to steady her hand, but then knocks. In the few seconds it takes for the door to open, she collects all her courage, puts on a smile, and waits.

Jen's exquisite face with full ruby lips, and those alluring blue eyes appear. Gisele, sensing a tingling starting to go through her body, averts her gaze. Noticing the sheer cropped Tee shirt that displays her well-shaped breast, protruding hard nipples, and bare mid-section with a t-shape belly button exposed helps increase her sexual urges. All inhibition is lost, catching the sight of the sexy denim frayed low-rise cheeky mini shorts with the shoestring lace-up on the sides showing off well-shaped tan legs. The voice brings Gisele's eyes back to gaze at a remarkable smiling face.

"Hey, come on in. Set the stuff on the coffee table, and I will get the wine." Jen divulges, turning to lead the way.

"Thanks." *Well, if she caught me ogling her, she didn't let on! Now leering at two round firm bare ass cheeks protruding out of the shorts swaying as she followed, did not help! If she turned to kiss me and asked to drop my drawers right now, I would. Get a grip, woman; you have a plan; don't screw it up.* "Did you want to put a cloth over the table before I set up?" Gisele asks, heading over and setting the case down on the floor.

Jen returns with the drinks. "No, just set it up. It will be fine."

Gisele, feeling nervous and excited at the same time, reaches for the glass. "Might need a few before the movie!" she voices.

"That's OK. I have a few bottles. You do look a little anxious! Don't be. I thought it might be porn related. Dan and I watched a few in our days." Jen smoothens out. "You sounded so aroused the other night that I just had to see what got you in such a state." A little smile comes across her face.

"Well, you could be a little shocked at what you see," Gisele warns. "But if you do get upset and want me to leave, all I ask is that you give me a chance to explain, as I value our friendship."

"OK, I promise! Now, please get the movie started. As I am getting curious now!" Jen murmurs.

"All right." She gets up, pulls the projector out of the box and extends the reels. Her hands shake a little, not knowing if from fear or being aroused at what might happen.

"Dam girl!" Jen exclaims, moving closer, "When you watch movies, you make sure it is authentic. That only makes it more tantalizing."

Gisele is acutely aware of Jen's thigh pressing against her as her friend leans over to observe the setup. Straightening up with the cable in hand, Gisele feels her arm brush against Jen's nipple. If this flirting keeps up, they might not even make it to the movie. Staring directly into Jen's eyes, she asks out loud, "Where should I insert this?"

"Oh, the TV is right there. Let's move the table so it reaches." Jen steps back.

Both girls, bending, grab an end. Gisele's focus shifts to Jen's fuller breasts. *Would love to kiss those.* Finishing the task at hand, she stands up and looks at Jen.

"Now remember what I said. Also, once the film is over or if you stop it before that! I'll need you to help me understand what is going on. The last part is important!"

"Yes! Yes! Now you got me a little scared as I cannot, for the life of me, think of anything that would be in that film that needs to be explained to you! But please hurry, as I am more intrigued than ever! Couldn't discourage me now if you try! Push play!" Seeing Jen sitting on the edge of the couch so intense, Gisele grins, switches the lever to start, and joins her. Out of the corner of her eye, Gisele watches Jen's face to see how she will respond. She braces herself for the outburst.

The big screen lights up. Showing a bay window with the curtains wide open, the camera zooms in, lighting Jen's dining table and living room. Seeing Jen's eyes go wide, mouth open a little Gisele holds her breath, waiting for a response that never came. *She is probably trying to figure out how her room got into an old movie.* Still focusing on the monitor, both women are trying hard not to make eye contact.

Now Jen and another man come into view. Jen tries to cover up a deep inhale. Gisele hears the sounds but is too nervous to look over in case Jen is mad. *Eye contact might set her off, and I will get thrown out. By not looking it will give Jen time to decide.* The tension in the room is high as both are too nervous to act.

The film plays on. Both women are preoccupied with the action on the screen, trying to figure out what the other is thinking! The screen shows Dan coming to the table and bringing snacks.

Gisele can't stand not knowing. *I have to say something!* "You want me to shut it off?" she asks, trembling, turning to look at Jen. The lust in those beautiful eyes was answer enough. Feeling Jen's hand press lightly against her leg, she inhales, expecting the worst.

Jen's voice is shaky. "Don't know how you got this! Right now, I don't care! Just remembering that night makes me so horny I can't stop watching. So, no!! We will discuss how this came about later, K?" Jen's hand glides slightly up the leg in a way that makes Gisele shudder.

Both turn back to the TV. The film shows Dan going into the kitchen. Jen's hand creeps under the table, unzipping the man's pants, sliding underneath, wiggling the cock out. Releasing it, she moves it to an extremely wet-looking pussy. Fingers parting the lips, enter, then slide out. Gisele's breathing increases rapidly, hearing Jen moan. The action continues as the soaked fingers proceed back to stroking an erect cock, making it glisten in the light. Returning with the food, Dan sits at the table. The activity under it carries on. The three sit there talking while eating. Jen is eating with one hand; the other is smearing pre cum over the head of the man's shaft. Now, both women are breathing in short breaths without taking their eyes off of the screen.

The image shows Dan getting up from the table and removing the dishes. As he enters the kitchen and is out of sight, Jen pushes the man's chair back. Her head goes under the table so her mouth can slowly slide over his cock.

Both women are beyond it! They let out a moan, not even trying to cover it up. They look at each other. Jen has one hand on her breast, rubbing the nipple and the other between her legs, rubbing up and down. Gisele has both her hands on her crotch and rubbing. The film was all but forgotten. Facing each other, they gaze into each other's eyes. Both know what is next. Simultaneously, they reach for the buttons on their jeans.

Just then, hearing the door open, the girls regain composure. Gisele gets up to shut the projector off.

CHAPTER 16

Gisele hears Dan's voice. "What are you girls watching? A soap ..." His voice trails off. "Don't shut that off!" He commands harshly!

Gisele stops and straightens up. This just got awkward. A little alarmed, she turns to Jen for support. Her friend's eyes are wide, her cheeks are bright red, mouth is open as if she is in shock. Gisele's stomach tightens. *What the hell is going on? I watched the film to the end! Dan is in the dam thing! So why the surprise?* Taking her eyes off Jen, she moves her head toward the voice and stops. She notices a full-length arched floor mirror positioned against the wall between the TV and dining table, capturing most of the arm and front of the couch. Jen can be seen sitting with her head turned toward her husband as his figure comes into view. He is glaring back at her.

Gisele observes all this, getting more anxious by the minute. Noticing the huge bulge in Dan's slim, blue, tight pants as he strolls over to sit on the couch just behind her calms her nerves. Arouse is good, she rationalizes, as Dan seems focused on her ass. Testing the waters, she switches from one leg to the other and watches the swell in his pants twitch a little, giving her hope. Glancing at Jen, who is now gawking at her husband's erection, her expression appears more relaxed. *Looks like her disposition has improved.* Processing all this, Gisele's tension subsides. As Dan sits back, his hand moves to his crotch, rubbing slowly, and his hard-on becomes more noticeable. He turns to his wife, then swiftly to the mirror, catching Gisele's gaze.

Gisele immediately whirls to face the TV, which is zoomed in, showing Jen still having the man's cock in her mouth and stroking it vigorously as if to make him cum. Despite the dire situation going on all around her, observing the sex act being displayed, Gisele's sexual urges resurface. Trying as hard as she might to suppress them just makes it more exciting as, at the same time her courtesy kicks in! *Wonder what Dan is thinking! Him being a lawyer, I can't imagine.*

Dan's voice softens as he inquires. "What do we have here? I know we do not own a projector. Certainly, my wife does not make porn movies to give to our friends. That leaves some questions unanswered. When was this taken? How did you acquire it? And the motive for subjecting Jen to this?"

Gisele turns towards the mirror, glares at Dan, and tries to answer, but before a word can get out, Dan raises a hand, stopping her. Stiffening, she just shuffles back and forth, not knowing what else to do.

Dan's voice turns stern, "Save it! Just keep watching the screen! I don't want to hear it! And here is why!"

Before obeying, still staring at the mirror, Gisele observes Jen with a surprised expression on her face, which is focused on her husband's now very noticeable hard-on as he rubs it, admiring Gisele's ass. But on the screen, as Gisele submits to the request, she sees Jen licking pre cum off the head of the man's cock. Gisele moans as sexual desire overtakes her, surveying the two Jens simultaneously! One on screen, one in real life, pushes her arousal to the peak! All apprehension leaves her. *I don't know where this is headed, but I am in.* Her subconscious comes forward. *It worked in high school; it will work here!* She waits!

The voice softens again, resuming, sounding more like a speech coming on. Gisele snickers. *Dam, lawyers! He is going to talk himself into coming! Well, that would put a stop to this charade!* Suppressing a laugh, she stares at the monitor that now shows Jen's head above the table. Rubbing her legs together to ease the tingling between them, Dan continues.

"I will try to construct what is occurring here. You brought the projector and film over. That means what, I don't know yet. Surely not for blackmail purposes! You and Bill have plenty of money. The only other scenario is to acquire the upper hand on my wife. For what motive? Pressure her to do what? Have sex! That would be redundant as Jen and I, on numerous occasions, tried to entice both of you into a foursome!" At that statement, Gisele starts to move her head to get a glimpse of the situation.

"Keep your eyes on the monitor!" Dan's voice rises a little. "Never mind trying to see what I am doing!" she pauses.

Gisele obeys, frowning at the tone, becoming agitated. *Who the hell does he think he is? Scold me already, and let this awkwardness end!* Her eyes still focus on the screen view of the three in the show at the table eating; her subconscious emerges, *just hear him out; do not irritate him. You started this!* Dan's voice interrupts.

"Now, where was I? Oh yeah, knowing that is of little importance right now because, let me reassure you, I will not let you coerce my wife into anything she is not inclined to do so! That is not going to transpire!" Dan catches his breath.

Gisele senses Dan's voice getting stronger, giving her the impression he thinks he is in control. *Let him think that, as he is used to being in charge. We will change that!* The lecture continues.

"I don't think you know who has the upper hand here. You own the film. I can only surmise that Bill filmed it. That said, you might go as far as to assume that Bill, being a journalist, is exempt from prosecution! That gives him the right to watch people having sex and make a movie of it. Well, you're wrong! That makes him a peeping tom!" Dan lets out a deep breath.

Gisele's head snaps to look in the mirror, and her eyes go wide. Standing there, not knowing what to say or do, she just shifts from one leg to the other, staring. On doing this, she observes Dan's cock pushing harder against his pants. Jen's hard nipples, parted legs, and hands slowly rubbing her thighs do not go unnoticed as she stares intently at her husband's crotch.

Is that a tiny wet spot I see between her legs? Dam! Both are enjoying my discomfort! I wonder, where are they taking this? Not caring, all caution gone in the wind. Well, will listen for now! Facing straight ahead, she waits for the speech to finish.

Dan resumes the rant. "Being a lawyer, I manipulate people all day long. So now I will educate you on how it is done! First, if this film ever got out, Bill's job, freelancing would be over. There is a law against this sort of thing. He would probably be incarcerated! There goes all your wealth and friends!" He pauses, waiting for a reaction.

Gisele shudders! *Now I am getting scared! What the hell did I do? Bill is going to kill me!* All the apprehension starts to return. *How did I not associate the films could be that of a peeping tom? Maybe because I couldn't conceive peeping as a bad thing. It was more conceived as laughable than harmful in my day. There were numerous other detrimental scenarios it could have been!* She sighs. *How the hell do I amend this?* Her subconscious comes to light; *look at him, you know what he wants! Same as the incident at high school! You will endure! Just let go!*

Gisele releases a deep groan. *Well, as long as Bill doesn't find out about any of this!* The whisper startles her.

"Now, if you don't want that to happen," Dan's voice softens. "We are going to play a little game, Dan says."

Gisele, hearing this, lets out a breath of relief. *No matter how educated or how high their status they hold, sexual desires cannot be neglected!* Relaxing her stance, arms loose at her sides she pushes the thought back, waiting for the instruction! *Will I obey them?* She quivers at uncertainties lurking around the edge of her subconscious.

Dan continues setting the rules. "If you follow all of the commands requested, you leave here with everything you came with. And this never occurred. But if you terminate the game at any time before it is concluded, the evidence is mine to present to the police at my discretion. Do you understand?"

The mirror portrays Dan sitting up, his right hand skimming over the swelling between his legs, waiting for a response. Gisele nods, intrigued, and then she is astounded, hearing his zipper being pulled down. Gasping, she dreads what is coming next! *Jeez, I have never cheated on Bill ever!! But what the hell am I to do?* She notices his hand emerging from his pants, releasing his cock while stroking it! She feigns shock, fidgeting just enough to make her hips jiggle before turning to focus intently on the TV. *Ah, that should do it.* In the back of her mind, a little voice says, *nice play!*

She is too frightened of the consequences if she doesn't comply! *Try to rationalize that I am being blackmailed!* Her subconscious kicks in, *but you started all this! Quit blaming others! But if it helps, use that!* Then, the realization hits her! *Oh, bullshit, you're so inflamed you can barely see! Couldn't stop now, even if Bill walked in on us! I am going to enjoy this! Then, ask for forgiveness if it ever comes to light! Now, let's turn the tide! I have to appear like I am resisting, as that is the part that excites him the most.* She shuffles as if nervous, but instead, she is more eager for the game to get started.

CHAPTER 17

The film now has advanced to Jen's head, going back under the table as Dan is taking the dishes back to the kitchen. Everyone in the room is focused on the action in the film. The only sound heard in the air is the clacking of the projector running. The silence between them speaks volumes! Gisele turns back to the mirror, which reflects Dan sitting on the couch straight up, face forward, eyes squinted, still massaging his hard-on. Peering over at Jen's reflection, Gisele notices that she is sitting apart from him and appears to be copying her husband. Gisele takes pleasure in the fact that both are admiring her. Upon closer examination, it is disclosed the two of them seem immersed by what is on the screen - Jen taking the man's cock to the base, one hand cupping his balls, fingers squeezing lightly as her head moves up and down.

Gisele solely centers on the two in the mirror, trying to envision their thoughts as they watch the action, weakening her knees. A shiver runs up her spine. Moaning under her breath, she says, "Let me join you two. I can't take it anymore!"

Noticing Dan's eyes shifting to capture her gaze, she blushes at the thought. *Can he read my mind?* Her body shakes, smiling; *that should get his blood going, thinking I am distressed!*

Dan, acknowledging Gisele, whispers, "Oh, Jen, this is for you!" His eyes still locked on Gisele's, slouching back slowly, he raises his hips and slides out of his pants and shorts. That forces Gisele's eyes to gape at his erection bobbing against his belly as it is released. Then back to Dan, who is making sure his wife knows, stares lustfully at Gisele's ass while motioning for Jen to move beside him. The mirror shows Jen gliding over and Dan sitting up; one hand goes to his crotch so the fingers can slowly slide up and down on his cock. The other goes and rests on his wife's hip, blocking her from touching him.

Every nerve in Gisele's body is screaming for release. Taking in the two on the couch, Jen glares at her husband. Dan tightly squeezes his erection, massaging it slowly, showing no shame. *He wants me. What the hell is happening? Is Dan punishing Jen? Or is this part of the game?*

Still not acknowledging his wife while ogling the tight-shaped ass in front of him, he continues massaging himself, flirtatiously whispering, "Dan says, Gisele, slip your jeans down but do not take them off."

Gisele stiffens, still watching the reflections. Hesitant, she unbuttons her jeans, fumbling slowly, seizing the waistband trying to act as if she is resisting. Wiggling as she bends, she pushes them past her hips, exposing two round, firm, bare cheeks. Covering the rest of the buttocks is a pair of white lace tanga panties. Letting the jeans drop to the floor, she straightens and stands there facing the mirror; the reflection of the four eyes on her makes her feel vulnerable. *Patience, girl, your moment will arise. What the hell am I supposed to do in the meantime?* Gisele's subconscious surface again, *be their play doll, and the control will switch!* A chill creeps in, unsettling, a warning shiver. *We'll see...*

The mirror catches Jen sitting close by her husband, with one hand between her legs, rubbing softly and enjoying the view in front of her.

The other shifts towards her husband, which is blocked by his arm. Gisele's attention turns the focus on Dan's action, trying to fathom what is going on! Her gaze fixes on his eyes, catching the way they linger on her, completely ignoring his wife. His hand continues to stroke himself, squeezing tighter as it slides up to the tip, turning a light shade of purple. The taunting goes on, but Gisele speculates for whom? *I am so stimulated it takes all my self-control not to turn and confront them! Ask if this a threesome, then let's fuck!* A thought emerges, *patience, patience this is working to your advantage!*

The huge looking glass is now cast back; Jen's head turns, admiring her husband's huge hard-on as he plays with it. Her hand disappears under the waistband of the shorts. Gisele comes to realize that Dan has not once turned away from admiring her nice tight panties covering her ass in front of him! She speculates that must be pissing Jen off, who is trying to get his attention.

To reinforce the thought, Dan is seen removing his hand, leaving his erection bobbing in midair. Giving the impression it is dancing, he admires Gisele's half-naked body - the jeans around her ankle, long shapely bare legs forming a firm heart-shaped ass.

The mirror now shows Dan embracing Jen's hand, hesitating before resting it on his cock. At the same time, he reaches over, placing his hand on her inner thigh, his fingers gently caressing her leg. This prompts Jen to slide her hand down and seize his balls, leaving the shaft on its own that is now bobbing without anyone touching it. Gisele, witnessing Dan's head snap towards Jen, snickers silently. *Must have squeezed a little harder than he liked!* Gisele observes Jen. Once Jen gets her husband's attention, she raises her hand, wraps her fingers around his cock, and starts jerking.

He is so hard that the head looks purple. *Now I am turned on.* However, her thoughts are interrupted.

"Dan says, pull down your panties just to the knees and spread your legs," he adds more instructions.

Again, trying to look like she is a little frightened, she slides the panties down as she bends, stopping at the knees and spreading her legs to hold them there. The reflection catches Dan admiring her ass and the swollen lips between her legs as she is bent over. His chest rises and falls in short breaths as he tries to control himself. His wife keeps pumping his cock, watching him closely.

Remembering the game, the next command comes, "Dan says, shuffle back towards the couch." Chuckling, he adds further, "Jen would like to finger fuck you!"

Gisele's legs buckle a little, hearing Jen and fuck in the same sentence! *And she is going to finger me!* There was no way to hide her desire now. She straightens up and starts shuffling backward till the back of her knees hits the couch amid the sets of legs waiting. *Couldn't stop now even if I wanted to!*

The mirror shows Dan's, not Jen's, hand resting on her ass, moving smoothly between her legs. Spreading the welcoming lips apart, he slips two fingers in. Gisele inhales rising on her toes as the hand thrusts up. *What the hell!* A light moan escapes her mouth. *That is it!* Her hips start to move up and down, pushing against the hand. At the same time, she sees in the mirror Jen turning sideways, bending at the hips so her mouth can slide over her husband's cock.

The head starts to bob between her husband's legs, in time with Gisele's hips. Without warning, Dan lifts his wife's head by her hair, leaving his cock standing in midair, forcing her to watch him fingering her friend. Gisele cums, observing the shock on Jen's face at the roughness, but the lust in her eyes tells a different story.

Gisele's heart pounds so hard she can barely breathe. She watches Jen held in place as Gisele's juices run down her husband's hand. *Now we're getting somewhere!* All the repercussions are squashed as her inability to fight her addiction surfaces. The obsession with foreplay heightens the sexual desire to peek for release. *Once that is reached, I want that arousal to go on for days! Well, a few hours would suffice! I would do anything to hold...* The line of thought is interrupted. Gisele is still fixated on the mirror, watching the two behind her interact.

The next command is whispered, "Dan says, hon, lose the shorts!"

The mirror now reveals Dan's fingers slowly tightening the grip that clasped the hair at the back of his wife's head, deliberately forcing her to face him as she pushes her shorts down. Gisele craving heightens at the sight of Jen's puffy, wet lips being exposed through the soaked panties. She is interrupted by Dan's movement. Staring right into his wife's eyes, he barks, "Dan says, Gisele, go on all fours, facing my wife!"

Gisele goes rigid. *What the hell did he say?* Avoiding their eyes, she shifts her gaze toward the TV. The film is close to the end. The image is the man's bare ass, his hips slamming against Jen bent over the arm of the couch. Not registering any of that and more concentrated on what is going on around her, bewildered, she stands there motionless. All her senses are alive with excitement as a thought surfaces. I*s this the dominant-submissive shit going on I read about!*

That just drives me to the edge! Calm down, calm down, think of something else you're going to make yourself cum! The image of her mother scolding her when caught with her friend from high school comes to mind. That helps her catch her breath. *No, there is something else going on here. Just comply and finish this!*

Obeying, Gisele's knees sunk into the rug, stretching forward her hands to feel the smooth softness of the sheepskin as they land facing Jen. The only thing in view is the top of Jen's head because she is on the edge of the couch, bent over removing her feet from the shorts. Rising and sitting back, Gisele notices Jen's breasts exposed, her nipples taut, and her T-shirt bunched around her neck. As Jen opens her legs, revealing a pair of soaked panties while locking eyes with her, a moan escapes Gisele's lips. Slightly shifting her eyes to catch a glimpse in the mirror of what Dan is up to behind her, Gisele gasps, seeing herself on all fours like a dog, panties around her knees and jeans encircling her ankles, while Dan sits beside his wife, softly stroking himself, leering at her with a smug expression.

With all the attention focused on her, she feels out of her realm, which gets her extremely inflamed. *What the fuck is all this about? Is this some kind of S&M happening? Some sort of way to punish Jen or dominate me? And if so, what for? How rough is it going to get?* A touch of fear comes over her which intensifies her enthusiasm as she waits for the next command. *Will I be able to obey to the end?*

CHAPTER 18

The reflections don't change for a few minutes. Dan strokes his cock as he turns his head to watch his wife. Gisele senses that Jen doesn't notice, her eyes locked on her new friend's position, one hand now on her crotch, fingers slipping under the edge of her panties, stroking softly. Gisele lifts her head to meet Jen's gaze, savoring the arousal reflected in her eyes. From behind, a command is whispered. "Dan says, spread your legs." Gisele, in doing so, perceives Dan's prying eyes. Then, another command is murmured. "Wider, as wide as you can!"

Gisele has never felt so vulnerable in her life—coerced into exposing her private parts for someone else's gratification. Wetness streaks down her leg. *The most astonishing humiliation of all this is that I can't hide how aroused I am—nor can I stop.* The next movement is Dan ignoring his wife as he stands, letting his pants drop to his feet. Moving behind Gisele, he slowly pushes his shorts down and steps out of them. Her eyes lock with Jen, and both come to the realization. *One, I am fucked, literally! Two, they are riding this out together to the end! Barring any extreme pain. Well, we'll see.*

The next command tears Jen's eyes away from Gisele to focus on her husband. Gisele lets her gaze fall to Jen's crotch. Seeing wet spots seeping through makes her shiver. Hearing the voice, she veers to look at the mirror. Dan stands tall in all his grandeur, cock erect, hands on his hips, eyeballing his wife. To Gisele, all this showboating was to cover up the uncontrollable lust that showed in his eyes. *Well, this is a goddam threesome, and none of us are quitting! So...*

All of a sudden, another command interrupts her train of thought. "Dan says, Gisele, crawl to my wife." Feeling his eyes are now fully on her, Gisele experiences a slight quiver with her head straight as she moves one hand and then a knee forward, then the others advancing catlike to Jen's open legs. Every muscle of her taunts, attempting to hold the panties from sliding past her knees. Within the short time it takes to cover the distance Gisele's head starts to swim, as different thoughts storm her mind anticipating the next move. *Not since adolescence had I indulged in this fantasy! Never once in my wildest dreams did I think that it was going to play out like this! Well, inching along my ass moving up and down, my aroused wet lips exposed, I think that will help Dan with his next decision!*

Gisele is halted as her face goes between Jen's spread legs. The aroma brought new heights of arousal she had never felt before. Hearing Dan come up behind her, feeling the sensation of his knees brushing the inside of her legs, she lifts her head to look at Jen. Her friend is staring elsewhere. Gisele then turns to the mirror to see what is going on behind her. Suddenly, she gasps, staring at the image.

Dan kneels behind her, cock in hand, aligning himself with her exposed entrance. Locking eyes with his wife, he presses the tip against her wet opening. He pauses, then places both hands on her ass cheeks and, with a wicked grin, squeezes them apart. His gaze is fixed on Jen as he slowly moves his hips forward, letting her soft lips part around the head of his shaft. Then, with a sharp thrust forward, it enters as deep as it will go and then holds.

Gisele lets out a low moan as her head rears back in pleasure at the intrusion. *Fuck me dam it, fuck me!* The force of Dan's sharp thrust forces her face against Jen's crotch. The wetness touching her lips filled her with a new desire for release. The movement of Jen's hips pushing against her mouth, then the sensation of hands touching the top of her head and holding her there, made her cum. Letting out a soft whine, Gisele feels Jen stir. She raises her eyes and catches Jen's gaze. Hearing her whisper, she leans back, lifting her hips toward the waiting mouth, all while keeping her eyes locked on her husband.

Gisele's desires resurface as the texture of Dan's stomach presses against her ass. He doesn't move, and feeling him inside ignites a deeper need, making her want to turn and look in the mirror. Kneeling between Jen's legs, hands resting on top of her head, he holds her in place. *What the hell kind of contest is this between these two? What is my purpose? The trigger! Calm down. Play it out. You know what you came here for. You can still salvage what you want.* However, her thought gets interrupted.

The next command comes in shallow breaths. "Dan says, Gisele, clean up those panty juices!"

Gisele holds steady as Dan begins moving his hips in slow, deliberate circles, gradually pulling back. Supporting his weight, he leans forward, sliding his arms beneath her to unbutton her blouse. As the material falls away, releasing two very firm breasts with erect nipples, he cups the bare breasts and pulls her body back as he thrusts forward. The thumb and forefinger pinch each nipple, rolling them gently. Gisele's eyes roll up in extreme sexual desire. *Jeez, does he have some moves? Maybe the size isn't everything! Naa! That isn't right!* Giving in, she knows everything from here on will happen robotically—she has no self-control left. Gisele, trying to obey the last command, feels her tongue meet resistance as Jen's crotch presses firmly against her mouth, hands holding her head in place. The tip of Gisele's tongue is at the entrance of her mouth, giving little flicks between the wet panty-covered lips. Sensing Jen quiver, sends Gisele close to the peek.

Then comes another command as he pants. "Dan… says, slide that tongue… into my wife's cunt!"

Gisele's body tingles! *Hoh… Lawyers do know four-letter words! Love that word!* Noticing that the hands have left her head, she lifts her own hand to slide the edge of Jen's panties aside, exposing her swollen lips. She begins placing tiny, rapid kisses along the inside of Jen's thigh, inching closer to her inflamed lips. Then, with a slow, cat-like lick, she traces her tongue along them, causing Jen's body to jerk in response.

The thrill Gisele feels prompts her to kiss lightly across the opening to the waiting lip there. She gives another slow cat-like lick and, with tongue still out, shifts to the opening to obey the orders. The tongue licks between the legs as commanded. Finished, a flood of juices flows over her tongue and in her mouth as it spreads the lips and goes deep inside. Gisele feels her discharge as thoughts flood her mind. *Is it the fact of watching her husband fuck another woman or my nose rubbing against that little erect button just above my mouth that made her cum?*

Dan's belly slams against her ass faster and harder, the sharp slapping sound filling the room. It's obvious to her—he's about to cum. She feels him pull out and rubs his cock between her ass cheeks. The warm sperm hitting her back and the balls spanking her pussy excite her. The feel of Jen's body quivering, and the taste of new juices lets her know it is coming to an end. She begins to pull her tongue back and lift her head but feels hands pressing firmly on the back of her head, guiding her back down—and she complies.

Jen's voice echoes, "Oh no! You are not done! Let us show him how to really satisfy a woman!" Thrusting her hips up, pressing the mouth hard against her, Jen glares at her husband.

Unconsciously, Gisele's tongue slides past very wet pubic hairs, parting the lips as it makes little circles inside. *What the fuck is going on! Am I their fucking slave?* The idea leaves her as she senses Dan entering her again. *Taking liberties, are we, Dan? Well, I will show these assholes how deviant I am!* With that, she rams her ass back hard against Dan's stomach; then, tongue extended, thrust forward, driving into Jen. She keeps that momentum up until feeling cum shooting inside her and Dan pulling out. *Now your turn, Jen! You don't know how perverted I am. No one does! I am going to finish it!*

Gisele kneels between Jen's legs, gaining confidence in the short span of time it took to change positions. Images of all the things she would try if she had a chance emerge. One quick peek in the mirror shows Dan's long, lean body stretched out against the couch spent. An evil grin appears on her face. *Oh, Jen, here I come!*

She slides her arms under Jen's legs, resting them gently on her shoulders. There is a hesitation as Jen's body stiffens. Slowly, she begins running her tongue down the leg, savoring the taste as she moves toward the inner thigh. When she reaches it, she turns her head, her tongue brushing over the delicate skin as she focuses on the right thigh. Pausing, she begins planting light kisses, gently licking her way back to the knee. When finished, she sits back to admire the work.

Looking up at Jen, Gisele begins to ask to expose her tits, but the moment her eyes land on her, she sees Jen pulling up the T-shirt around her neck, revealing her breasts, pinching the nipples, making them hard. The excitement Gisele felt at that moment knew no bounds with the realization she was in charge.

Bowing her head gently, taking the right plush lip in her mouth, she softly pulls on it, then releases it and does the same to the left. Without warning, she swiftly thrust her tongue in as far as it can go. A yelp-like cry escapes Jen's mouth. Her body convulses and then becomes still. Gisele was in heaven! Making her tongue do one more circle, she sucks it back in her mouth, producing a slurping sound. Holding for a second, then she slides it back near Jen's asshole. *Do you like cocks in there? Let's see what a tongue fucking does for you!* Driving it in as far as possible, she starts to move it around. Feeling it trying to pucker around her tongue, Gisele shoves harder, trying not to get pushed out. This skirmish goes on for a moment until Jen relaxes. Gisele, accepting the win, pulls out.

Moving her head up, letting the tongue worm its way to where the little button is waiting, she whispers silently, "Let's finish this fuck fest!" Licking it for a second, she then puts her lips over it and starts to suck on it as if it is a little cock. Jen's body gives a few small jerks, then stops. Wondering if her friend has passed out, she gives a couple more sucks before sitting back on her heels, resting her head on Jen's crotch. The click sound of the project still running gets Gisele's attention. Crawling over, she shuts it off, enjoying the thought that Dan's eyes are following her all the way.

"Let me go and get some towels so we can clean up," Dan whispers, stirring.

xxx

Returning, the three refresh themself as best they can. The hosts put on robes while Gisele gets dressed. Turning to the coffee table and starting to dismantle the unit, she glances at the mirror and catches Dan staring at her ass in the tight jeans. *Move one foot to the other to make the ass sway a little. Give them time, and the opportunity will present itself.*

Dan finally breaks the silence, "Nothing done or seen here today will ever be mentioned. Ever! Bill doesn't have to find out about it. Jen and I would still like everyone to still be friends." He finishes.

Gisele, putting the equipment in the box doesn't respond. *Let them sweat a little. Don't know about you, Dan, but I think Jen and I are going to be best friends!* Straightening up, she twists around to see a surprised look on Jen's face. Turning toward the source, she notices Dan with another hard-on. Gisele begins to chuckle. However, she picks up the box and heads to the door. With every step, Gisele endures as the anxiety increases! *What do I have to do?* The voice inside her says, *wait it out, it will come!*

The couple walks with her. Just as they reach the door, Dan asks, "Gisele, before I showed up, what was the reason for you bringing the film over? Come on," he urges, "After all that took place, nothing could shock us now."

A little voice in Gisele's head says, *is that so? Let's show them, girl.* Putting the box down on the table by the door, she turns to face them. A miniature smile forms.

"Shall we return to the lounge?"

CHAPTER 19

Walking back to the living room, Jen and Dan sit on the sofa. Gisele leaning against the coffee table, her hands clutching at her side, appears as if getting ready to give a speech. "Ok, I will tell you," *You'll see how devious I am! See if you can keep up!* Smirking, she continues. "I have always fantasized about Bill and I having a threesome with another woman but never acted on it. None of my friends are suitable as they have big mouths. Then fate intervenes. While shopping for a dress one day, I came upon the most tantalizing woman that I ever had the pleasure to cross paths with." Looking right at Jen, Gisele notices her blushing. Sensing a little pleasure at that, Gisele carries on, "That got me daydreaming about the threesome again. So, imagine how shocked I was when, at a dinner party days later, I was introduced to this same stunning woman. Well, I knew it had to be destiny!"

Looking at the other two, Gisele notices Dan's erection. *So we are not done yet!* Chuckling, she moves on, "Upon discovering the film with the same alluring woman starring in it, getting her ass fucked while sucking cock, I was aroused!" she pauses to let it sink in, then adds, "Oh, trust me, I watched it a few times while I schemed." Hopping up onto the coffee table, she sits, enjoying the attention and moves on. "Thought I would approach Jen knowing she was already into a threesome to see if she would like to join Bill and me." She glances at Dan, waiting for his eyes to meet hers, then silently locks her gaze on him.

Getting Dan's attention away from her chest, she resumes, "No disrespect to you, Dan, but I think Bill is homophobic, so I was only inviting Jen." She smiles and gets back to the story, "Didn't really know how I was going to proceed. Then, on one of my alone time, Jen called, interrupting me, sensing my mood, let's say asked if she could borrow the movie when I was done. Agreeing, I showed up here today to drop off the tape. When I got here, your wife invited me to stay. I never got to execute my plan because that is when you showed up." Finishing, the three sat in silence without moving a muscle.

Gisele is caressing her inner thigh for Dan's amusement while keeping an eye on Jen getting aroused, taking in the sight of the two of them flirting.

The little voice in Gisele's head says. *Don't quit now; I have gotten you this far. Tell them plan B!* Gisele hesitates, "Dan, could we have more wine? I will spill the rest of the plot."

"OK," comes the answer. As he moves to grab the drinks, Gisele catches him deliberately, letting the robe fall open and exposing himself. His delight is evident as he notices the two women stealing glances at his arousal. Returning to them, he saunters confidently, flaunting his erection, hands each of them a glass, and then settles into his seat, visibly gratified by their reactions. Gisele can't help but be impressed by his bold recovery.

With a drink in hand and everyone seated, Gisele begins. "Now, here is my dilemma! The more I watch the film, my fantasy changes from a threesome to me hiding to watch Jen seduce my husband. I want to experience the arousal of that at that very moment. That said, I didn't know how that was to come as we have never cheated on one another." Feeling the stares on her, the little voice kicks in: *don't think about it or voice it. Just continue.* "So, with all that took place here today, I would like to ask if you two will help fulfill my fantasy?"

Without hesitation, both answer together, "Oh yes!"

Dan chips in, "Leave everything up to me. I will make sure it happens," and with that, he begins to stand.

Gisele commands, "Be seated, Dan, as I have one last request."

Dan returns to his seat.

Gisele wonders how to continue as Dan and Jen, shoulder to shoulder, stare at her, waiting for the instruction. Breathing out heavily, she gathers up all her courage and starts, "I would like to, how to put this? Experience the sensation of watching! Besides, your husband is hard again, you can't leave him like that! I would like to watch while you jerk him off and have him cum all over those wonderful tits of yours!"

There is no delay as Jen moves her hand towards her husband, reaching over, grabbing out his cock stroking it slowly - all the while staring into Gisele's eyes, not saying a word. Gisele watching Dan being jerked off makes her passion rise. Jen leans toward her husband and raps her lips over the head of his cock, stroking faster as she sucks.

Gisele gets the feeling Jen is now just putting on a show as she reaches down, grabs his balls and squeezes so lightly, shoving the rest of the cock down her throat. That makes Gisele and Dan moan together. Observing Dan's hand reaching under his wife's bent-over body, he pushes aside the robe and starts to squeeze the erect nipples. Jen reacts by moving up and down faster as she sucks. *This is too much;* Gisele moves her hand between her legs as she watches.

Jen stops, raising her head and letting the cock slide out. Her tongue starts to slide up one side licking around the head, then spreads the little slit at the tip before slipping back down. Gisele, while watching, feels a twitch between her legs. She massages the clit some more. *Dam, she is good.* With eyes glued on Jen, Gisele wonders what she is going to do next.

Jen gets off the couch, gets between her husband's legs and starts to suck his cock again. At the same time, she makes sure the robe is out of the way, legs spread to give Gisele a good view of her ass and cunt.

Nice move, Jen. But it is the foreplay that I like. Watching is what inflames me, so I won't be joining in! But I will help with Dan.

With that, she raises a hand to one breast and starts squeezing and pinching the hard nipple through the blouse. Seeing Dan enjoying the show, she pushes the shirt aside, still working the nipple as the hand pushes on the breast. At the same time, she mouths, "I want to suck your cock!" Leaning back and spreading her legs, she slides her fingers over her crotch.

Watching as Jen's head rise, Gisele perceives that Dan must be ready to cum. Getting off the table, she walks over to get a better view, letting her bare breasts jiggle. Standing beside the two, Gisele glances at Jen working her magic. Reaching down, she lifts Dan's hand up so he can caress her breast, the palm sending shivers over her as it presses against the nipple, making her head bend back at the sheer pleasure. Lowering her head forward, taking in the action at her knees, she notes the cock is starting to throb as the fingers slowly slide up and down. Jen leans closer to see pre-cum forming on the tip so the head is resting between her tits. She squeezes harder, stroking faster.

All three moan as the warm, thick sperm shoots out the head, landing on Jen's breast and sliding down over a nipple onto the floor. Jen brings the cock to her mouth, licking the head clean for the show. She kisses it and then leans back on her heels.

"That was fantastic, you two!" Gisele breathes, leaning over Jen taking one finger and scooping a little cum off Jen's nipple while whispering in her ear, "I would like to fuck you again!" Straightening up, she licks the cum off her finger and takes a deep breath.

Gisele's face, taking on a stern look, addresses them for reassurance "Bill must never hear of what took place here today! Promise?" They nod in unison as Gisele steps back.

Jen gets off her knees, letting Dan rise from the couch. The host covers up as the three walk to the door. "I will leave everything here so you can come up with a plan, ok Dan?" Turning towards them, she catches Jen shaking her head and then stops.

Gisele ignores it while adding. "I kept up my end of the bargain. Please keep up yours." With that, she goes out the door and gets into the car. Feeling more confident, she murmurs, "You don't want to cross me! I survived senior high! This is a walk in the park."

xxx

Driving home, it was hard for Gisele to concentrate on the road. The fear of Bill finding out floods back, overwhelming every thought.

What if Dan lets it slip at one of their meetings?

Stop it! Clear your head! Sort everything out when you get home. Quit being paranoid!

Arriving home safely, and once in the house, she pours a glass of wine and heads upstairs to shower. *Clear your head, and you can resolve things tomorrow. Watching a movie tonight will help.* On that thought, she laughs. *That's what got me in this mess to start with!* Finishing washing up, she takes her own advice and grabs a glass of wine, cuddles with a blanket on the couch and turns on the TV.

Oh, I pray this works.

CHAPTER 20

Gisele's sleep doesn't come easy, and as her eyes open to the morning light, she realizes today will be no different. Her mind screams back to yesterday's events, trying to comprehend how everything went south. Feeling guilty, her mind begins to spin. *I never cheated on Bill ever! Didn't even cross my mind! Yeaaa, in fantasies, but not seriously! God dam it, what did I do? Then, to make things worse Dan insinuates Bill is a Peeping Tom as if it was a bad thing. He could even go to jail! Causing him to lose his job!* Shaking her head, she repeats, "What the hell have I done? I can't think of worse things it could have been!"

She goes to get a coffee. "I have to sit, calm down, and think this through before Bill gets home." Seated on the island, her mind starts to rearrange the reality leading up to the incident. "It worked in senior high; it will succeed again."

"Ok, ok, ok! This is not my fault! Bill was the one hiding something. As a wife, it was my duty to find out what it was to help me understand who I was married to. To that end I found out about the secret hiding place and the numerous films." She gets up and starts pacing; it helps her think. *Did I have to watch them? Yes, who could resist? Then, when I discovered Jen and Dan starring in one I just had to know if he was hired to film them.* She pauses for a moment, seeing the time, and replaces the cup of coffee with a glass of wine.

Sipping the wine, she starts to get excited, recalling that *I climaxed a few times to those viewings. Stop it, stay focused.* She resumes the task at hand. *I started to get curious if he knew them before we were introduced, as the film dates suggested it was possible. So, in trying to solve that dilemma, I approached Jen with the film. Discovered that, indeed, they did not, and that's when Dan got involved. That is when the blackmailing started, making me have sex with them! I had no choice but to give in so no one else would know of Bill's fetish. So, in reality, you're the cause of all this, Bill! You bastard!* Having solved who really is to blame for what happened seems to have freed her mind of guilt. The voice confirms her thoughts: *you are right; all this happened because of him not trusting you! Well, I will stop all this secrecy. And that will only happen if Jen and Dan can fulfill my request.*

Getting up, she starts to make a late lunch and decides *I have to Google Peeping Tom to see if what Dan implied is correct.* Once she finishes eating, she puts the dishes in the sink, heads up to her study, turns on the computer, and proceeds to search. After an hour of research, she sits back to reflect on what she read.

So, Dan is right: it is illegal, and you can get jail time. But highly unlikely to get caught as many believe it to be harmless, so they don't report it. The thought of the incident at college pops up. She smiles to herself. *Dam, I need more wine.* She heads down to the kitchen with what she read still on her mind. *Let's see what else, oh, the peepers start at a young age and get away with it, so it continues. It's not always sexual. Could also be to get the feel of power and control.* She ponders on that point for a moment but shakes her head, discarding the thought. *No, for Bill, it is definitely for sexual gravitation, as the sex is great when he gets home. So that should rule out that he might be inclined to move up to sexual assault. The science study concluded very few do.* Frowning, she pushes the darker implication of the act out of her mind. Chuckling, she thinks about the legend that labeled Peeper's Tom.

When Lady Godiva rode naked through the streets, the residents were ordered not to look out their windows. One poor soul defied the officials and was struck blind; his name was Tom. Laughing, she wonders out loud, "If that was true, wouldn't that be the first and last peeping tom!" She begins to laugh remembering what parents told their sons, "If you masturbate too much, you will go blind. Don't know if that applied to daughters; if so, well, I'd definitely need glasses!" That puts her in a better mood, so she decides to head upstairs to do more research. This time about her sexual urges and the thoughts she had that day.

xxx

Sitting by the computer, the soft glow of the monitor lights up her face. Her fingers hover over the keyboard as she brings up Google, unsure of what to search for. With a deep breath, she leans back, letting her thoughts wander to what happened and the emotions swirling inside her.

The moment I was with Jen was a no-brainer. Knowing I was about to have a threesome that drove me to the edge was not unusual. No, it is something else.

Something I never thought about or never thought I would be sexually aroused by it. Gisele focuses on a moment in time. An image emerges, and *that's it! Seeing Jen's head being pulled back by her hair! Not just that, but at the same time, being forced out of my comfort zone to do things I had no control over or the will to stop.*

With that image in her head, she types "sex control" into the search bar. The word "dominance" pops up, and she clicks on it, her curiosity leading the way. The response she gets makes her sit back in surprise. **"Dominance and submission, also called D/S,"** she reads aloud. As she scrolls further, her thoughts begin to swirl. *So, if I got this right, Dan would have been the dominant who is in the superior position making me the submissive or the subordinate.*

Startled by the sound of the car pulling into the driveway, she gasps. "Dam, time got away from me!" Glancing at the clock, she realizes it's already four o'clock—Bill is back from his trip. Quickly, she shuts everything down and heads to the door to greet her husband. *I must remember to research more to see if that is what happened.* Just as she falls into Bill's arms, her last thought is of Jen shaking her head that day as they said goodbye. *Hmmm, what was that about?* Before breaking the embrace, Gisele gives him a hard, long kiss and then steps back.

"Wow, you keep that up, and I won't have time to shower!" Bill teases, grinning.

Loving the response, she replies, "That wouldn't hurt my feelings in the least!" With that being said, she heads to the kitchen, chuckling to herself, "Ok, you have a shower, and I will start supper."

Bill strolls to his study as Gisele, while preparing the food, starts to wonder. *Did he get a film for his collection? Don't you dare!* She starts scolding herself! However, her inner voice has something else to say. *Oh, go peek; who will it hurt? Then you will know! That way, you will not have to sneak later!* Not being able to withstand the urge, she creeps toward the study. Upon reaching the door, she stops and presses against the wall. She tilts her head slightly, just enough to catch glimpses of Bill. With his back to her, he stands at the wide-open frame, carefully sliding a film reel into place. Gisele heart jumps into her throat. She is so excited she can hardly breathe! She starts to back away, relieved she is barefoot, inching her way back to the kitchen.

xxx

Standing over the stove, turning the meat, she feels the tingle down there and gets a little wet. *Jeez, you think after yesterday you would be sexed out. I got to be some kind of nymph.* Grinning, she decides to look that up later. However, Gisele's thoughts are interrupted by the feel of hands sliding around her waist up towards her breast. Leaning her head back on Bill's shoulder, she whispers, "Let's see if we can make it through supper! That will make the foreplay more intense later!" Embracing her tighter, Bill lets his hands move down to his side. She gently nudges him back and continues to attend to the supper while feeling Bill's crotch press against her, sending a shiver up her spine and leaving her wanting more.

Moving back, Bill moans, "Dam, you woman, all this teasing is going to make me cum before supper! Let me get the wine."

"Oh, come on, hon! How is this old mini front button dress getting you aroused?" she shakes her ass for emphasis.

"Because I know for a fact that you are not wearing any underwear! If I came over there and ripped the buttons off, you would be naked!" setting the wine down, ribbing, he continues. "But let's play it your way to see who lasts."

Gisele, beaming, brings the food to the table. Setting it down, she sits at the other end. *Love this man; he sure does know me.*

"Ok, love, tell me about your trip!" Gisele gives her husband her full attention.

Bill, dishing up, starts the story. "The first day and night was uneventful. More for staking the place out to find the best place to go unnoticed. You remember the night I called?"

Gisele nods her head. *Jeez, get to the good parts already!*

"Well, it's a good thing I stuck to my guns! With it was raining so hard, my two subjects stayed in. Let's say the pictures I captured put a new meaning in brotherly love." Grinning, he looks at his wife. "So, I think Dan is going to like what I found out. Whether they are related or not, either way, it says a lot about their character." Taking the last bite quickly, he shoves the chair back and stands up.

Gisele, not quite done yet, puts down her fork, "Oh, is this how it's going to be!" she pushes her chair back. "You will have to catch me first!" She starts running around the table. "Come on, big boy!" she taunts, dashing toward the stairs. As she unbuttons her dress, they race to the bedroom, knowing all the talking is done. She jumps on the bed and surrenders.

CHAPTER 21

The late morning sun shining through the window finds Gisele in the study, finishing up paperwork on the house she just sold. Closing the deal always puts her in a good mood. She starts thinking about when Bill came home a couple of days ago and how everything went as planned. They had supper together and talked about how the story was going. Then, went to bed and made love! *I enjoy the intimacy on these occasions when he comes back from those short journeys. The tenderness, cuddling afterward. Ahaaa... the bonding was great. Don't have many nights like that as he is not often away from home.* The little voice enters the thought, *what about the film he was caught hiding?* Before she can address the idea, her ringing phone brings her out of her daydream. She picks it up.

"Hello"

"Hi! It's Jen. Are you busy this afternoon?"

"Actually, no. I just finished my work, so I am free," she replies.

"Great, let's have lunch. I have some news."

Upon hearing that, Gisele becomes excited. "Where and when, hon?"

"The three D's, it has a great outdoor patio, located at 454 69th street, say one-thirty?"

"Ok, meet you at the diner." Gisele hangs up after saying their goodbyes. Intrigued, she heads to the bedroom to get dressed, trying to fathom how they've already put a plan together. *Can't even imagine what it could be!* She grabs the red button-front long-sleeve collar blouse she bought the other day from the closet. The one with round ivory pearl buttons—a single row just above the breast, running from each armpit to the V-cut. Double rows of buttons extend downward over each breast to the bottom of the blouse. Slipping it on, she reaches for her jeans. *Only bought it because after Googling BDSM, I think it will give me that dominant look.* Laughing, she throws on her jeans and glances in the mirror to confirm how alluring she looks. She grabs some heels and heads out.

Not knowing where to go, she types the address in the GPS. *That's what I love about this city being easy to navigate around. The streets go north to south or east to west, and not many one-ways. Not overpopulated either. Just right for my business.* As soon as she makes the right turn, the GPS announces, "You have arrived at your destination."

Seeing a sign that says "Parking in the Rear," she chuckles as she pulls in and parks. The word "rear" is replaced by two cartoon butt cheeks. "Cute!" she mutters with a smirk.

Entering the restaurant, she approaches the male host, all dressed in black - tight-fitting pants and a very snug short-sleeved shirt open to the navel to show off his smooth, shinny chest.

"I am supposed to meet a friend here. I think she is out on the patio."

"Ok, just this way, follow me."

Walking behind, she focuses on that tight butt. *If he is twenty, I will eat his shorts! That is, if he is wearing any.* The thought sends her smiling all the way to the patio.

As they pass by the tables, Gisele notices two things right away: first, most of the patrons are women, and second, the tables are spaced far apart, offering plenty of privacy. Not to mention how beautifully the empty ones are set. Each looked like a work of art, with polished silverware, crystal glasses, carefully folded napkins, and fresh flowers adding an elegant touch. *Dam, this is going to be expensive!*

The host pushes open two large glass double coors and steps onto the patio. Gisele follows, her attention immediately drawn to the sight of sunlight streaming onto a well-appointed bar on the left, adding to the place's allure. Spotting Jen, she waves to signal the host that she has found her table. As Gisele walks up to greet her friend, she stops short, noticing the look on Jen's face—wide eyes and a small, flirtatious grin playing on her lips.

"That is so suggestive! Are you wearing that blouse just for me? The red just yells out yes!" Jen pauses, still seated, mesmerized by Gisele's attire.

The host pulls the chair back for Gisele to be seated then leaves.

Gisele sits and looks at her friend, "I could ask the same! That silk white blouse opened just past the breast suggests yes!" Both blush and let out a little chuckle.

The waiter comes around to take their drink order. Jen motions for Gisele to go first.

Looking over the drink menu, Gisele smiles, "These are quite suggestive. But I think I will try the kitty nectar," she says, handing the menu back to the host. Gisele quivers as her eyes scan over the waiter's crotch. The bulge there suggested he was indeed not wearing underwear.

"Well, I would like to try girls' night out, thanks," Jen says, handing hers back as well as steering her gaze to where her friend is focused. Jen's eyes widen in acknowledging the same urge.

Turning her attention to Jen, "How did you find this extraordinary voluptuous place?" Gisele whispers seductively.

Jen smiles, remembering the occasion, and a sheepish grin crosses over her face. "It was quite flattering. A very attractive young woman approached me at one of my functions and gave me the address. I think she thought I was hitting on her."

Gisele raises her eyebrows, confronting Jen.

"Ok, maybe I was eyeing her up a little." They both laugh.

Jen's voice takes a more serious tone, "Ok, why did I ask you here? I was a little concerned about the other day. Just wanted to see if you were alright with what took place that afternoon!"

"Well, to be honest, I'm feeling a little guilty having cheated on Bill! But more apprehensive of him finding out!" Gisele confesses, watching her friend's reaction.

"Let's see if I can put your mind at ease." Pausing for a moment to choose her words carefully, Jen takes a sip, "Do you remember me shaking my head as you left?"

Gisele acknowledges she did.

"Well, I was doing so to let Dan know that it was inappropriate to invite you to stay for dinner. The man is a great criminal lawyer, but when it comes to social awareness, he is clueless."

Gisele's eyebrows knit together, looking puzzled as her friend speaks.

"I will explain. Dan relates life as if he is in a courtroom. So, to him, he presented his case and won. His reality was we had a threesome, no harm, no foul. I had to sit him down and explain, no! That you were blackmailed into participating, so in reality, you were raped!"

Gisele's eyes widen, and as she opens her mouth to speak, Jen quickly puts up a hand to stop her.

"Let me finish! So, I let him know that no one can ever find out what happened as we both will go to jail. That, my dear, should ease your mind on both accounts." Jen finishes, looking at her puzzled friend.

At that moment, Gisele is relieved the waiter appeared to take their order giving her time to gather her thoughts. As before, Jen urges Gisele to order first. Blushing slightly at the names on the menu—just like the drinks, they were all sexually suggestive—she scans the list before finally placing her order. "I will try the Cincinnati three-way," she says, grinning at her friend seductively.

Not to be outdone, Jen locks eyes with her friend and says, "And I'll try the In-N-Out Animal Style." She doesn't waver as the waiter takes their orders and walks away. Before Gisele can respond, Jen leans in slightly and adds, "So, with all that said and done, do you still want to go through with your plan?"

Gisele, drinking slowly, takes a few minutes to answer as she tries to suppress the shock at her friend's words. "Please don't ever use that word rape again, ever! It implies what we did was obscene, and for your information, it is not true. I am more inclined to go with Dan's version."

With knitted brows, she declares, "Oh, don't look so shocked! What was my motive when I arrived at your place, hmmm? To see if I could blackmail you into having a threesome with me! That said, is that any different than Dan's? So, to put all doubt out of your mind, I was so aroused when he asked me to crawl over to you that I had no willpower to stop, even if requested! So, no more talk about rape!" Still frowning, she picks up the glass of wine and drinks.

Gisele watches as Jen seems lost in thought, clearly recalling the moment. Finally, Jen smirks flirtatiously and purrs."Well, I don't think ask is the word you were looking for!" Gisele observes Jen fidgeting, taking up the conversation, "Oh love you don't know how close you were to succeeding! My husband had no idea about the first part of the film! Yea when having the desert, I was to stroke the man beside me as that was in the plan just to get him ready for the conclusion! But the blowjob was all me. That's why I quit before Dan entered the room. My little secret to keep the game thrilling and myself aroused."

Gisele, in horror, jumps in, "Jesus Christ! I didn't know! I would never in a million years have Dan see that film even if you had said no!" They sit in silence noticing the waiter bring drinks to their table.

Setting them down, the server says, "These are from the two ladies three tables back." Gisele's back is to them, but Jen waves in thanks. "What are these drinks called?"

"One is the Jam Donut Shot, the other, Wet Pussy Shot," the waiter replies.

"Ok, would you please take two glasses of Girls Night Out and tell them thanks, maybe another time."

The waiter nods and then leaves.

"I should have warned you that you could get hit on." Jen smiles, breaking the awkwardness between them.

Gisele turns to view which two women he is referring to. Astonished at recognizing her friend Susan, she turns away to face Jen.

"You seem a little flustered. What's up?"

"One of the girls that sent the drinks is an old classmate. When we were in college, six of us made a pact that no matter where life led us, we would meet at least once a month for brunch to stay in touch. And she is one of them."

Jen muses, grinning, "Let me get this straight. You six are college friends who meet up when you can but don't know each other?"

"We do but the more intimate stuff we keep to ourselves. Like, they will never know of my, let's say, indiscretion from the other day. We don't go to each other's homes or get involved in their everyday life. All I know about Sue is she let it slip that she married Rodger, who was in the same class as us, but that is it. The rest is left up to the individual if they want to reveal anything more. The talk is mostly about what wild things we used to do in college and things we should have done before we got married and life got in the way. Makes us feel young and adventurous." Gisele chuckles nervously thinking how stupid and immature it must sound.

"Would love to join your group! Sounds interesting." Gisele gets the idea Jen is trying to bait her as her friend purrs. "You could introduce me to Sue! Maybe I would discover what crazy things you two got away with," Jen's lips pucker, grinning, sending an imaginary kiss.

"Stop it, there are no outsiders," Gisele laughs, turning to the last of the hors d'oeuvre.

The waiter brings the food, sets it down, and walks away. Both girls ogle him as he goes.

Catching one another, they smirk before turning to the plate of food and eating in silence.

Finishing a bite, Jen breaks it. "The word is they hired a chef from France to come over to cook," Jen informs her friend, wiping the corners of her mouth.

Once done eating, she pushes her plate back, "That tasted fantastic! I believe it." Gisele responds, copying Jen.

Finishing the food and wiping her mouth with a napkin, Jen asks, "Would you like another drink? I will tell you the second part why I asked you here."

Gisele's brows rise in surprise at the statement and she agrees. Jen gets the waiter's attention. "Could I get a Butt Plug? And for you, Gisele?"

She hesitates for a moment, not wanting to be outdone. With a playful smirk, she looks at Jen and says, "I'll have the Clit Licking

Cowgirl 2, please." Gazing into Jen's eyes, she slowly licks her lips. A small voice in her mind whispers, *Where are you taking this? Are you really willing to step out on Bill? I don't think so!* Sighing, she sits back, waiting for Jen's explanation.

Jen, giving back a shy leer, starts, "Things are just about ready to put the plan in motion. Just thinking about it makes me a little wet! It took a while, but Dan thinks he got it figured out. The hard part was where you were going to hide so you could see all the action."

"You don't have a closet?" Gisele responds curious at what the answer would be.

"The thing is, Dan wants to play the same game as with the other men. It seems to make more sense." Jen shrugs. "So, we figured, let's build a bar. Now the problem is how to position it for the occupant's best viewing."

Gisele looks a little puzzled at that statement.

Jen notices the puzzled look and pipes up. "No, it is ok! Dan said he would make sure it would be big enough to fit you comfortably if we left the shelves out until they were needed. Everything is a go. Will start the project after this weekend as we have a function to attend this Saturday at Dan's firm."

Gisele wonders why, gazing at Jen. "That seems awfully expensive, Jen, for one night's use."

"Who says it's for one night only!" Jen adds with a suggestive grin on her face, "Not really, I always wanted a bar. Just didn't know where to put it and now we do."

"Well, I hope it is worth it." Gisele is appreciative of the effort they are enduring pondering on what could possibly be their alternative motive. She whispers. "And thanks."

"Just seeing the lust in your eyes makes it worth it already." Jen whispers, carrying on with the flirtation. The women, getting aroused, finish their drinks.

"Holy shit look at the time, I have to get home!" Gisele starts to get up.

"Why? If you don't make it home by midnight, you turn into a lesbian?" Jen whispers playfully.

Grinning, she replies, "I think you mean a pumpkin." Jen walks close to Gisele, caressing her ass as they leave, whispering, "Any time you turn into pumpkin, call. I will drop everything and be your pumpkin eater! " Then the hand falls away.

Oh, you like this cat and mouse stuff also, don't you? Well, the game is on. Gisele thinks, and a shiver goes through as she detects a wetness between her legs as they part ways. "You will be the first one I will call!" Gisele kisses Jen on the cheek before heading to the car.

Driving home she ponders over what Dan and Jen discussed after she left that day. *Better yet, what was Sue doing at The Three D's? To top that, what am I playing at?*

CHAPTER 22

The next day, sitting at her desk in the study, Gisele reflects on what had been discussed yesterday. So, Jen getting her hair pulled and Dan fucking me was her punishment because he didn't know what she had been doing in the first part of the film. Shuffling the documents, not really looking at them, her thoughts drift further towards that day. Dan commanding me to crawl on all fours and have sex with his wife was supposed to be my punishment for trying to blackmail Jen! Well, sorry to disappoint you. Instead of feeling humiliated, I've now uncovered a new sexual desire I didn't even know existed. Chuckling, she put the papers away, knowing she couldn't concentrate. She goes downstairs for more coffee and sits down on the stool, sipping from the cup. Why was Jen insinuating that I was raped! Well, I hope I set her straight with my explanation. The only good that comes of that way of thinking is I can hold that over Dan's head. Or, at the very least, convince Bill it was to save my marriage!

Standing holding the warm cup to her bare breasts, she strolls over to her favorite part of the house, the French patio doors. The window on each side protrudes out on an angle making an alcove to create a panoramic view. Standing there in just panties, the gray light of the morning surrounding her, she watches the light rain splash against the panes, and a warm sensation flows over her. Enjoying the moment, she remembers, "Shit, don't forget Bill made dinner plans," and breathes out. That gets her moving to the stairs, all the while pondering why Jen picked the Three D's restaurant! Was she testing me to see if I was into women more than I let on? What's that saying, 'Coming out of the closet!' She grins at the thought. Sorry, girl, I just like to experiment. I am not giving up on those seven inches for anyone. Then, remembering Sue being there, her thoughts drift in another direction. Well, that is going to make it awkward at the next brunch get-together. Suddenly, her phone buzzes. Checking it, she sees a text from Bill reminding her about their dinner date tonight."Shit,

" she mutters. "I'd better get my work done."With that, she heads to the study.

xxx

A few hours go by. With the work done, she goes to the bedroom to get ready. Once ready, she hears Bill come in and steps to the doorway, hollering, "What time is the reservation?"

"At seven-thirty. We have about an hour before we leave."

"Ok, just about ready."

Descending the stairs, she wears a Black deep V-neckline embellished maxi dress. A high slit on one side reveals her leg, while rhinestones form an intricate butterfly pattern—the wings extending from her breasts down to her hips, the tail cascading elegantly along the fabric. A shawl drapes over her shoulders, completing the striking ensemble.

Bill was waiting at the door, dressed in a casual cashmere black blazer with a black high-neck T-shirt and tight black pants. Letting out a short whistle, he leers at his wife.

Gisele, sensing the arousal in him and her own erotism, blows a kiss at him. Reaching the door and locking arms, they head to the car.

xxx

Arriving at the restaurant, Gisele thinks not as elegant as the three D's but impressive. Once shown to their table Bill orders a drink and starts up the conversation. "That story I am working on just got a whole lot crazier! Apparently, Dan's intuition that the wife's brother and sister did her in might be bang on! Which, I found out, the two are probably not even related to anyone!" Bill starts to laugh while having a drink and carries on. "Quite sure they are not even brother and sister! So, what is the scam? Here is the million-dollar question!" Finishing his whiskey, he orders another regarding his wife as if she had the answer. Scowling, he proceeds. "She tried to frame the husband for the murder! Thinking with the husband charged they'd get all the inheritance. How the hell does that work? You would have to be a relative or, God dam, that is it, at the very least, in the will." He pauses to take a drink, looking smug.

Gisele, with excitement in her eyes, gazes at her husband nodding acknowledgment in all the right places! *I have been on enough of these dinner outings to know he loves these, what he calls 'Our quiet time.' Or what I like to call the sounding board.* The voice comes to the front, *you have your agenda on these nights! You're so bad! I do! Love these nights out!* Gisele throws a lustful lock at her husband and leans forward to let him know all her attention is his. She orders him another drink.

Waiting for the waitress to remove the empty glass and set down the full one, Bill continues to wrap up the story. "They live in a trailer park in Dillten." Bill stops, hearing Gisele snicker."Oh, just because they have a trailer, that makes them trailer trash. Next, you will be hating renters. " Bill starts to laugh. "Don't forget where you came from, missy."

Gisele smirks. *That is not what I was chuckling at. Watching you ogle the waitress's big breast as she puts down the drink and enjoying the hint of her nipples erect, pushing against the uniform. With your eyes, following that nice round ass as she walks away was arousing me! That is what I was admiring! Oh, she is getting a big tip!* Gisele sniggers and *so am I*, and hints to her husband to continue.

Bill carries on with a glint in his eyes. "Was to follow up on the story in Dillten and stay overnight, but I put it off until Saturday. Just need a break and some time with you."

"Hmm-hmm,"

Gisele orders another drink. She knows how this is going to go, as her plans for the evening are falling into place nicely. Bill goes on about how it is going to be the story of the century and his big break. Listening, she keeps ordering drinks for him and ginger ale for herself, sticking to the scheme.

With the meal finished, Bill is well intoxicated. Watching his eyes drooping he appears to be ready to fall asleep. Gisele motions for the bill and pays the tab. With his arm around her shoulder and hers around his waist, she helps him to the car and drives home. Once there, she leads Bill upstairs to bed. The long hours and the drinking take their toll. That was what she was hoping! Flopping Bill on the bed, he passes out.

Gisele, standing by the bed looking down at Bill, smiles as she realizes that her mission has been accomplished. Seeing him there, she gets turned on as the idea of what is going to happen next materializes. *You don't let this happen very often but when it does, I am taking full advantage of the situation!* She starts to remove her gown, and with that done, she attends to Bill.

With the blazer and t-shirt discarded, she huffs *isn't as easy as it looks in the movies*. She muses on this for a moment before leaving Bill on his back and moving to the foot of the bed. She bends over and unbuckles Bill's pants, pulling them over his hips and then off. With a big grin on her face, gazing at the bulge in his shorts as she knew it would be, she gets wet. Standing there in just her panties, debating whether to leave the shorts on or take them off, she finally whispers to herself, "For this occasion, I think off." Sliding a hand over the bulge, she gives a little squeeze before moving up to the elastic band. She watches the shaft twitch as the short glide over it while being removed.

Gisele goes to the side of the bed and crawls in beside Bill. The heat from his body as she presses her breast to his side, crotch against his hip, sends a warmth through her. One arm snakes over his hip, and her hand slides down to the base of the shaft. Gently cupping the balls for a second, two fingers encircle the erection, lifting it off his stomach. Slowly fondling it, she savors the moment. *How do I get off that? My fingers can barely close around it at the thickness it gets as I stroke.* Standing Bill's cock straight up, she begins to stroke faster, her movements intensifying as her arousal grows.

"What are you dreaming about, or who that gets you so hard?" She whispers in his ear and tightens her grip as she tries to imagine. The sensation of feeling the thickness as her fingers slide up to the head and back down is just about too much to bear. The desire to climax is hard to control. Removing her panties, she sits up and straddles that massive cock. Lowering slowly down, letting the pulsing head spread her lips as it enters. As her ass touch Bill's legs, leaning forward with both hands on his chest, she starts to rock back and forth.

Staring into that oblivious face under her, she accepts the power she has over him. She murmurs while visualizing, "Jen could be fucking you, and you wouldn't know the difference!" She breathes. "I would be sucking on her tits while she fondles mine." That was it. Gisele starts convulsively while climaxing, inhaling deeply. Sensing Bill is ready to explode, she slides off, kneeling on the bed beside him and grabs his cock, jerking it slowly. Increasing the motion as she feels it start throbbing, she squeezes it harder as her hand slides up and down. Gisele quivers orgasmically when the thick sperm shoots in the air and lands all over Bill's stomach and on her hand. "You can't get any more stimulated than watching that."

She gets up and grabs a hand towel to clean Bill up, then lies back in bed, her mind drifting. *How long will it take Dan to piece the plan together?* The thought lingers as she falls asleep, trying to imagine the details playing out in her head.

CHAPTER 23

Waking to the brightness of the morning, Gisele panics and shakes Bill, shouting, "Bill! Bill! Bill! Wake up! It is 8:30! Take a shower, and I'll put the coffee on and start breakfast."

By the time Bill comes downstairs, everything is on the table, while Gisele is still darting around.

"Calm down, hon. I did want to get going early, but it was no big deal. I will have to stay overnight no matter what time I get there today." Bill frowns, "Sorry about last night, love. The alcohol hit me harder than I thought."

Gisele sits at the table, reflecting—it was a great night. Though out loud, she says, "That's okay, hon. It doesn't happen often. You can make it up to me when you get home," she reassures him with a smile.

With the meal done, Bill gathers up his cameras to get ready to leave. "That is a promise. And oh, thanks for helping me." He pauses while he grabs his coat from the chair. Gisele stares at him! *Maybe he wasn't asleep!* Bill goes on, confessing, "Talking over the story with you last night helped, love. I did not imagine the angle could be one of them is in the will. It makes more sense now." Pulling the coat on, he goes over, kisses her and then walks to the door.

Gisele walks with him to the door and throws her arms around him. "Glad I could help. I am going to miss you!" she says, kissing him and then steps back.

"Miss you too," he says before walking out the door.

Clearing her mind, Gisele gets another coffee and strolls over to the French doors. Standing there, taking in the view as light rain splashes on the panes.

"To hell with it." She lets the robe slip from her shoulders, dropping it to the floor. Sliding her panties down, she steps out of them and pushes the doors open, walking into the morning light. A sigh of relief escapes her lips as the rain showers over her, washing away the tension in her body.

She strides to the patio railings, leaning against them, surveying the world around her. "This makes me feel so alive," she murmurs, her thoughts drifting to the events of the past few days.

Can Dan genuinely make it happen? Can't even fathom how he would approach Bill, let alone convince him. Suddenly, her mind switches to something different. *I have to explore this D/S activity to see how I can make that happen in the bedroom. Or if I want to really get aroused if that was what was going on that afternoon.*

Then there is Jen. Just something is off about her. Doesn't talk much about herself or what she does. Hmm will keep an eye on her. She lingers a little longer, savoring the feeling of the rain washing over her body. The past evening enters her thoughts.

Smiling, she says to herself, "How that man doesn't wake up is beyond me." She starts reminiscing about the first time it happened. Standing there by the bed with Bill passed out, she remembers how furious and turned on she was all at once. Her eyes had caught the bulge in his pants, and throwing caution to the wind, she'd reached down, pulled him out, and ridden him like an animal.

She chuckles at the memory, recalling how his head had just lolled from side to side—he hadn't even flinched. Over time, she'd grown bolder, taking every opportunity when it arose. Last night had been number five.

Straightened, Gisele heads back in. Picking up the clothes on her way, she heads to the laundry chute to throw them in. "I am going to be a goddam nudist today." She goes into Bill's shower and grabs a towel. Drying off, she steps over to the desk. "Is there anything new, I wonder?" Grabbing the pick, she opens the frame, peers inside, and finds nothing new. Happily, she closes everything up. Putting the pick back, she heads upstairs to her study.

Turning on the computer, she opens Google and types in Dominance and Submission. The search displays a lot of different choices to explore. Getting lost in the material, she loses all sense of time until she starts to feel hungry. She gets up, shuts down the computer, and goes to the kitchen, "Well, that is a lot to take in and is very sexually suggestive. It's starting to get me aroused. I better make lunch so I can calm down." The rest of the afternoon consists of cleaning up and weighing the pros and cons of the Dominance and the submission roles. And most importantly, trying to decide which one she would be best at!

xxx

Supper time rolls around to find Gisele sitting in the living room, a freshly delivered pizza in front of her, looking for a movie to watch. "Dam found it!" She whispers as the title 8mm comes on the screen. Once the movie begins, she becomes shocked at what it is about, shuts it off halfway through, and eats in silence.

Finished, she gets up to do the dishes the movie still in her head. *Never thought of snuff movies! Are they even real? I don't even want to know.* After finishing up, she decides to read a book to get the movie off her mind.

xxx

Curled up on the couch, the book still in her hand, she glances at the clock. *It is 11 o'clock. I should head to bed.* Reaching the bedroom, she lies on top of the bedcovers naked, allowing the night breeze from the open window to ripple over her. Not wearing any clothes sure has its advantages. Not sleepy, but a little stimulated, she meditate on what to do.

Then, an idea comes to her! "It said D/S can be conducted over the phone. Can I be authoritative enough to pull this off?" *Hearing Jen's voice while I masturbated and watching her in the film gave me such a fierce orgasm! Wondering if just hearing her voice will do the trick! At the very least, I will discover if I have enough confidence to be a Domme! I will win either way.* Recalling that Jen is at a function, she picks up the phone, a thrilling sensation surging through her, and wonders if Jen will answer.

"Hello," Jen answers.

"Hi, how is the party?" Gisele replies, trying hard to steady her breathing being caught off guard hearing the voice on the first ring.

"Going great! Dan is over there in the corner, flirting with a couple of women. Looks to me like he has a real hard-on. Can't wait to get that in my mouth. As for me, I just got done flirting with a guy who was brushing up against me. I could feel his cock on my ass." she laughs. "Felt like he wanted to go a little farther, but he wasn't all that big." she giggles.

"Now you are making me wet," Gisele chips in. "I am just lying on the bed, ready to enjoy myself, thinking of you. Thought I would like to hear your voice before I start! But you just gave me a better idea! Let's get Dan off instead!"

"What!" Jen exclaims.

Gisele keeps talking before she chickens out, her voice getting stronger as she explains. "I want you to walk over there and hand Dan the phone. Say someone wants to talk to him. Then turn, face the woman, back up against Dan's crotch, putting one hand behind your back, and start jerking him off. Imagine how much longer he'll last if he cums once before going home." Gisele's hand moves down her stomach, letting her fingers twirl the pubic hairs as the excitement increases, waiting for a response.

Jen, sounding unsure, responds, "But the women will know what I am doing!"

"Oh, I am sure they will." Gisele is trying to be commanding: "And you make sure they do! Look them right in the eyes, letting them see your lust! They will either get very aroused and want to join you, or they will walk away. We win both ways." Gisele says, her voice having a harsh tone.

"Oh, shit, I am getting so horny thinking about that woman in the blue top, big tits eyeing up Dan! Let's do this!" moans Jen.

Gisele is forcing the sexual urges she feels back on Jen; giving in to the demand is just about impossible! Wanting to embrace the full power she seems to have over Jen, Gisele nervously tries to make her voice more forceful! "Ah, just one more thing Jen! Lean your head back towards Dan's enough so you can hear what I'm saying. That way, you will know that I am getting your husband to imagine fucking me while you jerk him off! All the time, getting the three women wishing it was them!" She stresses strongly, "Got it!"

For some time, there has been no answer. All she hears next is, "Dan, someone wants to talk to you!" and the sound of footsteps echoes next.

"Hello." Dan answers.

"Hi, Dan!"

Gisele's body is screaming for attention! Moving one hand down between her legs, she massages her lips to ease the craving and continues with a seductive voice, "I was just headed to bed and was thinking of you, so I thought I'd call and say goodnight." She hears Dan breathing heavily.

That is her cue as she imagines Jen embracing his cock and starting to rub it. Gisele can hear Jen's heavy breathing over the phone. Gisele wonders if Jen is that turned-on or if the show is more to entice the ladies! She continues knowing Jen now can hear her.

"I am on my bed with my legs spread, thinking of how you had me on all fours. How you came up behind me and rammed your cock in me." Oh, shit, is the quiet response from Dan. Hearing that, Gisele slips one finger into her.

Faintly, she breathes, attempting to moan and continues, "Fucking me so hard my tits were bouncing. Then, when I looked into your wife's eyes and saw how surprised she was that you were pounding me from behind!" Gisele moans, thinking, *I can barely speak.* But she forces a throaty tone, "Dan, let me describe what I am doing while I recall that day! I am massaging my breast, skimming over the nipples, getting them erect! The other hand is reaching for the vibrator wishing it was your cock!" Hearing Jen inhale and Dan's heavy breathing drives Gisele wild. In the most flirtatious voice she could muster up, she says, "I am spreading my legs! Can you hear the vibrator as I slide it between my legs? Dan! It is entering me. I am fucking it! My ass is thrusting up, trying to shove it in deeper!" Gisele moans into the phone, then murmurs, "Oh Dan, I wish you were kneeling over my head so I could slide your cock into my mouth."

She hears his breath start to quicken. *Almost there,* she thinks. *But it is Jen's voice I want to hear when I cum. Must slow things down.* Switching tact, her voice gets stronger.

"Dan, just think of those women watching as your wife gives you a hand job." She moans again and purrs. "They have to be so wet. Fuck, they probably are thinking how great it would be to be sucking your cock right now and tasting your sperm!" That is all it took. Dan's breath came in gasps. Gisele senses that he is coming. *Ah, my work is done here!*

"Oh, Dan, I'm cumming!" she moans, slurring her words for effect. As he nears his finish, she hesitates before whispering, "Can I say good night to Jen?"

"Hello"

Gisele's voice shifts, trying to sound like it is giving approval. "That was excellent!"

She attempts to sound more domineering than she feels. "Now describe what took place as I masturbate! Christ, I was just about to cum hearing your voice. Now tell me what the women's reaction was. They stayed; I take it?" Gisele can barely hold back the urge to climax as she listens.

"Oh, they stayed all right. As soon as they knew what was going on the three moved in closer in a circle around Dan and me. Immediately one started to touch my ass. The one in the middle, blue top, big tits, just stared at me. I think she was cumming. Must have had a vibrating egg inside her." Jen giggles. "The one to my left moved around closer so she could reach out and grab my hand to help me jerk Dan off. Her hand was high enough on mine. I knew that she was feeling his cock as well. Then when she tried to smother her pleasure, I knew she felt the cum through Dan's pants!" Jen pauses, breathing heavily.

Gisele shakes as a heavy gasp escapes her lips. The thought of Jen hearing her climax sends a deeper shudder through her, amplifying the pleasure and making the release even more intense.

When she tries to talk, heavy breaths escape between her words.

"Thanks Jen... best... orgasm... ever!" Gisele hears a whisper

"Is that your friend?" one of the ladies asks.

"Yes."

"Describe to me what is going on!" Gisele demands on the phone.

"The girls are helping me walk Dan out. As he has a big wet spot on his pants. You know how much he cums. He is in the middle of our group." Both women laugh. "Who knew people like this were at these parties! Found three at once!" Jen insinuates, giggling.

Gisele hears them shuffle. "Oh, you knew, just too scared to find out which ones they were!" Gisele answers harshly. "Just need a little encouragement, that's all."

"Indeed!" Jen answers, adding, "We will have to invite you and Bill to some of these parties. Shit! We are outside, I have to go. Will see you soon. Oh, by the way, if you like that role, take more control. Love ya!"

With that, the phone goes silent.

What the fuck? Gisele can feel her face flush. Sighing, she hangs up the phone. Stretching out on the bed, she lets the thoughts flow over her. *Phone sex is fantastic!* She breathes in at the thought. *Did Jen know all along what I was trying? Hmmm, did I succeed?* And that was the only concern she had right before falling asleep.

Roger D. Ewen

CHAPTER 24

On Sunday, Gisele wakes to the sound of the door closing.

"Shit, Bill is home!"

Lying on the bed naked with the vibrator beside her, she quickly gets up, grabs the toys and shoves them into the drawer. Seeing sunlight coming through the window she realizes that it must be late morning. Once she's done, she heads to the shower. *I really don't want to get caught enjoying myself.* She chuckles, her mind wandering. *Not that I think Bill would mind knowing I masturbate— he probably does it himself. But I like to keep it a secret. It makes things more interesting. And besides, some of the things I think about... well, I definitely want to keep those to myself.* She smiles. *After this weekend, maybe I'll have someone to share them with.* Getting out of the shower, she throws on some panties and a tee shirt and heads downstairs.

Bill is just coming out of the office.

"Good morning, hon." Gisele goes and hugs him. "Want some breakfast?"

"No, it was a rough night. Two different scopes. Just got one out on time. The other is for Dan. I am going to get some sleep, then maybe eat, ok?"

Thank God, she thought. *I'm still sore from last night. Besides, I got work to do. I would like to sell that listing before the weekend. I want to be free by then.* Grabbing a coffee, she heads to her study and gets the listing. The young couple interested in the house can be persuaded to buy the place. It is in their price range. The house is a little big, but it suits their needs now and in the future if they decide to have kids.

Her mind drifts to what's coming on Saturday night. *Cut it out,* she thinks. *Don't want to ruin it.* Focused, she muses on her plan to get the house sold.

xxx

A few hours later, Bill comes into the office, and she glances at him.

"I'll make something to eat,"

"Ok," he replies, following her out the door.

Gisele, feeling his eyes on her, says, "Don't you be getting any ideas. You know I have a showing on Wednesday. If I sell it, you know how I get. So, save your energy till then." She laughs.

"Ok. Hey, you still going out with the girls next Saturday?"

"Yeah, why?"

"Well, Dan asked me over and said Saturday night was the only night he would be free. He hinted that there was a big scoop he thought I would be interested in! It could be big!" Bill adds.

Gisele feels the tingling. *It is really going to happen.* She controls her voice. "You don't want to miss that dinner. It could be a big break. Besides, if I can get out of the party early, I will see if you are still there and come over. If you have already left, I will just come home and make it up to you, dear." She passes him the sandwich she just made.

"It is a deal," Bill replies while grabbing the sandwich off the plate. "Well, I am off to the office. You better sell that house! " Smiling, he goes out the door.

Gisele thinks, *oh, I am going to sell it alright, and then you are going to get the fucking of your life!* Cleaning up the kitchen, she starts to plan. *On Monday, I will go to the property to make sure everything is in order. Dust a little and make sure the locks are working.*

Once finished, she heads upstairs, her mind on Jen's last remark. Going to the study sites she opens Google. *Maybe I am not strong enough to be the Domme. Let's see what submission is like.* With her mind focused, she types in D/S and studies the results that are displayed on the screen.

Not clicking on any choices, Gisele reflects on the day she was made to strip and crawl around on all fours like a dog. *Jeez, I get excited just imagining it. Never felt that aroused ever! And when I climaxed, it was so intense.* Then her thoughts shifted to when she was trying to control Jen on the phone. *It was fun and stimulating but not nearly as fierce as the latter!* With that thought in the back of her mind, she clicks on Wikipedia Female Submission.

Reading through the pages once again, she detects a little thrill coming to the part that highlighted spanking! *Dam forgot all about game night. Dan spanking me as one of the choices he had got me wet. Hmmm, yep, I do want to learn more. What is this about the switch where the person can play either role?* Hearing the car pull in, she shuts things down. *Dam, I'm not even dressed!*

She heads to the bedroom, stripes out of the underwear, throws on the front button one-piece dress, and hurries down to meet Bill.

"Hay hon, go sit in the living room while I get you a whisky. Just starting supper got tied up," *I wish*, she chuckles and continues, "with work." She strolls off to get the drink and returns, handing it to Bill.

"What a day!" He starts.

You tell me! Gisele smirks. "Let me get supper started and a glass of wine, and then I will sit with you." She moves toward the kitchen, puts supper on, gets back to the couch, and sits beside Bill.

"Going over all my notes, I was right. Neither one of them is related to Miss. Beaumont, you remember the dead wife? Apparently, and this is from Dan's source, the woman in question her parents had a small estate in Dillten. That is where, as a young lady, she resided before marrying. Being on her own as her parents traveled a lot, she hired a cleaning lady to come in every few days. Now things were working out until, on one occasion the help showed up with a few bruises around her eyes and seemed to have trouble holding on to things as she cleaned." Bill stops to take a sip and collect his thoughts.

Gisele is quite intrigued with the whole thing and sits there staring at her husband. "Are these people dangerous?" she asks, eyes wide.

"No, no, let me finish. When Miss. Beaumont found out about the abusive husband and that the young woman had a child, that is all that she had to hear—insisted the cleaning lady, who wasn't much older than herself, to kick the husband to the curve and move in with her. To make a long story short everything was going as planned until the girl's mother never returned from one of her cleaning appointments. Miss. Beaumont spent a small fortune on a private detective. But all that was ever known was that an unidentified burnt body was found in a ditch outside of town. Never heard from the child's mother again, so she raises the girl on her own." Bill takes a break and drinks.

Gisele hears the timer go off, letting her know dinner is ready. She shows a little disappointment at having to interrupt. "Tell the rest over dinner as it is ready." Getting up, she walks to the kitchen with Bill in tow.

With everything set and the food dish up, Gisele stares at Bill with a frown. "Well, tell the rest, did the husband kill her? Come on, quit teasing me. I like it during sex, but now it is just annoying!"

Bill laughs, "Ok, I will finish. I guess as the girl got older, a few squabbles occurred between the women. So, when she was old enough to find her father, that was the last anyone heard from her. In the meantime, Miss Beaumont married and neglected to mention to her husband any part of that life. I only found out about the girl from a forty-year-old newspaper. And that was just by luck! Imagine the husband's surprise when he found out!

"So, with that information, we think that the girl, now a woman, is in the will. Now, we can only theorize the rest until Dan can confirm the will. Either everything is left to the girl, which would indicate the husband didn't have a reason to murder his wife, and the woman did. Or the will is split, and anyone or both parties involved is unhappy with the cut." Dan stops and leans back in the kitchen chair.

Gisele realizes she has hardly touched her food, being so captivated by the story! She also knows that most of this will not appear in the paper for liability reasons. *I love being in the now. Partly because I know things as they happen. But most of all, the intimacy felt in how much Bill trusted me!* "So, you are telling me that the girl went to find her father with the knowledge he might have killed her mother! That is insane!" Gisele voices, staring at her husband in surprise.

"Remember, she might not have been told the story about her father. The only scenario Dan and I can come up with is that she met some scum who told the story to convince her that the best plan of action to get all the money was to kill the old lady before the will was changed! That's all we got." Bill gets up and helps clean the table.

Gisele accepts that is all he is going to say. She finishes washing the dishes and then joins him on the couch. She sits there with a sitcom playing on the TV with hardly any interest. *I am more curious about the film you hid. Would love to see what is on it!* Leaning her head on Bill's shoulder, absorbed in her thoughts, she looks at her husband, pondering what his response would be when confronted with the proposition next Saturday night. *Will he hate me? Leave me!?* She shudders at the idea! *I wonder if phone sex is cheating! Naaaa, probably the same as watching porn.* Dismissing her thoughts, she turns her head to watch the show.

CHAPTER 25

Monday finds Gisele outside at the property, straightening the sign. She steps back to admire the headshot, a satisfied smile playing on her lips. With a nod of approval, she continues up the steps to the house and types the code into the padlock. Once inside Gisele inhales, sending a warmth over her while strolling through the vacant rooms, lost in thought. *I love the feeling of the emptiness; it's so intriguing. Imagine what kind of people lived here. What were their sexual preferences!? As I walk into the bedroom, it's kind of erotic picturing that! The older houses are more interesting as you can fantasize about ghosts watching you!* A chill runs through her. *Never told anyone, but the first day I stepped into an empty house, it was so electrifying! So sexually arousing! I knew right there and then what my passion was! What's that saying, "If you love what you are doing, you will never work a day in your life!"* Sighing, she continues to dust. The phone ringing brings her out of the daydream.

"Hello," She says.

"Hi, are you free tomorrow? The girls would like to get together." Betty inquiries.

"Would love to! I was just thinking about you guys. Same place, same time?" Gisele asks.

"Yes," Betty replies. "See you there. Bye!"

"Bye." Poor Betty, every time there is a meeting, she has to phone. Returning to her inspection her thoughts are drawn back to musing on who lived here. *What devious secret the walls would reveal if they could talk.* Entering the last room, she starts a fantasy of her own. The fading light of the day breaks her illusion. Finishing the dusting, Gisele takes a quick look around before heading out.

xxx

At home, Gisele is roaming around the kitchen preparing the meat for supper. Thoughts of Saturday emerge, and a dread comes over her. *I always had the assumption that the sex act was going to be the problem. Jeez! What is wrong with me? People finding out he is a Peeping Tom is going to crush him.*

"You self-centered bitch!" Gisele breathes. She begins to panic. *What did I do? Well, the ball is rolling, and there is no way to stop it! The cat is out of the bag!* Hearing the door open, she pushes all the negativity to the back of her mind. That just prompts the voice, *calm down, you will make it work! You turn it around in high school! You will do the same here!* That settles her down.

"I am in the kitchen, hon," Gisele calls out. With that, she prepares for the rest of the evening.

xxx

The next day Gisele is getting ready for the brunch meet. The thoughts about Saturday go out of her head, and she focuses more on arranging things for Wednesday. The clock strikes noon, and that gets her moving to get ready to meet the girls.

Arriving at the patio the group is sitting at the same table, close to the restaurant's entrance. That gets Gisele to reminisce about the first time she came here. *"Why do we have to sit so close to the entrance? We are not alcoholics!"*

"Well, we are not camels either!" Janet had replied, and everyone began laughing, and with that, the thought fades.

Strolling over to the table the girls simultaneously holler, "GISELE!"

"What are we doing today? Reminiscing about old TV sitcoms!?" Gisele responds, laughing with the others. *Looks like they got here a little earlier than I did.* Once seated, the women get back to chattering.

While waving to get the attention of a waitress Gisele notices Susan's attempts to get hers. *Hmmm.* With drinks ordered, Gisele acknowledges her, prompting Susan to stand and announce she's heading to the bathroom, gesturing for Gisele to follow. Once there, Susan confronts her directly.

"You're not going to mention anything about our meeting the other day, are you?" Susan asks timidly.

"Of course not! I was there as well, don't forget." Gisele softly replies reassuringly.

"Thanks. I know in this day in age, it is nothing. But would like to keep that side of my life private." Susan considers for a moment. "I have never seen you there before."

"I never heard of the place. One of Bill's freelance client's wife asked me to join her there out of the blue." Gisele surveys her friend, musing about what it might be like with an experienced woman. "Can I ask…for my own personal reasons, does your husband know?" Gisele, sounding as respectful as possible, asks, her face showing a curious frown.

Susan, with an inquisitive look on her face, answers. "Well, he is not oblivious…How do I put this? We have an open marriage." Susan laughs at that. "But neither one of us knows it." She says, still trying to cover the laugh. "Rodger has his little rendezvous, and I get to step out with my friend." Noticing the confused look on Gisele's face, she resumes. "Everything else we have together is marvelous! So why wreck a good marriage and lifestyle over different sexual preferences? Oh, before you ask, we pretend not to know to make it more intriguing!"

Gisele opens her arms, and Susan walks into them. Hugging, Gisele whispers, "Thanks love. You help me more than you know." Letting go, Gisele watches as Susan heads to the door. *That is one nice ass.*

Right on time, Susan turns around, "If you ever want to experience real sexual pleasure, please call me!" She opens the door to walk through but stops, "And please bring your friend!" The door swings shut behind her.

Gisele, looking in the mirror, fussing over her hair and make-up, ponders. *I might have given her the wrong impression.* The voice comes to the front. *Maybe she knows you more than you think!* Dismissing the thought, she heads back to the table.

xxx

Upon arriving, they see the women chuckling amongst themselves. Sitting down, she observes Janet facing her two fingers pressed to her lips, tongue sticking out between them. "Oh, don't be vulgar!" Gisele whispers, laughing.

Jennette speaks up. "Don't pay any attention to her! Her mind is in the gutter after the little tidbit Betty revealed about her sex life while you two were gone." Gisele, catching Susan staring at Betty, turns her head towards Jennette, waiting for more.

Betty, grinning, stands up, encouraging her to continue, "Go on, fill them in! I will finish the story when I get back." Turning, she heads to the washroom, a chuckle following.

Jennette, sensing that was her cue, sits back, and her eyes gleam. "Well, Betty and her husband have this game they play. Apparently, she sits him on a kitchen chair naked and ties his hands behind his back then!" Drawing a breath, she continues. "If I heard right! She puts a cock ring on him! She said it helps make the erection harder and last longer!" she murmurs, and as no one interrupts, she carries on. "Once he is hard as a rock, she just strolls around her husband teasing. Until neither one of them can take it anymore, at that point, she straddles him. This is her words, not mine!" Jennette, inhaling, continues. "Still tied, she rides him like an animal!"

Gisele, scanning the table finds everyone having a sly smile. *Probably wish they were brave enough to do that. Or wondering how meek little Betty got so adventurous!* Her thoughts are interrupted once Betty returns,

"I assume everyone is caught up." Pulling out her chair, Betty sits. "Ok, I swear on my mother's grave, this really happened. You might think I got this from one of those Penthouse Forms we used to read back in the day. But girls, this really occurred!" Betty whispers, leaning in with an earnest expression on her face.

Susan speaks up. "Jeez, what could you possibly wish for more than having your husband tied to a chair, naked or otherwise!" She hesitates before continuing. "Now you can go into the living room with a nice glass of wine and watch your favorite soap opera in peace!" Everyone starts roaring out loud.

Gisele thinks *only you would think of that. The rest of us like the latter.* Starting to feel less anxious about her situation and the upcoming events on Saturday, Gisele feels glad she could make it today. Like the rest, Gisele excitedly waits for Betty to continue.

"Ok, ok. If everyone is done, let me go on. You won't be laughing then." Betty takes a deep breath. "One afternoon, I was over having a few drinks with my neighbor. She is a good friend and we got around to generally talking about what excites us in bed. Yeah, maybe we had more than a few. Anyway, for the life of me, I don't know what got into me, but I told the story I just finished telling you guys!" Taking a drink, she smiles. "My neighbor just sat there gawking as if I, on those occasions, performed some magnificent feat! Sitting there all proud of myself at her praise I didn't see what was coming. Both of us didn't say anything for a minute just drinking until she spoke. *How would you like to heighten the sexual experience she asked.* Just staring, I let her continue. *Now, it is just an idea. But what if, on one of those times, you blindfold your husband, and I come over and give him a blowjob!* Recognizing my surprise or shock, my neighbor hurried on. *I won't touch it, only my mouth to suck him off!* This is for your pleasure, not his, as the only thing he knows is you sucking him!" Before Betty could resume, a voice interrupts.

"Holy shit!" Shirley blurts out, surprisingly.

Gisele is taken aback by the outburst along with the rest of the girls as Shirley never expresses herself at these functions. Everyone glances at her, and then the group, chuckling, turns their attention back to Betty.

Chuckling herself, Betty moves on. "At first, my thought was no way. But the more the idea stuck in my head, the more I liked it. So, we agreed and set the plan in motion. The opportunity presented itself two days later. There was my husband tied to the chair naked, cock standing straight up in midair, hard as a rock, so I suggested the blindfold. He balked at first. But when I introduced the idea of how arousing it would be not to know what was going to happen next, he agreed. I grabbed his erection, stroking it. Then mentioning how he could imagine being with any movie star he desired to clinch the deal. Once the blindfold was in place, I called my friend.

"Arriving barefoot and with a robe on, she opened the door. All the while, I was talking to my husband so he couldn't hear my neighbor's footsteps. Things like, what are you fantasizing about? Oh, I know that girl in the horror movie we watched the other night. Her running away in just panties and tits showing through her thin t-shit! Falling on all fours, and the camera zooms on her ass as she crawls away. Noticing my friend removing her robe, getting on all fours in nothing but panties started to creep toward my husband, whose cock was now throbbing. You know, girls, I knew right then this was all about me! My knees were weak, and I could hardly speak anymore, watching as her breasts swayed as she crawled closer.

"Then, I went quiet as her mouth opened to let the head of my husband's erection slide in! Now, with her hands at her side and head bouncing, I couldn't take any more! Standing close to her, putting one hand on the back of her head and the other around the base of the throbbing cock I started jerking him off until the sperm was shooting into her mouth! That was the second time I had come! And true to her words, she released him with a lick of the tongue to get the last drop off the tip and started to crawl away. That prompted me to start talking again. Saying things to keep his mind swimming with desire! *How was that young girl? Does she suck cock as you imagined! Did she take out her tits for you to feel?* Seeing my friend was out the door, I knelt in front of him, removing his blindfold and looked up at him, licking my lips, standing untying him. We finished up the old-fashioned way." Betty, with a satisfied look on her face, raises the glass to her lips and sips.

Gisele, mouth open, staring at Betty notices the rest of the girls were also wide-eyed. *Are they as wet as I am? Is this the same meek Betty from college? Who knew?* Seeing Shirley fidgeting, she smirks, fully aware of how she feels. She is about to comment, but Betty is already raising her hand to order more drinks.

Janet tries to protest. "It is getting late; we should get going."

Betty encourages them to stay. "Just one more. Let me tell you the kicker! Even I couldn't believe it!"

Gisele and the girls eye one another, bewildered. They shake their heads in agreement and sit back, waiting for the drinks to arrive.

Betty's voice, getting a little shaky at this point, continues. "A couple days later, my husband and I were invited over for dinner at my friends. There we were, sitting at the table eating. Peering over at my friend's husband, I gazed right into his eyes as he put food into his mouth! I was thinking, *do you know your wife had my husband's cock in her mouth!* I wet myself right there! The desire I felt lasted all night. I really think my neighbor thought, at the way I was acting we should reverse the roles." Betty pauses for effect. "But if she only knew, I kept glancing at him, visualizing him not knowing, as I remembered watching his wife swallowing my husband's sperm! There is no greater arousal than that! Dam, I am bad!" Betty sighing sits back with a very huge grin on her face.

Jenette interrupts, looking at her watch. "Well, it is late, and I must get home. I have something to take care of. Let's pick this up again next time." With that, they finish the drinks and stand.

Gisele, with a sly look, watches others do the same. Standing up, she says goodbye and walks out to the car. On the way home, her mind gets flooded with thoughts. *When did our brunches turn into revealing our dark secrets? Christ, next, we will find out Shirley is really a vampire!* She chuckles. *Isn't that what happens in movies?*

With that thought aside, she drives the rest of the way, listening to the radio.

Roger D. Ewen

CHAPTER 26

Evening finds Gisele curled up on the couch with a hot pizza in front of her and the TV casting shadows on the wall, lost in deep thought. *When the hell did Betty get so adventurous? She was so meek in college. And when did she discover S/M? And how the hell did I miss Susan coming out of the closet?* The voice interrupts. *Don't forget Janet's secret romps. Hmmm. Well, to be truthful, my story would probably shake them. I wonder what circumstances caused them to realize who they were!* Getting up from the couch and cleaning away the food, Gisele shrugs her shoulders. *To hell with it, I have my own issues.* Remembering her husband will be working late, she decides to look up the use of cock rings before he gets home.

xxx

Up in her study with Google on the screen, sitting at her desk, her mind wanders. *Ok, everything Betty said is true. The only thing I found more interesting is that it can intensify the orgasm for both parties. I am all in for that! But how the hell am I going to introduce all these ideas into our love life?* Hearing Bill pull in, she shuts down the computer and goes downstairs to greet him.

Saturday night, things might go my way.

xxx

The next morning, she finds Bill already gone. She gets up and heads to the shower, her excitement buzzing at the thought of closing the deal. The cool rush of water sends a shiver down her spine. As her hands move to wash her body, a mischievous thought crosses her mind. Sliding her hand lower, she pauses, tempted to tease herself with just one finger. *Noooo! It would be better to be vigilant at the showing.* She quickly washes up and gets out. She dries herself and heads to the study. The only thing she had to do was keep from masturbating every time she thought of what might take place Saturday night and plan for the sale pitch. The former was harder than the latter. But she succeeded. She knows Bill is busy trying to get things done before Saturday, so she keeps her hands busy typing up other sale documents on other houses. Once finished, she goes and gets dressed.

Finding a white blouse that opens just above the navel—no bra— so when she bends over, they could catch a peek at her nipples. The pants are white too. No panties. They're tight enough to give the impression you can almost see through them. Getting a look at her round ass, the fabric clinging perfectly but dark enough in the front to hide her pubic hair—just barely. It gives the illusion that if you look hard enough, you might see more.

Gisele giggles and says, "Oh, how I love showing my body off!"

Now, it's not like she seduces her clients. She just gets them aroused. Let them think about what they want. She is very good at reading people, and she plays on that. She didn't become the best realtor in the city by just looking sexy.

Arriving early, she checks the place. When she hears the couple arrive, she opens the door.

"Welcome. Come on in." She says with a big smile on her face.

The young woman standing in front of her wears a deep blue V-neck satin blouse, showing off a pair of perfectly firm breasts. Her nipples stick straight out as if desperate to escape. The micro-mini skirt barely covers her round, toned ass.

Gisele feels a slight tingle. Since that day with Jen, she sees women differently—more intensely, more curiously.

The young man beside her wears a formal light gray shirt, open at the neck. His tight gray suit trousers leave little to the imagination, highlighting a very impressive semi-hard-on.

What the hell were they doing before they got here? Gisele can only imagine.

Ah, later. She pushes the thought aside—for now.

Gisele steps aside, widening the door. In a very pleasing voice, she says, "Let me show you around. This hallway leads to a very spacious living room to your left that leads into the dining room. Down the hallway, there is also another opening to the dining area."

Gisele glances at the couple, who seem far more interested in flirting with each other than in viewing the house. She considers suggesting they get a room and come back later but decides to wait and see where this might lead. Who knew that it would turn our to be the best decision she ever made?

Walking into the kitchen, Gisele points out. "The kitchen comes with all the latest appliances."

The young lady strolls over to the stove and bends down to check out the double oven.

As if she cooks with those nails! Gisele smirks. Then she notices the skirt rising, revealing a very bare tan ass. As the woman moves her hips, Gisele sees a glistening between her legs. *This girl is soaked.* Then it dawns on her. *I have already sold this house, and they are here to christen it.* She feels a tingle and a wetness emerge at both thoughts. She looks over at the young man. *If his trousers were a little lower, the head of his cock would be sticking out.* Gisele starts getting wetter. *I got to hurry and finalize this deal and get home.*

Gisele encourages the couple. "Shall we move on to the other rooms? You will find the sleeping quarters very appealing."

Moving on to the upper level where the spacious master bedroom, walk-in closet, master bathroom, and jacuzzi are. "As you can picture, there is enough free space for any occasion."

Gisele glances at the couple, gauging their reaction. The young man stands close behind the woman, who admires the jacuzzi. But her hand—subtle, deliberate—is behind her back, stroking his cock.

Voyeurs.

They want her to watch. They want an audience.

We'll see about that.

Breaking up their little masturbation fest, Gisele clears her throat and announces, "There's one more floor to show on the lower level."

Leading them down to the last floor, she describes the remaining rooms. "Down here is a large showroom. As you see it is set up in somewhat of a theatrical theme." Pointing to the left. "Off to one side is the laundry room," she walks while motioning, "and to the right, two other rooms. These two areas can be turned into playrooms for adults." Gisele, pausing to let it sink in, continues with a sly grin on her face, "Or later, bedrooms. It is up to the owner's discretion."

The woman turns to the man. "Stan, I want this house! It is us!"

"Well then," Stan says, turning, " Gisele, we will take it and pay the asking price."

"Ok, fantastic, let me make a call and go straight to the office to get it off the market!"

The couple looks a little disappointed that she will be leaving but says nothing. *I have to get out of here so I can get home and have a cold shower!* With that, she heads upstairs, hesitating. *Did I hear a light moan from the woman? They can't wait till I get out of the house.* She smiles. *Ah, being young.* With that thought, she heads out the door.

Getting into the car, Gisele phones the office and lets them know that the sale is final. While the other hand slides down her pants as she spreads her legs. "Oh, just one finger. I need to cum!"

With that, she starts to rub the clit, pushes the car seat back and lowers the backrest. Stretching out as much as possible with two fingers, she spreads the swollen lips and then slides them in. Moving in and out slowly thinking of the couple in the house. *He is probably behind her; the young lady is bent over the island in the middle of the kitchen, her skirt lifted, and he is sliding his cock in that soaked pussy.* She imagines herself watching them from the kitchen doorway. Getting in position, Gisele slides her pants down past her knees so she can spread her legs more. Moving her hand back, she continues to masturbate. Her fingers work faster than before in rhythm with the imaginary cock pounding the bent-over woman. *There is no stopping now.* She visualizes the man thrusting harder as he is about to cum and making the woman's body jerk forward and her ass shake.

Gisele pushes her fingers harder and faster. She feels the building of the orgasm. Her mind races, picturing the young woman turning her head, catching sight of her standing in the doorway—pants down, fingers deep inside her. The thought pushes her over the edge, and she can't hold back any longer as she cums. Letting out a long sigh of relief as her fingers get soaked. With the orgasm subsiding, she breathes. "And that is why you have leather seats." She laughs.

Pulling her pants up and adjusting the seat back to the driving position, Gisele starts the car. She checks the mirrors and lets out a gasp, "Wait, did I just see two heads pull back from the upstairs window!?" she blushes. "Were they watching me this whole time?" The thought gets her a little aroused. *Maybe I am the one who is the voyeur.* With that, she pulls out of the drive.

Now, on the way home, Gisele enjoys the lingering thrill of fantasizing about the couple—how their eyes followed her, how she caught them watching.

Was he fingering her while they watched?

The thought sends a fresh wave of excitement through her.

Stop it! She scolds herself.

Focus. Think about how to work this into our fun night. Then—Goddamn it, that's it!

A plan starts to take shape.

CHAPTER 27

Arriving home, Gisele is beaming. I need to take a shower and think about how to present this game to Bill! And what to wear for a fun night. Maybe try to duplicate the young lady's outfit from today. Drying off, she heads to the bedroom. Ruffling through the closet she grabs a white see-through blouse and short skirt - no panties or bra. Taking one last look in the mirror, she is impressed that the outfit still fits. With newfound courage she goes downstairs, thinking if this plan goes right, it might help Bill enjoy Saturday night. Fussing over the stove, nerves on end, a few ideas start to take shape. I will wait until we're upstairs to ask! Naa, when done supper maybe! Quit it! Stick to the plan from the drive home! Don't chicken out now! With that, she sets the table. Hearing Bill come through the door, she greets him by throwing her arms around his neck. She gives him a hard, long kiss, sliding her tongue over his lips. Feeling his response helps quiet her nervousness.

Still hugging him, she utters, "Hurry and shower. That way, we will have time for a drink before supper." She gives him another light kiss before letting go, hand glazing his crotch.

Bill reaches for her waist, pulling her tight to him. Feeling his erection press against her thigh, he moves his head forward and plants little kisses along her neck. Reaching the ear lobe and nipping on it, he whispers. "Maybe I will take you right here!"

Letting out a heavy moan, easing him back, with a slight laugh, Gisele whispers back, "Well, if I give in to you, we both will miss out! Now go have a shower! I have more adventurous plans than a quicky!" Turning to attend to supper, she feels a light slap on her ass as Bill walks into his study to shower.

"Make that a cold one!" Giggling, Gisele shouts after him. All the self-doubt leaves her as the sexual urges take over. She grins ear to ear. This is going to work just fine. She pours the drinks, forming the story in her head while she waits.

Bill enters the kitchen wearing a black shirt, a few buttons undone, and very tight black pants - enough to show off his semi-hardon. Bringing the drinks, Gisele motions for Bill to join her on the island.

Sitting, her skirt rises enough to expose curly pubic hairs. Realizing this, she implements the plan. "Hon, I would like to try something a little different tonight. How about we have a fantasy night!?" Noticing her husband's eyes are averted to her crotch, she spreads her legs a little to show how wet she is! Ahhh, I love the foreplay! Now his eyes are moving back towards her face, but not before taking in the firm breast and the erect nipples pushing hard against the blouse. As their eyes meet, she recognizes that lust and continues.

"The night will be like this! When we sit down for supper, the game will start. You ask me how my day went, and I will start the fantasy. Some will be true, but other parts won't be. This game will last until tomorrow. No question till then! What do you think?" Without waiting for an answer, observing his face and the huge bulge in his pants, Gisele stands, walks to the table, and prompts Bill to follow. Once they are seated and the meal is dished up, the game begins.

Bill anxiously begins. "Well, hon, how did the sale go?"

Gisele takes a big breath, leering at her husband. Nervous about how to begin, her heart races. This is the first time she's ever dared to reveal one of her fantasies out loud. With the sexual sensation wanting release, she breathes out and begins. "My day went great! A little more unusual than any I closed before, to say the least. But I made the sale. The young couple arrived on time. The young lady was dressed kind of like how I am now, and the young man was about how you are now. Now, this is when it gets bizarre! Once I proceeded to conduct the viewing, the woman, at any chance she got, kept bending over to show off her nice tan ass along with exposing a very swollen pink wet pussy." Gisele, burning with curiosity, glances over at her husband, seeking approval that she is on the right track. The arousal drives through at the sight of her husband rubbing his cock as he listens.

With newfound courage and in the most flirtatious voice she can muster, she breathes out. "Noticing how hard he was, I thought that the guy's cock was going to jump out of his pants. That got me a little wet, also! Oh, all this teasing went on through the whole showing of the house. She would brush against her husband's crotch, and he, in return, brushed up against a breast or her ass! By the time they said they would buy the house, I was soaking wet! I had to get out of there so I could find a place to finger myself till I cum.'"

Pausing here to take a drink, she notices Bill is hardly touching his food.

At that thought, she is fighting the urge to go over and suck him off! Steadying herself, she pushes the temptation aside and carries on. "Finally, the opportunity came so I could excuse myself. Rushing up the stairs and reaching the front door, I could hear the couple coming up behind me! With my hand on the doorknob, I refrained from opening it, as the woman's voice was clear! Get that cock out so I can suck it! Removing my hand, I snuck down the hall, trying to find a good spot to hide so I could spy on them. I was so turned on by the thought I knew there was no turning back. Making my way toward the kitchen where the sounds were coming from, I found a place where I was sure they couldn't see me, but I could view all the action. By the time I got there, the woman was on her knees, sliding her husband's cock out of her mouth. Standing up, she turned around so that he could bend her over the island. Raising her skirt, the young man started to slide two fingers slowly into her cunt. Leaning against the wall, I, in turn, slid my hands down my pants and copied the man's movements!"

At this point, Gisele breaks off to steady her breathing. Taking deep breaths, she moves one hand under the table while continuing to eat with the other. Peering over at Bill, she sees him eating with one hand. Hmmm, wonder if his cock is out or if he is just rubbing it over his pants! Pushing the thought away and getting her control back, she continues the fantasy as she rubs her wet lips between her legs to ease the ach.

"Then, with the other hand, the husband slowly slides it up and down her back. Then over the crack of her ass, he inserted a finger slowly into the opening, all the while with the other hand finger-fucking her. My knees gave up a little while watching this! Sliding my pants down a little so I could reach back to finger my ass thinking all she needs now is a cock in her mouth and every hole would be filled! Quivering a little at that image, I noticed the guy removing his fingers. Holding his cock he slowly started to enter her. Then, holding her hips, he gave a hard-forward thrust! He slowly pulled out and drove it in again! That made the woman's ass and tits bounce. He continued doing this to the woman's sheer delight.

"Preoccupied with pleasing myself, my fingers shoved deep inside me. I lost all awareness of where I was! I don't know how long the woman was observing me in the doorway before I noticed but when I did, I froze! Turning red, I started to pull my pants up but stopped as I noticed the woman waving me over. With my wet pussy showing, and I don't even remember when I undid my blcuse, but there I was, tits exposed, nipples hard as a rock standing there, unable to move, just staring! As our eyes met, we both knew where this was leading, no turning back. With pants still halfway down, I shuffled more, then walked over and stood beside the young lady.

"After staring at every inch of my body, she said to turn and face my husband so he could admire that beautiful body of yours. Turning, I faced him. He didn't even miss a beat as he looked at me. That must have been his cue to pull out. As his hard cock stood in mid-air soaked, the woman stood, turned, and knelt in front of her husband. Staring up at me, she said, Grap his cock and stroke it until the cum splashes all over my tits! Looking into her eyes, I reached over and started to stroke the husband's cock. With each stroke, the cock throbbed, trying to push my fingers apart. The more it did, the harder I squeezed. He was trying hard not to cum. Then I felt the pulse quicken at the same time, I felt a hand slowly sliding up my leg. As the husband started to cum, the wife's fingers entered me. Looking at her kneeling, fingering herself and me, with sperm splashing on her tits and my juices dripping down her fingers—that was all it took! We all came at once!"

Gisele is pulled from the fantasy as she hears a noise. Bill rises and moves toward her, his fly undone, cock out—standing straight up, twitching.

She has never seen it this hard before.

Did it get bigger?

Pushing her chair back from the table, she spread her legs so her husband could see she was fingering herself.

She says, breathing a little hard, "Don't touch it. Let me stroke it until you cum all over me!"

Standing in front of her, with his cock just inches away from touching her lips, she starts to unbutton her blouse. She moves her head forward, letting her lips slide over the head and down the shaft. Feeling his cock start to jerk in her mouth, she quickly pulls her head back. Moving her hand from between her legs, she grabs his cock and starts to stroke it slowly. Before she knows it, the sperm begins shooting out the head in thick, short streams.

Watching that and feeling the cum splash down onto her tits, she quivers, sensing herself coming without even being touched. Squeezing tight and sliding her hand back and forth, she reaches up with the other, cupping his balls, trying to get more cum to splash on her. This experience is so thrilling! Enjoying the feel of the warm sperm sliding down her breast and over her nipples, she takes a finger rubbing the thick liquid between her breast and over the nipples and stares up at Bill! She brings the sperm-covered fingers to her lips and sucks on them. Leaning back in the chair, she is surprised to see Bill still semi-hard.

"Let me clean up, and then I will help you with that," she starts to say, but Bill cuts her off.

"No need." Taking off his shirt, he slides his pants down, steps out of them and reaches for her. "Sex is like gardening. If you're not getting dirty, you're not doing it right!" With that, he helps her out of the chair and steers her to the stairs.

Once in the bedroom, he lays her on the bed. Gisele notices he hasn't removed her clothes. Is that what turns him on—her lying there half-naked? She watches as he straddles her, pushing her unbuttoned blouse farther apart. His hands glide over her breasts as he leans in close, whispering in her ear.

"I am going to eat you till you can't cum anymore, then fuck your brains out! But before that starts, you will have to tell me more about your fantasy!" With that, he starts to move lower down her body, kissing it as he goes. Coming to the skirt, Gisele feels it being pushed over her hips. His hands spread her legs as his head lowers between them. He starts planting tiny kisses on the inside of her thighs, moving toward her juice-covered lips. Sucking some pubic hair in his mouth, he stops. His tongue darts out, sliding over one very swollen lip.

Gisele places her hands on top of Bill's head, pushing down as her hips rise to the growing passion. Breathing heavily she starts to think of what to say. I have to get this right! Plant the right seed, and Saturday night will go smoothly! Years of fantasies while masturbating kick in, and she presses on.

"Thinking the game was over I started to reach down to pull up my pants. The woman stops me. We are not done, are we? she asked. Step out of those pants! Seeing me obey, she stood up and leaned over the island again. Immediately the husband moved behind, spreading her legs and sliding his cock in. Pulling it all the way out and then slowly back in. Watching this, I felt a tingle. Then I heard her voice. I know it is me you wanted, by the way, you were looking at my ass earlier in the day, so if you want a taste of this! You will follow my orders! She paused, waiting for an answer. Shaking my head up and down, all I heard was, I can't hear you! Murmuring, yes, she went on. When my husband finishes, I am going to stand and go over there. Lie down on the floor with my legs spread. You are going to suck all the cum off my husband's cock while eyeing my wet hairy cunt! When done, he will come over and start fucking me. I want you then to come over and kneel over my face so I have access to yours. This was all relayed to me while her husband pounded away. With the last order conveyed, she stood. Her husband's cock was just standing in midair. Hard as ever throbbing!

"Walking over and kneeling in front of him, I slowly engulfed his erection. Not being that big, I could feel his balls touch my chin as I slid all of him down my throat. Remembering the woman's request, I started to pull my head back until the head of his cock was pressed against my lips! Extending my tongue, I started licking! All the time, my eyes were on the woman in the corner with her legs spread, exposing her hairy cunt, ready to be fucked! No sooner was my mouth off his cock, the young man obliged. He strolled over, kneeling and started fucking her! That was my cue to kneel over the young woman's face. Which I did."

True to his word, Bill attends to her needs all through the storytelling. But now, this is where fantasy and reality collide. Every time Gisele mentions the woman's tongue spreading her pussy lips and entering her, she can feel Bill doing the same. Narrating the woman sucking on her clit, Gisele's head pushes backward, and her hips push up as Bill does the same. Finding this driving her over the edge, not to mention fascinating, makes her wonder how far she can take this. Trying hard to breathe, being in this heightened sexual arousal, she attempts to paint a picture! "The woman moves her head back, extending her tongue as it slithers over the Gooch till the tip is at the rim of my ass! Swirling it in circles before slipping her tongue into the opening." Upon hearing that, Bill's tongue pushes into her ass. As her body shudders, Bill pushes harder. That is it! I am about to cum. And then she climaxes! Even before she can recover, all she hears is Bill rising off the bed and then the command.

"Get on the floor, on all fours!"

A little fear runs through her as the thoughts scream in her head! Did Bill find out about the day with Jen and Dan? We have never done it this way before! Surely Dan wouldn't have told! He promised! With all this in her head, she climbs off the bed. And if he did know why wait till now? She goes on all fours. The image of being in this position heightens all her senses to a pleasurable ach! Then, not knowing what is happening mixed in, drives her to the top.

There she was, her blouse undone, tits pointing to the floor, bare ass in the air. The next thing she feels is Bill kneeling between her legs, spreading them as her skirt lifts over her back. He grabs her hair and pulls her head back, making her body move back. Then Bill's huge cock parts her pussy lips as he enters. The sound of her ass smacking against Bill's belly grows louder as he thrusts harder, faster—chasing his release. Her body trembles, overwhelmed, begging for more.

How many times have I cum?

The thought shatters as his cock pulses and thick, hot sperm floods deep inside her. Being done, Bill pulls out and collapses on the floor, exhausted. With the last quiver leaving her body, Gliese does the same.

"I'll shower in a minute." She whispers as she lays her head on her husband's shoulder, eyes fluttering, falling asleep.

CHAPTER 28

Gisele wakes up the next morning on the bed, somewhat cleaned up, with a note resting on the pillow beside her. Picking it up, she reads it.

"Last night was fantastic. Let's do it again sometime. Love you."

Smiling, she climbs out of bed feeling so alive and excited at Bill's words. She heads to the shower, murmuring, "Now that is encouraging!" In high spirits, she finishes showering and gets dressed.

However, she decides to stay just in panties and heads downstairs. Putting on the coffee, she moves toward the island to sit and begins reminiscing about the events of last night. *What processed Bill to even imagine I would consider an act like that! And the hair-pulling! Where the hell did that come from? Thought that was just a Dan thing!*

Searching for answers, she tries to picture something she might have conveyed during the fantasy! *Nope, nothing at all. And there definitely was not any hair-pulling!* Hearing the coffee is prepared, she goes and pours a cup. Standing, eyes squinted, deep in thought, she strolls over to the French doors, cup pressed to her lips. *It doesn't matter. Last night went a long way to help nudge Bill into accepting Saturday night.* Then, the past month emerges!

Tried blackmailing and had a threesome, but not with my husband! Made out with a woman! Well, ate her out! Gisele chuckles while continuing through the list. *Had phone sex, then last night, I told a fantasy story while having sex. And last but not least am orchestrating a plan so that my husband is forced to have sex with another woman while I watch. What the hell is making me so ventured? It started when I found out about Bill's little secret and watched those dam films!*

"Shit, that's it!" Gisele gasps, returning her thoughts, catching him hiding a film and her on all fours getting her hair pulled! *He caught something on film that aroused his curiosity when he was in Dillten! So, when I suggested fantasy role-playing, Bill saw the chance to inject his twisted urges into the game! There is no other explanation.* Pacing in front of the windows with a newfound resilience, she gulps the coffee down. *Hmmm, maybe I don't know my husband as well as I thought! Undoubtedly, I have my secret urges.* A sly smirk forms as she steps into the warm morning light.

The voice comes to the front, so *the threesome you had added nothing to help with the wakening.*

Oh, it was always in my fantasies! But acting them out in real life never once crossed my mind. I think maybe my mother was right: I am oversexed! Grinning, she heads upstairs to dress. Musing to herself, *I have a showing today and another tomorrow. Then, I'm free for the weekend.* The thought lifts her mood, setting the tone for the rest of the day.

xxx

On Friday, Gisele wakes up kicking the blankets off. She stretches her hands behind her head, daydreaming about how to start her day.

210

One, I am getting rid of these panties. Two, no shower. I am going to swim in the pool instead! That thought makes her feel like some kind of a rebel. Lying there, indulging in the dream, she remembers the showing. *Dam, I should cancel!*

Then the voice surfaces, *you never canceled a showing ever! Remember the time you were too sick to even get out of bed?*

Chuckling, she recollects that day. *There I was, a mask covering my face with a scarf wrapped around my head. I wore extra clothing to make sure the clients didn't catch what I had! Applied so much lotion to my hands that they glistened!* Remembering that day, she begins to laugh out loud! Imagining all they probably saw were two eyeballs staring back at them. Reflecting on how ridiculous the situation looked, she recalls what had put her at ease: the woman who showed up was covered head to toe in black clothing, with only her eyes visible! She grins, remembering how, even when she was fully covered, the gentleman still followed her around as if she were the Queen of Sheba. Well, that was until the lady gave him a light tap on the ear. After that, he kept his eyes firmly to himself.

She swings her legs off the bed and sits up. *The only reason I remembered that is because I can't imagine her doing something like that in her own country.*

Reflecting on sealing the deal, *the only reason I could surmise closing the sale at the time was I kept my distance. Never crossed my mind until later that the woman might have conceived this to be out of respect and not to keep them from getting sick.* Smiling to herself, she reflects that, either way, she had managed to gain a few more clients. She ponders for a moment—*maybe I should dress like that if the opportunity ever arose.* Taking a deep breath, she decides it is inappropriate and dismisses the thought.

Sliding off the bed with a heavy sigh, she goes to the study to check on the time the showing is scheduled. The phone rings, and she hurries towards it.

"Hello"

"Hello, Miss Fairchild!" The client says, breathing heavily. "We hate to do this, but we are unable to make the appointment today. Our son had a mishap at school, and we have to take him to the hospital." The client continues rapidly. "We really want to purchase the house! Is there anything we can do to hold our spot till we can rearrange a meet?"

Gisele controls her excitement at the good fortune. "Yes, under the circumstances, this is what I can suggest. You transfer ten percent of the asking price to my company, and I will relay this to the seller. If they agree, I will accept the transaction; that way, you will know you still have the first bid."

"Thank You, Miss Fairchild! We will do that right away!"

"Ok, let me look after this and you take care of your son." Knowing the sellers are in the Bahamas and don't care if the property gets sold today or next month, Gisele continues, "Here is what I will guarantee. If you buy the house, the money will go towards the down payment. If you decide for some reason not to and knowing your situation, the money will be returned. This transaction is just a formality for the seller."

"Oh," they say, sounding a bit shocked, "You are the best in the business, and now I know why. Bye, and thank you!"

Gisele, excited, hangs up the phone and bounces down the stairs to make coffee. Standing there, thrilled by the outcome, she marvels at how effortlessly situations come alive the way she envisions them. First, the threesome, then phone sex, the role-playing game, and now wanting to cancel the showing, and it happens. That conjured up the idea that maybe she is the one making it happen by thought. A warmth flows over her as that brings up the memory of sitting with her father on the couch watching TV. The intro came on. "There is nothing wrong with your television set. Do not attempt to adjust the picture. We are controlling the transmission." She tries to call up the name of the TV series, but she is interrupted as the coffee finishes brewing.

Pouring a glass of orange juice and a cup of coffee, she heads out to the pool. Walking into the sun brings a murmur to her lips. "Love being naked."

Setting the drinks on the small table, she leisurely enters the water. She dives forward, swimming a few laps before pausing to take a sip from her drink. Once finished, she leans back, closes her eyes, and floats peacefully, enjoying the tranquility of the day. Sensing she is not alone, she opens her eyes and spots Raul at the other end of the pool, his back turned toward her. In the deep end, she treads water, letting it cover her body.

"Raul, what are you doing here!" she commands.

Not turning around, he answers back. "It's the last Friday of the month. I'm here to clean the pool. I will leave."

"Shit!" She recalls all the girls' scenarios of the lonely housewife and the pool boy! Turning red at the idea of how Raul must conceive this, she calls out to him again, "No, if you get the bath towel from the chair on the island in the kitchen, I will be out of your way."

Seeing the towel being dropped, Raul turns to go back around the house. Gisele starts to apologize. "I am so sorry! It will not happen again, I promise!" Getting out she calls out to Raul that it is safe to continue his work. "There will be a tip on the poolside table for your discretion and the respect shown towards me." With that, she enters the house, still steaming on how stupid it was to forget what day it was.

She heads upstairs, gets dressed and is a lot calmer. Her little voice starts. *You are only upset and embarrassed at becoming aroused at seeing Raul in a tank top, with very dark muscular bare arms showing. Fantasying what his chest might look like if he turns around. Then imagining him getting horny admiring your naked body.*

That and recalling Janet's transgression didn't help. Gisele dresses and enters the study to finish up some loose ends. Once done, she leans back, letting her mind wonder at what is going to transpire on Saturday.

CHAPTER 29

Gisele is fidgeting around the house, trembling at the thought of what is going to happen after tonight. She tries to calm herself down. *I am so glad Bill went in early as he usually works in the study on Saturday. This will give me the solitude needed to prepare myself for different situations that might arise this evening. That became more apparent while we hugged at the door! Seeing the excitement in his eyes as he remarked that he wanted to have things cleaned up at the paper before the meeting with Dan tonight.* Fear rises as she kisses him, aware of the two unfolding narratives. His— a fantasy built around some elusive scoop that may or may not fall into his lap. And then there's hers—the one meticulously planned for weeks, the one that is about to become reality. Sighing, Gisele pours some coffee, the anxiety building. *I pray once he is presented with the opportunity, he doesn't become infuriated! With all my heart, I want him to be too aroused to be upset. Because when finding out what he is really there for could blow up in my face!*

Then, remembering, she tries to suppress the excitement bubbling inside, knowing exactly what is going to happen. Watching him leave through the door that morning, she acknowledges to herself… *Well, on the bright side, there's a big scoop. The headline will read!*

"Peeping Tom In The Neighborhood."

Laughing at the irony, she muses—*the downside? He wouldn't be able to print it. After all, the story is him.* Gisele tries to make light of everything to ease the queasiness she feels. Pacing with coffee in hand, she goes over the reasons the idea was started in the first place. *Just wanted a goddam threesome! Consequently, finding out that Bill likes to spy on people got me speculating about how that could be desirable! Eventually leading me to brood over Bill and me with another woman! Jeez, could there have been a better way? Stop second-guessing; you're nervous, not knowing how Bill will react, which excites my senses with a whole new set of sexual cravings! Oh, he will go along with it, I am sure. But what about later is what I am really worried about! Trying to rationalize, discovering I was involved, what would be his defense? He is the one having the threesome; he is the peeping tom! I only ask to watch, duplicating what he did a million times before! To see if I would be into peeping! I wonder if that would make me a Peeping Jane!* She shakes with laughter, more probably from the stress than the joke. One way or another, it will be interesting.

All that did was bring a whole new line of thought. Gisele reflects on how *it would feel if someone found out I was a peeping Jane!* Mortified at that thought, she shudders! *I got so engrossed with my own sexual gratification with no regard for the consequences or Bill's welfare! He will be humiliated being found out, and that is huge!*

There will be no coming back from that! Oh, for my sake, I pray that Dan can persuade Bill that only the four of us will ever know about his indiscretion! And the world will not find out about this! Besides, we find it more sexually stimulating and that it is nothing to be embarrassed about. We all have hidden erotic urges we would not like the world to know. I don't know if Dan can pull it off. But for all

216

our sakes, he'd better. At that, Gisele smirks, *that lawyer better have one very convincing closing argument!* Noticing the time, all this worry got her hungry. She goes into the kitchen to make a sandwich.

Finishing up lunch, she gets a glass of wine and takes it to the patio, and disrobes, stretching out on the lawn chair. With the warmth of the sun hitting her body, she lets out a heavy sigh! *It is the titillating fear driving me to new heights of arousal! Frightened by not knowing the outcome, brings me a new sexual craving of excitement I can not shrug off! How do I fight these intense urges? With all my senses on fire, the burning between my legs! I do not have the willpower, or if truth be told, I do not wish to stop it! For there is no foreplay in this world or the next that could bring this kind of extreme sexual appetite that is running through me! This is once in a lifetime!*

"Oh, shit!" Gisele breathes, hearing the door opening. "I will endure the ramifications no matter what!" she whispers, smiling rising to go greet Bill.

Gisele comes from the patio just in her panties and a drink. She throws her arms around, kissing him. "Hi, hon. I poured you a drink. I have to get dressed. The girls should be here in a minute to pick me up." She says and steps back.

"If they can wait a little, I have something in mind," Bill responds, grabbing the waistband of her panties and pulling her against him.

Gisele smiles, allowing her to be dragged over to him. Putting her hand on his crotch, she says seductively. "You keep that big boy hard until I get home. I'll have something for it to do then. You do know it is all about the foreplay, right?" she adds, drumming up all her willpower not to shove his hand down between her legs. Instead, she lifts it off her waist and backs away. Noticing his eyes, taking in the camel toe and the wet spot on her panties, she grins and heads to the stairs.

Bill stops at the door to the office. "You keep greeting me dressed like that. One day I will just rip those panties off and fuck you right here in the hall!" He declares, laughing playfully.

Gisele turns at the bottom of the stairs to face Bill. With a taunting grin, she utters, "Oh, you could try!" Stretching the waistband away from her belly, teasing. "If it wasn't so close to you having to leave, I would double dare you!" She spins around and scoots upstairs, beaming. *After all these years, he still lusts after this body!*

xxx

Once dressed, she strolls downstairs wearing a short skirt, no panties, and a see-through blouse with no bra. *Didn't take long to dress. But I only linger long enough, so he might not have time to jerk off before it's time for him to go!* Smiling to herself, she sticks her head into the office, just far enough so he can't see what she is wearing. She didn't want him to think she was out looking for some strange stuff. Well, to be fair, she is, but with him!

"The girls are here, and it's just about time for you to get going."

"Ok, have fun. I will let you know when I am home." Bill replies.

"I will call you before heading home to see where you are," She calls back, stepping out the door.

Outside, Jen is waiting. Getting in the car, the women drive off.

"Nice outfit. Jesus, your nipples are really hard," Jen comments, smirking.

"Well, that's not all. My pussy is just as soaked." Gisele answers. "Can't stop thinking about watching your mouth slide over my husband's cock."

"Ok, let's stop talking about it before I cum!" Jen squirms. "On a more serious note. Are you sure you are ok with this? I've been wanting to try and get that huge cock in me ever since I saw how long it was. Nothing more!" Jen declares.

"I was dreaming about a threesome for a very long time. Now that it might come true, there is no turning back. Let's just see where the evening takes us." Turning her head toward Jen, she continues, "Come Sunday, we will pray that we are all kosher with it!"

With that, both women laugh. Driving the rest of the way in silence, both are lost in their thoughts.

CHAPTER 30

Pulling into the drive, Gisele catches Dan standing in the doorway. With the car coming to a stop, Gisele comments. "He is a little enthusiastic!"

Jen laughs. "That's an understatement. Caught him jerking off this morning, so asked him what the hell?! He said he couldn't help himself thinking of you and me making out! So, I said if he described his thoughts, I would give him a blowjob. I was swallowing cum at the point where he was describing me fingering you while you stared at his cock, wishing you could suck it." Jen is still laughing! "I came a little myself."

With a big grin on their faces, the girls get out of the car. Dan, walking over to them, escorts the two smirking ladies into the house.

"Gisele you better get into your hiding place. Bill will be here soon." Dan instructs ."There are some toys in there as well. In case you need them. Oh, don't worry, they are brand new. Jen made sure to sanitize them."

Remembering what was revealed in the car, Gisele, still looking at Dan, reaches for Jen. Putting one hand behind Jen's head, the other around the waist, she kisses her fully on the mouth, tongue sliding past open lips. After a moment, she pulls back, satisfied with the response and moaning, and says, "Oh, I will need them!"

"Ok, you two cut it out! I can't have a hard-on while talking to Bill! Who, by the way, will be here soon! So, Gisele, get hiding!" Dan commands, leading Gisele toward the newly built bar.

Gisele balks in mid-stride, utterly captivated by the magnificence and beauty of the bar cabinet before her. *It must be six and a half feet in length if not seven.* The front half was rectangular, and the top and bottom were sold mahogany. The middle was a dark glass, almost black, going all the way around to the ends to shape the bar. The cabinet was a work of beauty in itself! Set back against the wall, it was half in length, all made of mahogany. It stood at least eight feet in height and had beveled mirrors. Gisele feels a nudge pushing her forward as Dan slides one side of the bar out.

"You can admire it later! But we have to hurry. Bill should be here any minute!" Dan insists, helping her bend down to crawl into the hiding space.

On all fours, Gisele realizes that her short skirt gives Bill a glimpse of her bare ass, and a low groan escapes him. Hearing it, the memory of being in this position before, with him behind her, sends a rush of heat through her. Gisele flirtatiously spreads her legs apart, pretending she is having trouble getting in, but really to give him a better view of her pussy. *Ah, that should do it.* Finally, she is in position. Dan moves the bar back into place.

Gisele is overly impressed also with all the trouble they went through to ensure how comfortable she would be while being concealed. The bottom was covered with a soft futon and two plush round cushions to rest her head. A couple of different types of dildos lay beside them. Gisele, looking out through the dark glass cover in the middle can see the couch clearly. Moving her head, the underside of the dining table comes into view. Grinning, she surmises this must be like looking into an interrogation room through a one-way mirror, just like in the police movies. *This is going to work fine.* The sides are wide enough so she can change position easily. The opening in the backside has a small fan on the outside pushing cool air in.

"Well, these two will stop at nothing, trying to get what they want. Or, in this case, what I want!" She murmurs to herself.

Leaning back, she removes the skirt. "Won't need that or this." She begins to remove the blouse when the door charm rings. She freezes, doubt setting in! The thought of all the things that could go wrong comes to the surface. Contemplating the situation she is in, all apprehension subsides.

She murmurs to herself. "What am I supposed to do? Jump out bare ass and say what? Just checking out the bar!" Holding back a laugh, Gisele starts to make herself comfortable, remembering the old motto.

In for a penny, in for a pound, they say.

Besides, by tomorrow, I will either be single or a new chapter of sexual adventures will start. Hearing "Come in, Bill." her mind drifts back to the moment. Gisele is surprised at how well she can hear the two men as they walk past.

"Would you like a whisky, bourbon, Gin, vodka?" Dan asks.

"Whisky straight, please," Bill replies.

Watching the two as they go into the living room, the end of the couch, coffee table, and loveseat come into view. Her eyes go wide, noticing that there is no projector on the table just a small box. *What the hell is going on?* Gisele feels a little panic set in, feeling trapped. *Is this some kind of double cross? Am I the one being played?!* That thought brings the excitement to new heights! She now focuses on the two men with newfound interest.

Bill is motioning to sit in the big chair as Dan turns toward the bar to get the drinks. Gisele catches a deep breath as he gets close. She can see his face as clear as day, then just his crotch, his semi-hard-on visible as he stands close, mixing the drinks."Can they see me? He looked right at me!" Then the paranoia subsides as Dan turns walking back with the drinks. Gisele, watching as Dan hands Bill the whisky, her muscles tense. Knowing what's coming, the fear fuels the excitement as she anticipates Bill's reaction.

Dan begins. "You are probably wondering what the big story is. We will get to that soon enough! But first, I am going to tell you a little story. It is somewhat personal! But in the end, you will see why I needed to tell you. Jen and I have sexual fantasies that we like to bring to life in our own home. Now, if what we do during these endeavors comes to light, it would be no big deal except for one individual who was participating without our knowledge. How did we find out that there was a fourth person?"

Gisele draws in her breath and gradually utters, "Here we go!" Breathless, she gawks out the glass.

"One night after one of our play dates was over. We were getting ready for bed. Jen turned to me and said I get the feeling someone is watching us. Not that I mind. It really turns me on. But if a person is watching, we should find out to see if he or she will join us. Or at least offer them a drink. We both laughed at that and retired for the night." Dan pauses and offers Bill a refill.

"Sure," Bill replies.

Gisele releases a heavy sigh as she lies on her back. Prompting up the pillows, her one hand strokes the pubic hair, and the other brings the glass up to take a sip. *Dam, they are right about lawyers. They are long-winded.* With that, she lies back as she hears Dan's voice.

"So, to continue, I decided to install a security camera right where I thought the perp would be. Sure enough. Jen was right. Now, being a criminal lawyer, I have the means and resources to find out information and retrieve objects I want. That brings us to the USB drive I want to show you and the reason why you are here!" Dan moves to the equipment.

Gisele starts to wonder why Bill hasn't acknowledged that he's the one Dan is talking about. *He always loves playing the long game. Maybe he's pretending to help Dan figure out who it could be. Or perhaps the camera, unable to get a clear shot of the perp, was there to clean up the image.* She watches intently as Dan walks to the table and inserts the drive.

"I am only going to show you part of the video that my associates acquired. Then we will talk."

Lying there, Gisele can only imagine what is playing. A hand starts to move between her legs, a finger toying with the entrance. *What parts is he showing? Is it Jen's head under the table, mouth wrapped around the man's cock? Ohhh,* she moans. *Or forward it to where the guy has his cock shoved up that magnificent ass?* Gisele's finger begins to move in and out as her ass rises slowly. Just when she is about to climax, the sound of Dan moving, the dying hum of the equipment, brings her back. *Aahh, the moment of truth.* Gisele doesn't realize she is holding her breath until she gasps for air. *Jesus, did I go too far? Will he storm out? The only thing so far is that I wasn't indicated.*

Now, she just listens.

Dan turns to Bill. "By the look on your face, we both now know who we are talking about here. No! Don't get up! Finish your drink and hear me out."

Gisele has her face pressed against the glass, trying to get a better look at Bill. His face is flushed. She doesn't know if it is from embarrassment or from anger. But at last, she watches as he settles back in the chair and takes a sip.

Dan, at that point, continues. "Well as friends, we go out to parties together and dinners. But I guess Gisele and Jen meet up during the day for coffee, and they talk about more than what they are going to make for supper. Then, on one occasion, as I understand it, the subject got around to their sex life. Which got your wife describing how well-hung you are. That, in turn, got my wife fantasizing if she could get a cock that thick and long in her ass. The more she thought about it, the more obsessed she became. That's when she came to me with her problem." Dan halts here to observe the effect this was having on his guest and then offers. "Can I get you another whisky? Then I will get to the point."

Bill accepts the offer.

Returning with the drinks, Dan picks up where he left off. "So, Jen and I came up with a plan to see if we could get you two into a foursome! Well, as you know, that didn't work. But all that rubbing and flirting and rejection just made Jen want that huge cock in her ass that much more. The more my wife stewed over this, the more it consumed her! Then, one evening, returning home she came running all excited, meeting me at the door. She said *I got it, honey! I knew I recognized Bill from somewhere! You still have that camera from the old place. The one we used when we wanted to catch that peeper!* Assuring her, I did. We went and retrieved it. On viewing it, to our surprise, there you were, staring back at us! So now that brings us to the here and now. I will get us refills before continuing." Taking the two glasses, he heads to the bar.

Roger D. Ewen

CHAPTER 31

Gisele is in awe. "For one second, I almost believed that's how it happened," she murmurs to herself. "Now I get why everyone thinks he's such a brilliant lawyer! I swear, a judge could witness someone killing their wife and still preside over the case. By the time Dan's closing statement is done, the man would be declared an innocent victim—and the judge would think he did it!" She grins, a rush of admiration spilling over. "I love you, mister!"

All the tension drains from her body, replaced with pure excitement, knowing she's in the clear. The only thing left to face is Bill's response. Gisele stretches, easing her aching muscles and sneaking a peek at Dan's crotch as he moves away from the bar.

Returning, Dan hands Bill his drink, "Where was I? Oh yeah, seeing you on camera. We came up with a plan. Jen and I agreed at the risk of losing two great friends and a colleague we would confront you, giving you two choices. One, you could get up and leave and I will take the footage to the police, and you will lose everything. Or you play out what is on that USB stick, and you will get the equipment, the thumb drive, and a signed document stating you were blackmailed! And retain me as your lawyer; that way, I cannot reveal what I found out. If I do, we both will lose our careers."

Gisele's heart stops, watching as Bill leans forward and picks up the paper. Gisele notices Dan take a step back, anticipating a different response. She watches closely, ears alert, as Bill sits back to read the document. She holds her breath, tension mounting, and then exhales in relief when she hears his answer.

"Ok! Looks like I have no choice. I have never cheated on my wife. If you knew her as well as I do, you would know why. With that said, and you holding all the cards, I have one request." Bill glares at Dan, a stern warning forming on his lips. "The only way my wife finds out about this is if I tell her, agreed?" With Dan nodding in acknowledgement, Bill adds. "When do we start?"

"Now." Dan summons Jen, "Could you come and join us, please?"

Gisele's heart is racing so fast she can hardly breathe! *I have never been this excited during foreplay ever! This is like when you are preparing to watch a porn movie, but a way more advantageous! It is live, and your husband is one of the stars. Stop it! You don't want to climax before the show starts!* She lays back, getting in position for the best possible viewing ever and reaches for the large dildo. "Now I am ready."

Seeing Bill stand, she notices he has the biggest hard-on she has ever seen. Her breath catches as a wicked grin spreads across her face. "You bastard," she sighs, biting her lip. "This is going better than I ever hoped for." The anticipation coils inside her, tightening with every passing second.

Spotting Jen entering the room, Gisele's head jerks back as Jen throws a quick glance toward the bar. *Jeez, have to get used to this glass. Makes me feel as if I was standing right beside her!* A yearning fills her, viewing the outfit that is being worn for the game. A see-through blouse, unbuttoned to the navel, clings to her body, her erect nipples pushing straight out. The short skirt barely covers her hips, leaving little to the imagination, stealing one's breath away. It's time to stop thinking and just enjoy.

Jen strolls over, standing next to Bill putting a hand on his shoulder.

"You two go sit yourself at the table while I go finish making dinner." Dan offers.

The pair moves to the dining table. "Can I get you another drink, Bill? I am going to have a glass of wine before dinner." Jen inquires.

"Sure. Oh, I left my glass on the coffee table," Bill answers.

"That's ok. I will get you another one from the bar," Jen calls back and heads to the bar, all the while staring straight into the glass in the middle of the bar. On reaching the counter, Jen presses herself against the glass, making sure the front of her skirt is raised. She ensures that her pelvis is pressed against the glass with one leg to the side. Gisele is now staring right at one very hairy and wet pussy. *Oh, is that your way of letting me know how aroused you are, realizing you are going to have my husband's cock up your ass as I observe! Or maybe you are teasing me, knowing how much I would like to have my head buried between those gorgeous legs, licking you clean! Being fully aware, I can't! Either way, I will get my chance to pay you back!*

Then the skirt falls into place, the back of Jen's skirt swinging as she walks back to the table. Realizing how close her face is to the glass, she draws back, getting comfortable again, laughing. "Just like watching a movie." She mumbles, viewing the two as Jen hands Bill his drink and then sits beside him.

That prompts Gisele to lean back down. *I didn't notice in the film I watched that there were only three chairs at the table. Hmmm.* The only view she is focused on now is under the table. Jen and Bill's chair face her.

"Let the show begin!" she breathes.

Jen's legs come into view as she sits beside Bill. It doesn't take long for her hand to reach Bill's crotch and unzip him. Having trouble, Gisele watches as Bill helps, undoing his belt and then pushing his pants down. Doing so, that huge cock springs out into Jen's waiting hand. Her fingers can barely encircle it as her wrist starts to slowly move up and down, fingers squeezing at the same time, trying to get them to meet. She watches as Jen's legs spread and her skirt rises, the other hand sliding down. Then a finger starts stroking up and down her pussy, in sync with her other hand. The hairs and lips start spreading as two of Jen's fingers slide in and out slowly. A loud moan can be heard. *That is it!* Gisele reaches for one of the dildos and slides it into her as she watches. *Am I going to climax before the good stuff? Oh, hell, I have the stamina to cum more than once!* At that, her attention is drawn to Jen's chair. It moves back, and her head comes into view. The mouth opens to engulf that huge head, prying the lips farther apart as Jen forces them to slide further down the throbbing shaft with her fingers still stroking between her legs.

Gisele grins, thrilled, as Jen's head stops and moves back up a little. *Oh, that's reassuring she can't take it all either!* But suddenly, she gasps at the sight of the fingers sliding down, and so does the lips. Slowly, that huge cock slides deeper into Jen's mouth, inch by inch, until it presses down her throat. *God, dam it, she swallowed the whole thing. How the hell can she do that, I can only get a quarter of it in. She will have to show me how to do that!*

With that, Gisele's body begins to jerk as she shoves the dildo faster in and out, eyes closing, thinking of her and Jen sucking off her husband. Climaxing, she doesn't see Jen's head move above the table and the chair being pulled back in as Dan enters the room with the dish of food.

As her eyes slowly open, all she sees now is three pairs of legs under the table and Jen still stroking that huge cock as they talk.

Jen's hand moves up from the base, and fingers are spread apart as they reach the throbbing head as the pre cum is being squeezed out. Gisele's body gives a last small quiver as she takes in the scene.

The three seem to be chatting away as if nothing more is going on. Gisele relaxes a little. *God dam it, when are they going to quit this shit and move to the couch? I need to get into the action! Get something going!* As if Jen could read her mind, the hand moves from Bill's cock to her spread legs. One finger, then two, at last, three slides in her cunt, moving in and out. Once her hand is soaked with warm juices, she reaches over and starts stroking that huge cock once again. Observing this, Gisele feels herself getting aroused again. *Oh, I am going to be sore tomorrow! I better pace myself.* With that, she just rubs her pussy softly as she watches.

Jen's hand disappears from under the table. Bill's cock is just standing straight up, glistening in the light from the precum and Jen's juices. Gisele fidgets, wondering what's going on, and then it hits her—they're recreating the dinner from the video. An image forms in her mind, and she snickers. *What the hell is Jen eating with that hand? Finger food.* She laughs aloud.

"That's rich—finger food!"

Unable to see above the table, her imagination runs wild. The movement from the table snaps her back to the moment, refocusing her on the scene playing out before her.

Dan's legs disappear from the table. Moments later, Jen's head comes into view as she swallows Bill's cock right to the base. *May you choke on that, you bitch!* Gisele smirks. Jen slides her mouth back up to the head, sucking on it before gliding down to the base again. Bill's legs twitch involuntarily. Gisele experiences a pang of jealousy. *I really got to learn that.* Bringing the huge dildo to her mouth, she tries to imitate Jen but starts to choke right away. *Dam it.* Before she can try again, she notices Jen's head move up, making a plopping sound as the lips come off the head, then out of sight. Dan's legs are once again under the table. Bill's cock has Jen's fingers around it once again, being stroked.

Gisele starts to get impatient again. *Now, what is keeping them?* To help her calm down, she thinks about the tape again.

First, the making of the dinner so Jen can be alone with the guy. Then the three eat. Then, clearing off the table. The preparation of the dessert. So, Jen can be alone again with the man. Then eating. God dam, I can't take this anymore! As she is squirming, trying to control herself, there is movement from under the table. The three chairs push back, and the next thing Gisele sees is the three of them coming in front of the bar. Jen leads Bill by his cock as she walks over to face Dan. Her husband immediately unzips his pants.

Hmm, I guess we are skipping dessert this time. A smile forms on her face.

Dan's cock is out by the time Jen gets to him. Not letting go of Bill, she then grabs the hardon in front of her with the other hand and starts to kneel. When she is even with the throbbing tip, she lets go moving her head forward, slowly opening her lips to start sucking the head. Then, she slides down the shaft to the base. All the while slowly sliding her hand up and down Bill's cock.

Gisele moans, her eyes locked on Jen kneeling between both men—her lips wrapped around one cock while her hand strokes the other. The sight sends a deep shiver through her body. Noticing this, she starts to fantasize about having two cocks at the same time. Her hand starts to slide down her inner leg over her swollen lips while staring at Jen's bobbing head. Dan's balls are kind of bouncing off Jen's chin. Watching that, she laughs. *So that is where that saying comes from. Never thought of it before.* Then her eyes veer over to take in Bill, standing like a statue, hands by his side, his huge erection throbbing, spreading Jen's fingers apart as she jerks him off!

Gisele's heart starts to pound. *This is it. Jeez, I am going to have a heart attack! I am so excited I can barely breathe.* Moving her hand away from her crotch and resting it on her chest, she begins to think. *Calm down you have to concentrate so you can pick the right moment to reveal yourself. Too soon or too late could spoil everything. Then it hits her. I know exactly when to come out.* Her heart slows down, and she gets comfortable, ready to watch the live porn show that is unfolding in front of her.

CHAPTER 32

Jen's head move back to let Dan slide out of her mouth. Seizing his erection and stroking it, she slowly turns her head to Bill's throbbing shaft, deliberately kissing, then licking the tip. A moan can be heard. Moving her head forward, with her lips barely open, she forces the head to part them. Once her mouth has surrounded the head, she stops to suck. Sliding it further past her lips, she halts to enjoy the feel. This, Jen repeats until all of Bill is engulfed! Jen suddenly returns to the tip, her tongue extending as she licks slowly around the head, her eyes flicking toward the bar. With her mouth wide open, she thrusts sharply down to the base, the force causing his balls to graze her chin. She begins bobbing her head swiftly, sucking as hard as she can, maintaining an intense rhythm. Bill's hands move to the back of her head, holding it still as he tries to control the movement, his hips thrusting back and forth, sliding in and out with a deliberate, steady pace.

Gisele is lying stock-still! Fixed solely on the action on the other side of the glass, she takes in a sharp breath as she tries to breathe. The dildo is lying between her legs, untouched in fear she would orgasm if moved. *I have got to try and hold onto this extreme sensation as long as possible! Never in my entire life have I been driven to this kind of supreme erotic state!* The voice emerges: *what about the time when you were still in high school?*

Not even then did I enjoy this kind of arousal!

Gisele stirs, changing positions to relieve the pressure on the aching muscles. That lets her collect her thoughts. She murmurs to herself, "I do not remember none of that being in the film." she holds back a laugh, "That was all to show what a great cocksucker she is!" She puts a hand to her mouth to muffle an outburst. "Well, this just confirms it, the bitch!" She mumbles, watching Jen sliding Bill out of her mouth as her head turns to stare straight at the bar. A wicked grin forms on her lips.

Fighting the urge to masturbate, Gisele observes Jen rising between the two men, squeezing both cocks that are still in her hands. Standing, she steps forward and releases them. She sets out in the direction of the couch, signaling for them to get rid of their clothes. Gisele realizing she still has her blouse on, starts to remove it while ogling the two men undressing. As the men finish, standing together, they are unaware that they are facing the bar. A grin starts to form on Gisele's face. *You really do not realize what a difference seven inches make until you observe it next to one that is not. Dam, I am a lucky lady!* The blouse is removed; her eyes follow the two attractive buttocks flexing as the boys go to stand by Jen.

No sooner does Dan move to the couch and out of sight. All that can be seen of him is one leg on the floor beside the arm and the other resting up on the back of the couch. Gisele can only imagine what Dan looks like from the video. The camera angle offers a different perspective than looking out from under the bar through the glass at the arm of the couch. But that doesn't restrict the view of the action unfolding at the other end.

Bill stands sideways, facing Jen. Her back is against the couch, facing forward, eyes locked on the bar. Gisele savors the image of Jen's nude body—every curve, every detail.

Bill remains still, his erection standing tall, while he enjoys the feel of Jen's firm breasts, her hardened nipples pointing straight at him. Then, there's movement. Jen reaches over, fingers grazing Bill's balls, drawing them toward her. His shaft twitches in response, bouncing with anticipation.

That was more for my benefit, Gisele thinks. Then it struck her! *Bill has never, all through this, reached out and tried to touch Jen's private parts. Not once! Oh, you will get rewarded for that big boy!* Suddenly, there is more movement.

Jen's hand moves away as she keeps her gaze fixed on the bar. A subtle, almost hesitant smile plays on her lips as if seeking reassurance. To Gisele, it's the look of uncertainty—of someone teetering on edge, unsure whether to step forward or retreat. Not sure if she can do it. Or how much is it going to hurt? Then it is gone as Jen faces the couch and bends over the arm. The skirt just rises to reveal that nice round, smooth ass and those beautiful swollen lips. *Looks like this girl is going to explode at any time, as some wetness can be seen on the inside of her legs.*

Gisele now can only picture what Jen is doing as her head disappears out of sight. Bill's naked body is the next thing she sees as he starts to move, standing behind Jen, stooped over. Now all Gisele sees is Bill's back; her eyes move, focusing on that nice tight ass and those big hanging balls as he positions himself between Jen's spread legs. Then everything goes still!

Gisele's eyes widen! As some of the passion is replaced with fear, she murmurs to herself, "What the fuck! Are you considering changing your mind? What the fuck am I to do!" Gisele agonizes over the situation. All the panic subsides as she realizes that the slight hesitation was Bill trying to arrange his body so he could kneel, pressing his face between Jen's ass cheeks. Once arranged, the head starts to move up and down.

Ha, you remember the video and the man getting the ass ready for penetration. I bet you are letting your tongue get a taste of that juicy pussy while you're at it. Letting out a small breath as the dread lifts, Gisele's legs relax as she circles the dildo over the little button, sending a twitch through her body as she watches.

Bill's head moves up Jen's body as he rises. At full height, Bill's feet move to push Jen's feet apart. Spreading her legs wider, at the same time, his thighs press forward a little. Then a little more! Watching this, Gisele can only imagine that big cock's head spreading that ass wide open! The third push brings Jen's head above the arm and into sight. Gisele wonders if she is going to yell, stop or just gasp for air. Bill's hips move back, and at the same time, Jen's head moves out of sight. Then Bill swiftly thrusts forward again. This time, Jen doesn't raise her head.

Observing the steady rhythm of Bill's hips, Gisele starts to get ready to make her move. Every nerve in her body is taut. Slowly pushing the bar sideways, she crawls out onto the floor. Keeping an eye on Bill all her muscles tense. So far, so good. Nervous, her mind tries to compensate. *What was that joke?*

A man and a woman are having sex on the railway tracks. The man is cumming! And the train is coming! And the train is the only one with brakes!

Letting out a little chuckle while creeping forward on weak knees, one foot in front of the other, she tries not to make a sound. Every sense is heightened - the echo of Bill's belly against Jen's ass and the balls slapping those swollen lips between Jen's legs.

Gisele is now only a few inches away. *I have never been this sexually aroused and so frightened at the same time!* Creeping closer, with the thought in her head, *this is it!! Point of no return! A new beginning or the end!*

Moving her head closer to Bill's ear, breast pressing against his back, she whispers. "Don't stop! Everything will make sense after!"

Bill's head snaps toward the sound, locking eyes with his wife. The look was that of a child who just got caught with his hand in the cookie jar.

"Shh," she whispers as her hand reaches up and touches his face, pushing it gently back to face the front. *Boy, did I pick the right moment! Bill never even missed a beat.* Gisele then bends over the arm, and when she is even with Jen's bobbing head, she breathes, "Lucky Bitch! Both holes filled! Let me see if I can help fill the last one for you." With that, she reaches over and pinches one of Jen's very erect nipples that are being pushed outward by the breasts being squeezed against the arm.

Feeling Bill's hand on her ass, she whispers again to Jen loud enough for Dan to hear. "I think my ass is going to get finger fucked while yours has a big cock in it." Hearing a moan, she turns her head toward the sound and meets Dan's eyes. His eyes look glazed over as he must feel like he is in heaven. *Well, that is all going to change when I get my revenge!*

CHAPTER 33

Gisele, upon straightening up, feels Bill's finger slide out of her ass. She notices his hand move back to Jen's hip to pull her into him as his thrusting seems to intensify. Moving her hand between Bill's balls and those swollen lips, she easily slides two fingers in as that pussy is soaked. She starts fingering Jen as much as possible with the balls restricting her hand, and just like that, the promise is kept! At the same moment, she whispers to Bill, "Lucky girl! Every hole is filled." Sensing the balls tightening, her hand pulls out and moves up between Bill's belly and Jen's ass. *Shit, he is going to cum any minute. Please hold on a little longer!* She tries to think of something else.

That got Gisele panicking some that he might not last until she gets her revenge. Reacting quickly, she pushes back on his belly until his cock slides out. Seizing her husband's cock, she yanks it even with Jen's exposed, wet lips and gently tries to tug it forward. Bill hesitates and shakes his head no. *Aah, so Dan mentions the no pussy fucking allowed.*

Gisele mouths, "It is ok. Jen wants this, please!"

Putting the free hand on his ass, she pushes gently forward. There's only a flicker of hesitation now—Bill is too far gone, offering no resistance. He lets the pressure move him into her. The head starts to stretch the lips apart. Thinking Jen never had anything that big in there... However, her thought is interrupted by Jen's struggle. It wasn't just because of Bill's big cock, but rather because Dan was trying to rise.

Gisele catches sight of the expression on Dan's face—dead set on getting off the couch! Meanwhile, Jen struggles to push him back down, pressing both hands against his chest. Cock is still in her mouth as she sucks, and that sets Gisele into action. Quickly moving to the side of the couch, she throws her body weight over Dan's chest just above Jen's hands. This means that her tits are covering Dan's face forcing his head back down. Struggling for a few minutes, Dan's body finally relaxes. Noticing Jen's hands move back to fondle Dan's balls, the other seizing the throbbing shaft, Gisele lifts her weight off and slides along the couch. Causing her hard nipples to slide down Dan's face to rest gently on his chest. Her face is even with his as they stare into each other's eyes. It seems like an eternity, but Dan's eyes finally reveal what Gisele is thinking! "What's good for the goose is good for the gander!"

Gisele, still holding Dan's gaze, spontaneously reaches over and pinches one of his erect nipples. Squeezing tighter, she watches as Dan tries to muffle the cry as she slowly lowers her head and flicks the tip of the other nipple before she starts sucking on it. Dan's hips start to push up to get farther down Jen's throat.

At that moment Gisele finds out something more about Dan. *This is the first time you haven't been in control! And you love it! You want someone else to be in charge! You want to be dominated! You welcome the pain! Well, I think Jen and I can help you with that!*

The theory is interrupted by Dan's body tensing! Turning her head to peer at Jen, she notices Jen's throat starts to contract to swallow as Dan starts to cum! Gisele quickly stands to move beside Bill as he is pulling out. Her fingers immediately encircle his shaft and start to jerk it slowly, then faster, as she feels the throbbing increase. Trying to see how far she can make the sperm shoot up Jens's back, Gisele's heart quickens as the warm, thick fluid streams out.

Her knees go weak at the sight of it getting into Jen's hair and onto her back. Her fingers squeeze tighter to get every last drop as the liquid flows over her fingers.

Gisele releases her hold as Bill steps back. Stepping aside herself she sees Jen start to straighten up and Dan getting off the couch to stand. Jen and Gisele move close together, holding their breath waiting on what might come next!

"Well, I have towels and bathrobes in the other rooms so we can clean up, and then we can sit by the fireplace to have a drink before the evening ends," Dan announces as he gestures to the others to head into the other room. The men hesitate to let the women go ahead.

Gisele smirks. *Ah, we know you want us to believe you're being a gentleman, but we all know you just want a good look at our bare ass.* Chuckling, she adds a sway to her walk, making her hips bounce. She glances over at Jen, noticing her stiff movements. *Thought so—you must be too sore to care.*

As the girls enter the room, Jen beams, immediately turning to throw her arms around Gisele's neck, resting her chin on her shoulder.

"That was amazing! I never had anything that big inside me! Then, when you started to finger me! With every hole filled! I was just about to pass out!"

Gisele was kind of listening, but her mind was concentrated more on how Jen's warm breast felt pressed against hers. With her arms around Jen's waist, hands creasing the lower back, Gisele is tingling. She wanted her hands to slide farther down but knew it was too soon. Jen is still babbling as she breaks the embrace; just at that moment, Gisele moves her crotch to press against Jen's.

Jen, arms extended with both hands on Gisele's shoulders, gazes into her eyes and continues excitedly. "Then, the sensation of Bill's throbbing cock at my entrance, I knew it was all you. I knew you would want revenge! I certainly did! Don't know how you managed to encourage Bill to shove his huge cock into my pussy knowing the consequences!" Jen takes a breath, "but when it started stretching my cunt all I could think of was how was I going to repay you! I don't even know if it all would fit! I just know when he hit the end, I orgasmed, barely realizing Dan was trying to rise until I could focus again! I was just about to shit! The rush I got from the fear he might get loose and the extreme arousal of Bill fucking me, WOW! There are no words to describe that sensation. But I am sure glad you intervened!" Jen drops her arms to her side. Breathing heavily, she waits for her friend's response.

Gisele reaches for Jen's hands now that she finally can get a word in. "First, as for the repaying part. If you can arrange to have that husband of yours long tongue between my legs would be payment enough! But for now, a kiss would be sufficient!" With that she pulls Jen towards her, pressing her lips on Jen's mouth. Then they step back as both women shudder. With a slight frown, Gisele presses on. "On a more serious note, do you think the guys are having it out in the other room?"

"No," she says. "If Dan was going to retaliate, he would have done it right there. Besides, I gave him the look! Letting him think that this was my payback for doing it to me!"

Gisele thought it was something else but said nothing.

The women finish cleaning up and put on their robes. Entering the room, they find the guys sitting by the fire in their robes. Bill, with his whisky and Dan, with a glass of champagne, both laughing.

"Welcome back, girls." Dan greets them, "Didn't think you were ever coming out!" Both have big smiles on their faces.

Gisele thinks, *Me either. I was a little scared but said nothing.*

She sits beside Bill, accepting the glass of champagne offered to her. Jen settles next to Dan, taking the drink from his hand. The four of them sit in silence for a while, each lost in their own thoughts.

Gisele scans their faces. *I wonder what's going through their heads. Do they think we were in the other room comparing notes? Maybe they imagined we were enjoying each other instead.*

A sly smile crosses her lips. The thought of having Jen to herself lingers—until Dan's voice snaps her back to reality.

"Well, I guess we should address the elephant in the room!" The other three tense up. *Dam, here we go!* Gisele inhales, indecisive on how she is going to react when the next words are uttered.

CHAPTER 34

"Well, Bill! You probably have a lot of questions, such as, why is your wife here? What happens next? And ones I haven't thought of." No one says a word. All eyes are on Dan. Seeing how he isn't interrupted, he continues. "I'll answer the first one. Once we discovered it was you spying on us, Jen got excited." Dan looks at his wife and puts his arm around her. He turns back to Bill and carries on. "We started figuring out a plan on what our next course of action would be. Once the scheme was in place, we put together how to persuade you to participate in our little game; Jen said she wouldn't have any of it if Gisele wasn't informed! Well, I figured it would be an excellent time to put our strategy into motion."

Gisele tense as Dan pauses to take a drink. A tingle goes through her watching Dan's eyes focus on her. Then she relaxes as he continues.

"So, we approached your wife to let her know of your indiscretion. Once we revealed that you were spying on us, and before she got into trying to convince us, we were mistaken. We let her know we had evidence. Naturally, she insisted on us producing the proof. Upon showing her part of the tape of you caught on camera, the swearing and the threats started!"

Gisele scans the room, especially trying to read Jen's reaction during all this but she keeps staring at her husband with admiration as he talks.

"Now, reading people is one of the skills I use every day. Interpreting your wife's actions, I realized that she wasn't mad at what you did. But more pissed at keeping it from her. So, I gathered the rest of the performance was for our benefit. Having all that information I interrupted her and pretty much delivered the same blackmail speech I gave you."

Gisele watches as Dan pauses to take another sip, more to gather his thoughts than to quench any thirst.

Then, a notion hits her. *Damn it—Dan's yarn is so convincing, I'm starting to believe it really happened! God damn it, I'm a victim!*

She bites back a guffaw, forcing herself to keep listening.

"Well, your wife accepted everything as you did, but she had a proposition of her own. She would like to watch you fuck my wife without you knowing. Well, you know the answer to that!"

Gisele mouths the words "Thank you" to Dan. *What a goddam good storyteller he is. Probably what makes him such an outstanding lawyer.* Looking at Jen, she notices a big smile on her face. Gisele sticks out her tongue as the yarn goes on.

"As for the next question. You held up your end of the bargain and more." The women hold their breath until they hear the next words. "So, you have all the papers which are signed. No one gains anything by exposing you. Just the opposite! We all lose. With that said, I do not think it is fair that we know something incriminating about you, and you know nothing about us. Let me fix that! I will start."

Gisele peers at her friend. *This should be intriguing.* She smiles, tugging the robe tighter around her before resting her head on Bill's shoulder. Her eyes flick to Dan, eager for the yarn to begin.

"One weekend, my parents decided to take a trip. Leaving me and my sister to watch the house. Yeah, you know where this is going. Anyway, my sister decided to throw a party. Being of age, she could buy liquor, so the stage was set. Saturday evening, all her friends showed up. That is when the drinking started. I had a few to get my courage up to approach a few of the girls who came without boyfriends. Being only seventeen, my advances were futile! As they were older and with my boyish good looks, I appeared more like twelve and, in my drunken state, acted like it, so they thought I was adorable but not fuckable!" Dan chuckles as the others laugh. He takes a drink and then continues.

"So frustrated with the results, I proceeded to get intoxicated. Finally, not being able to stand anymore I staggered to my parent's room as I knew my sister told everyone that it was off-limits. There, falling backward onto the bed, I passed out. Didn't know how long I was out, but as I was coming to my senses, I heard the door open. Then, I heard a male's voice. *You promise I could fuck you in the ass tonight! The female whispered, shut the door! Someone is in here!* There was silence for a moment except for the shuffling of feet. Thinking they were coming toward me, I closed my eyes. Don't know why; it was too dark to see anything anyways. Just thought it might help them leave if I didn't acknowledge them. Instead, the girl responded with, *Only if you let me suck this guy off while you do!* Hearing, *Ok!* my cock went as hard as a rock."

Gisele leers over at Jen, thinking he probably just about shot his load, knowing he might get a blowjob. The grin on Jen's face reveals she is thinking the same. The story goes on.

"During all this, my mind, in its drunken state, was trying to figure out who the girl was. She sounded like someone I knew! I lost interest, sensing my pants being unzipped. Then my cock was wiggled out. The fingers that encircled it started to jerk me off. When I felt soft, warm lips inclosing the tip, that is when I started to fully come awake, and the fog cleared! It was my sister! I was about to reveal myself when I felt the lips being pushed over the head. That is when it registered; he was fucking her in the ass, causing the mouth on my cock to slide over the head and down. With her hand stroking faster as she sucked, I didn't care anymore. It was my first blowjob, and I was going to enjoy it—no matter who it was! It didn't take long before I was cumming! Sis was swallowing it all to the sounds of the guy moaning as he fucked her. Finally, the mouth was removed, and the sound of pants being zipped up rang in my ears. Then the door opened, and they were gone. There I laid all by myself, cock hanging out with the guilt seeping in that I let my sister blow me!

"I don't think my sister ever found out it was me in the bedroom. But for me? Every time I saw that ass in tight jeans. Or any time she would run from the bathroom to the bedroom in her panties, I would run to my room and masturbate. This finally faded as I went out with other girls. They say you never forget your first blow job! I didn't! Then Jen came into my life, and well, here we are!"

Dan stops to look at the others. With a concern expression, Dan adds. "I always felt uncomfortable about the incest. I would be embarrassed if anyone found out about me fantasizing about my sister like that. So that's my story." Dan, creasing his wife's leg, addresses Jen. "Let's hear your most intimate experience that only you have knowledge of."

Roger D. Ewen

CHAPTER 35

Gisele turns her eyes toward Jen along with the other two. Still, images of Dan and his sister send an ache between her legs. Not knowing if the threesome was making her tingle or the thought of the incest! *Well, it is most likely caused by Dan's hand moving up his wife's robe!* Gisele eyes avert back to Jen's voice as it interrupts the spectacle.

"I was sixteen or seventeen years old, still in high school. My best friend and I had a pact that one weekend, I would stay over at her house and vice versa. This one particular time, however, we got into a fight. Probably over a boy, as we had just started noticing them. So, I went home after school instead of going to her house. I ran up to my room and cried myself to sleep! Just kid's stuff, really. Waking up around supper time, I thought I should go let my parents know I was home. I headed to the stairs. I started down the spiral steps but stopped dead in my tracks! The sight at the dinner table had me scurrying to hide myself from view behind the banister. There, at the supper table, was my mother with her blouse open, my dad sitting next to her, and my bare-ass Aunt standing beside him, which I noticed first. My eyes then took in mom's bare breasts jiggling due to her arm's erratic movement as her hand was under the table!" Jen hesitates long enough to have a sip of wine.

This gives Gisele time to survey the room. Dan's hand was rubbing his wife's leg almost to the inner thigh, causing the robe to reveal some of Jen's pubic hair. Shifting her eyes, she gets a glimpse of the bulge rising under Dan's robe. Staring at the sight, she rests her hand on her husband's leg and shudders as the tip of his cock jerks against her fingers. She turns her head towards Jen in time to see the glass move away from her lips as she presses on.

"Now my young mind knew about sex from the magazine we took from my best friend's dad's hiding place! And this was called a threesome! Mom was jerking Dad off while he, in turn, was stroking my aunt's naked ass. Getting that same feeling that I came by looking at those pictures my body couldn't move! Being so fascinated by the action, I kept watching, hands resting in my lap! My Aunt moved around the table to the opposite side, facing my dad. Going on all fours, she crawled under, and the only thing sticking out was her ass and legs! Dad then pushed his chair back to reach under the table. Not being able to see, I slid down farther, just enough to see under. There, Dad's one hand was on my aunt's bobbing head. The other was between Mom's spread legs, fingering her.

"I was so stimulated I didn't realize when my hand started moving under my dress! I pushed my panties aside to rub my aching clit. My eyes moved up to look at Dad. His head was pushed back, eyes closed. Looked like he was in heaven! Then he moved, startling me. *Let's move this into the other room*, he had said. That was my cue to get my ass back upstairs before I got caught. To say the least, I finished what I started in my room." Jen, finishing, moans at her husband's touch.

Dan whispers, "Divulge the rest so they can understand how you got so gifted."

Gisele knows exactly what he means—and so does her husband. With a smirk, she waits for Jen's next move. Jen looks nervous, trying to decide if she should proceed. She gazes at Dan. He reaches up, touching her hand for reassurance. That's all it takes.

"As the days passed, I kept picturing that evening. I was focused on how happy Dad looked getting a blowjob. The more I thought about it, the more I wanted to try it. Not to state the obvious, I started hanging around boys. Now, not being very knowledgeable in attracting them. It didn't come easy. I did not wear makeup or have any kind of a figure. But eventually, one succumbed to my advances. Things didn't go well at first. On date one, he was shooting his load all over my clothes before my mouth could even get close." Jen says, smiling a little at that as a chuckle leaves her lips.

"The second date, my lips just got to the tip. I had to turn my head to the side before the sperm shot into my mouth as he was cumming too soon. Eventually, things got better. Now word got around that I gave head, so that increased my popularity. To be clear, I never let them cum in my mouth, just jacked them off to finish. Not to mention, I couldn't get by the gagging I felt when I tried to slide all of it in my mouth. Then fate intervened." Jen hesitates, looking at Dan for encouragement. To Gisele, she seems to be apprehensive.

"Go on. You think it is easy for Bill that we know about him. You have nothing to worry about!" Dan's soft voice seems to motivate her to continue.

A little anxious, Jen complies. "One day at school, a boy and I were in the boy's bathroom. I just got him in my mouth when the door opened and closed. *What are you two doing?* The voice frightened me. I just about bit down on poor Tom's cock. There was Tom and I so terrified that we couldn't move. I was on my knees with a cock in my mouth that was going soft! Tommy was standing bare ass cheeks for all to see with his pants around his ankles. Miss Ames, our teacher, came into view as she came over to stand beside us! *Don't stop on my account,* she commanded as her body knelt. Her hand went under my chin, moving past to fondle the hanging balls, making Tom instantly hard, filling my mouth. I felt a hand on the back of my head gently pushing it forward, then with fingers wrapping in my hair and pulling it back. Her hand left the balls to allow the fingers to encircle part of the shaft my mouth wasn't covering. Slowly, she started stroking it! I sensed what was coming next as the throbbing increased! I tried to move my head back but couldn't! Her hand held me firm. As the sperm spurted out into my mouth, my instincts took over, and I tried to swallow but started gagging.

"Feeling the hand move off the back of my head, I drew back, letting the rest of the thick secretion run down the corner of my lips onto my clothes. That was the first time I tasted cum, and did I ever love the sensation! At that point, Miss Ames stood there as Tom was sliding out of my mouth. Skimming her fingers over my lips and staring into my eyes, she said, *now, not a word of what happened here. That way, you two will not be expelled. And your parents won't find out.*

"Bringing her hand up to her mouth, she licked the specks of cum off her fingers. With that, the bathroom door opened, and Miss Ames walked out. Leaving poor Tom with his pants still around his ankles and me kneeling, sitting back on my heels, staring up at him—neither of us was sure what to do next. Finally, Tom reached down, pulled up his pants, fastened them, and held out a hand to help me up. As I stood, warmth flooded my cheeks, burning with embarrassment. Tom just turned not saying a word, and walked out. Coming to my senses, I went over to the sink, cleaned the mess off my blouse, and then left the washroom, entering the hallway as the recess bell rang! After that, I was so frightened of being caught again things slowed down. Oh, don't get me wrong, I didn't stop. You know how obsessed I get. I just had to find a new rendezvous." Jen pauses to sip some wine.

CHAPTER 36

Gisele is so taken in by Jen's narrative she doesn't realize her eyes are gazing at Jen's crotch. Observing as Jen's husband's hand moves smoothly between her parting legs, causing the robe to fall open, she sees that Jen is returning the favor as her hand disappears under Dan's robe, stroking him. Registering what is happening, Gisele raises her eyes to her husband's face, detecting his hand sliding under her robe and stroking her nipple. Inhaling at the touch and knowing her husband is leering at Jen's exposed pussy she slips her hand into Bill's robe, copying Jen. Squeezing her husband's cock, praying that this better get juicer, she peers into her friend's eyes and breathes, "Please continue."

Jen, taking a quick sip, obliges. "After a few weeks, I was getting frustrated at not improving. As for the experience, it was getting more along the lines of Wham bam, thank you, ma'am! And well, truth be told, the boys were trying to push me into going all the way, which frightened me at that time! So, in despair, not obtaining any pleasure, the boys were starting to scare me! Not to mention, I was not really improving in the blow job department I lost interest and was going to move on. That is when destiny took over. One day after class, as I was gathering my books off my desk, Miss Ames called out to me. *Jennifer, can I see you for a moment* she said. My heart stopped. I stood by the desk holding my breath, so scared she was going to bring up the bathroom incident! My eyes were darting around watching the other students leave as I was trying to avoid Miss Ames.

"I see that your grades are dropping, Miss Ames pointed out, walking towards me. *If it is ok with you, I would like to get the principal and your parent's permission to tutor you after school.* Sensing her standing in front of my desk and the scent of her perfume, I just kept my head down, fidgeting with the books on the desk. She told me that she was already helping another student. And it won't be an inconvenience. *What do you say?* Relieved and still feeling embarrassed about getting caught in the washroom, I just responded with okay. I grabbed my books and quickly left the classroom. The weeks that followed left me apprehensive about what subject my teacher was revering to and the torment that I had to face her one-on-one!

"True to her word, one Friday afternoon, Miss Ames reminded me I had to stay after class. I was dreading the thought but since I promised, I was going to keep it. Best decision I ever made in my life! When class ended, and there I sat, waiting for the kids to leave so I could start my lessons. *Grab some books and meet me at the teacher's lounge,* she shot at me, heading out the door. Little startled at the comment and confused, I picked up the books; doing as asked I caught her coming out of the lounge with her coat and handbag. *The lessons will be at my house. It will be quieter there.* I was informed as we left the school."

Gisele notices Jen's head lean back as the story suddenly comes to a halt. She takes in a deep breath, slightly gasping at the pleasure Dan's hands are bringing to her. Her raspy breaths give Gisele an idea of how high the heat is between them. Another jolt runs through her as Bill pinches her nipple, and Dan leers at her when the robe falls away from her other breast, exposing it! *Dam it, Dan! Let her finish.* She moves Bill's robe and caresses his cock.

As if Jen could read minds, she brings her head forward and proceeds. "Once in the house, she instructed me to put my books down on the aisle in the kitchen. *The other student will be here shortly. There are snacks and drinks set out. Help yourself.* That's all she said, walking out of the room. I just sat down and helped myself to the snacks when in walked Thomas. I wasn't too surprised as he failed this grade a couple of times. That made him older than the rest of the class. Strolling to the aisle, he had a big grin on his face when he noticed I was there. We sat, not really saying anything to each other, munching down on the chips and drinking the pop that was provided, waiting on our tutor.

"Well, let me tell you, I was just about to spit everything all over poor Thomas. In walked, Miss Ames wearing this see-through jumpsuit covered in small white stone buttons! It hugged her body like it was a second skin, showing off one magnificent figure. She didn't even acknowledge we were there and strolled over to the fridge; her smooth curved swaying ass could be seen as plain as day. Thomas was now leering, cherishing the view. Not to say I wasn't! The difference was he didn't look shocked. As for me, I could feel my cheeks burning! They must have been red as beets. Eyes wide, mouth hung open, I could only imagine what I looked like. Not moving, both of us were gawking as Miss Ames opened the fridge and bent down to retrieve something, causing her lushes round ass to protrude in the air! That exposed the swell lips between her legs to be seen as a wet spot appeared. The image of my aunt crawling under the table came to mind. I creamed my panties right there! Straightening, Miss Ames shut the fridge, turned to face us with a drink in her hand and sauntered towards us, those large breasts bouncing with every stride. Nipples pressed hard against the fabric as she moved closer. I tried to look away, but it was useless—the moment the dark pubic hairs came into view, my gaze was locked. Finally, tearing my eyes away, I fidgeted with my books, my mind briefly drifting to the thought of Thomas having a hard-on. That thought vanished in an instant as Miss Ames's voice cut through the air. *You won't be needing them on what I will be tutoring you in!* she stated, coming to the edge of the aisle, resting her waist on the edge, leaning a bit. She got her breast to bob more for Thomas's enjoyment than mine! Miss Ames's head turned and touched my hand to get my attention. In a soft voice, she said, *Now, Jennifer, you are getting quite the reputation around school! Not a good one, I might add. I couldn't put my finger on it until the bathroom incident. Getting caught never even frightens you enough to stop. Yeah, I know you just changed secret places. That got me thinking as to why! So, I figured it wasn't the sex part of the act you enjoyed! You wanted to learn something but didn't really know what. Well, hon if you let me, I am going to help you discover what it is! As for Thomas here, that is a different matter.*

"Shifting her focus on Thomas, taking a drink, pressing her breasts up on the counter to expose them more, still teasing, she continued, *a few girls came to me complaining he was trying to touch their ass or breast against their will. Had words like rape and forced upon in the same sentence. I assured them that was not what rape was but was more in the line with groping! And I would take care of it as long as they didn't take this any further. I would talk to him. They agreed.* Miss Ames paused as her fingers stroked the bottle of vodka cooler on the table before bringing it to her lips to sip. You can well imagine I was wondering where this was going. I observed that Thomas was ogling Miss Ames's tits. Her, in turn, seemed to be edging him on! I was more focused on what the teacher's intentions were going to be

264

when I was interrupted. *So now you two are going to help one another. We will help Thomas curve his urges. He, in turn, will be the tool that helps you reveal what knowledge you seek.* With that, we were led into the living room. On the floor by the electric fireplace was this huge white fur rug." Jen pauses as Gisele puts her hand down to feel the rug under her. *Sheepskin, I bet.*

"I have the jumpsuit also," Jen informs her as Dan stares at her. So, she continues.

Gisele chuckles at that, picturing Jen sporting that kind of outfit.

"Here, we were instructed to remove our clothes before stepping onto the rug. Feeling uncomfortable with the whole being naked thing, I hesitated. As with all the blowjobs I gave, not once were my clothes removed. But catching Miss Ames standing there waiting in that see-through outfit and Thomas, with his pants unbuckled down to his knees, I thought, what the hell. Besides, it would be a little awkward to back out now. So, as I was removing my clothes, I kept an eye on Thomas being a little self-conscious. This soon disappeared when he was down to his underwear. You could see the bulge they were hiding. My eyes grew even bigger as they were pulled down. Standing straight up was this thick and longest of all penises seen by me! I couldn't stop staring as I started to get aroused! However, Miss Ames's orders startled me. *Jennifer, you kneel. Thomas, would you lie on the rug flat on your back?* Turning my attention to her, now naked, did as I was asked. Thomas, stepping out of his shorts, laid down at my knees. All I could do was stare at that huge cock bobbing in mid-air! As soon as we did what was asked, Miss Ames knelt on the other side of Thomas, knees spreading apart, drawing the jumpsuit tight to her crotch. Exposing thick lips between her legs made Thomas's cock jerk up in little spasms as his head was turned to stare at the opening."

Gisele, hearing a deep intake of breath instead of words, watches Jen's body shiver as Dan slips two fingers into her opening. Gisele's own body responds, feeling her pussy flex at the sight. Turning toward Dan does nothing to ease the heat coursing through her as he leans back on his elbows, robe parted, lost in pleasure. Her gaze flickers to her husband, his grip tightening around his own need as he watches, waiting for Jen to continue.

CHAPTER 37

"There was the three of us! Thomas was breathing heavily, sandwiched between the teacher and me, waiting on one of us to embrace his throbbing cock! Miss Ames, peering into my eyes, obliged. With an open hand, she pushed the hard shaft down, resting it on Thomas's stomach, rubbing it gently as she spoke. My attention immediately went to watch the teacher's hand, a wetness forming between my legs. *Now, Jennifer, you will have to get used to the taste,* she informed me, still attending to Thomas's needs. My focus then went from the hand that was flat on Thomas's cock, softly sliding over it, to the movement of the teacher's knees shuffling up towards Thomas's head. Those moist lips seemed to be opening and closing as she shuffled, calling out for attention as they reached their destination. Miss Ames's hand never left Thomas's cock!

"There I knelt on the other side of Thomas naked, too young and insecure to move. My own urges screamed for attention. All I could do was stare at Miss Ames's crotch, her knees spread, nestling the top of Thomas's head between them. Then, her fingers made a circle, sliding over the head and down the shaft, urging the erection to stand straight up. It took all my concentration not to touch myself as I watched that hand stroke that huge shaft. Pre-cum was glistening on the tip! Then, Thomas was cumming, all over Miss Ames's hand, up Thomas's chest. All over his belly. It was the most sperm I had ever witnessed. I noticed a little wetness on the crotch of the suit as the teacher stood, licking her hand clean. Looking at me, she said, *Now, Jennifer, clean up the mess with your tongue."* I was so aroused I didn't hesitate. My tongue went from the base of his cock all the way up the head. Then, onto the belly to his chest, lapping up every drop. When I knelt back on my heels the teacher let us know that was the end of lesson one and we could go home.

"As Miss Ames left the room I stood retrieving my clothes. Thomas was still stretched out on the rug by the time I was dressed. Walking out of the house, I headed home. The thought of Thomas just lying there crossed my mind, but I let it slide, grateful for the solitude. Still, I couldn't shake the annoyance of not getting to play with Thomas's erection. The tutoring continued after school at Miss Ames's house. I got so excited just thinking of seeing my teacher in that white beaded jumpsuit; how I loved that suit! Not to mention having Thomas naked in front of me! We did everything demanded of us. But the tutoring got more focused on me as it seemed Thomas's urges were being taken care of by my session." Jen's voice rises, "So I thought!" she says but doesn't elaborate.

"The first few lessons were me kneeling, giving Thomas a blowjob. Miss Ames would sometimes intervene to instruct new techniques, like rolling the tongue around the head while it was in my mouth. Or squeezing the balls at the right moment to heighten the climax. Or squeezing the penis where the head meets the shaft until the urge to ejaculate passes making the sex last longer. These teachings were easy and fast to learn. As I still choked at the shaft going to the back of my mouth, Miss Ames would encircle Thomas's cock withdrawing it from my mouth before he could ejaculate! She proceeded to jerk him off, his thick, creamy sperm shooting across my tits. She instructed me to rub it over my nipples while she watched.

I loved those sessions. Then, three weeks before school ended, after class, Miss Ames advised me, *I am going to add tutoring days to teach you what you really wanted to learn.* Now I thought, how is that a bad thing?

"Well, to my dismay, Thomas wasn't needed. I didn't have to get undressed! Miss Ames's attire was the see-through jumpsuit. I always wondered why since Thomas wasn't there to arouse, but never asked. Everything was focused on my mouth; how to concentrate on something other than gagging whenever my finger went down my throat. This practice went on for a few days. When that was accomplished, we moved to using a dildo. Now, when at first, I saw how thick and long it was, I got a little nervous. Once feeling and stroking it for reassurance, I found the texture to feel like a real cock. Bringing it to my mouth, I curled my lips around the head. My hand seized the artificial balls so I could urge the dildo further towards the back of my throat. All the while, Miss Ames, stroking my throat, told me to relax as I tried to get that thing farther down without gagging.

"Miss Ames continued to instruct me, *Stop trying to suck the dildo! Let those lips loose! Relax your mouth! That way, your throat will widen.* Coughing, I withdrew the dildo in frustration! Miss Ames didn't even flinch. Her arm was still around my shoulder, her fingers still caressing my throat in her soothing voice; *now, now, my child, it is ok. Catch your breath and stay calm.* That was it! Not wanting to let the teacher down, I let the instructions run through my mind. Everything then came to me. Bringing that silicone toy to my mouth, as the dildo passed my lips, I didn't let them surround it. My mouth opened wide, and as the head reached the back of the throat, my thoughts went elsewhere. My mind was fixed on that see-through jumpsuit and how those stones must feel against the teacher's hard nipples and rubbing between her legs. With that, my mind kept imagining that it was Thomas going down my throat. And then it happened! I felt the silicone balls of the dildo hit my chin. It was amazing! So excited, I slid the toy back, then thrust it forward till the balls once again rested on my chin. Repeating that several times as if I was given head. That thought made me cum. Slipping it out, I rested my head on Miss Ames. Those stones felt warm on my face as I pressed into those luscious breasts, and she just hugged me tighter. Tears ran down my cheeks at the thrill I felt at pleasing her!

"After a few minutes, my breathing slowed. Miss Ames, breaking the embrace, spoke. *Now, girl! One more time.* Standing, extending a hand, she waited. Reaching up and embracing her hand, I was so taken in by how magnificent and beautiful this woman was standing in front of me. How much I adored her to the point of arousal! As I stood, my eyes captured the teacher's steamy blue eyes. I inched my face towards her with the illusion we would embrace and kiss. To my dismay, Miss Ames, at my touch, turned, leading us to the living room."

Gisele, stroking her husband faster, let out a loud moan that halted the tale. Seeing Jen's eyes light up at the response, Gisele closes hers to let Jen continue.

"Halting by the fireplace just shy of the rug, she informed me. *You can disrobe or leave your clothes on, whatever makes you more comfortable.* She did not wait for an answer and instructed, *Thomas, would you come in here, please?* Now, how he was so available intrigued me! But not as much as his naked body showing a very huge, stiff hard-on as he walked in. The thought passed as he was now standing in front of me, cock twitching, wanting attention! Leering at that glistening cock, my hand reached for it and started stroking as I dropped to my knees. So, titillated by the wetness I felt, it didn't even register why. Not even when pulling it towards my mouth, my tongue licking the head, tasting the sweetness of the moisture. That taste drove me crazy. With lips apart, mouth open, I shoved my head forward, forcing it in further. That was all it took for Thomas. His hands grasped the hair at the back of my head as his hips pushed forward, slowly shoving his cock even deeper. All senses in my body were tingling. I never felt so aroused! My pussy was screaming for attention. With my head held in place while his balls hit my chin Thomas feverishly started to fuck my face. Now I don't know what made me cum!

"Knowing that cock was throbbing so far down my throat, the sight of Miss Ames standing beside Thomas as his hand slowly glided up the inside of her leg, and the sensation of flesh slapping against my chin all blended together, sending a shiver through me and blurring the lines between memory and desire. But by the time the sperm was shooting down my throat, my panties were soaked with cum! I now knew the pleasure I was seeking. And that was how I got so gifted! Oh, and my first orgasm!"

Gisele feels the warmth on her hand and opens her eyes, her gaze drifting to her husband. She follows his line of sight—the source of his release. There, on the rug, hips arching to meet his thrusting fingers, Jen lost in the same intoxicating rhythm. Her legs spread, quivering as they push up against the hand between her legs. Diverting her eyes away from her friend's arched back, she leers at Dan, the robe wide open, his cock shooting sperm in the air all over his wife's hand. Noticing Dan's gaze locked on her jiggling breasts as she brings her husband to release, she quickens her strokes. A rush of pleasure washes over her, knowing just how much her body aroused him, as the last of her husband's release spills into her grasp.

It seemed to Gisele it only took a moment, and it was over. Surveying the quiet room, removing her hand from her husband's robe, she observes Bill as he gulps the last of his drink. Dan is rising, closing his robe with a very satisfied grin on his face, still ogling her breast. Gisele pulls her robe together, covering herself. Gazing into his eyes, she lets him see the pleasure she feels.

Dan shifts the attention to Bill. "How about the two of us go and clean up and refill our drinks? And in the meantime, that will give the ladies time to freshen up."

Walking to join Bill, who now was standing, he adds. "Then, if you two will retire to the couch and loveseat to get comfortable, I will retrieve more champagne." The two men walk away.

Gisele, being careful not to touch the rug with her wet hand, stands. Peering down at Jen, who has a mischievous grin and eyes that are sparkling, holds out her other hand to help her up. "Oh, I know you didn't have to tell the story in such elaborate detail. But sure, I'm thrilled you did!" Gisele reveals, leering at her friend. "But hon!" Whispering, she adds. "I have one question: during all that tutoring, not once did popping your cherry come into question?!"

Jen, with a devilish smirk, says, "Well, love, give me a taste of your husband, and I will reveal all!"

Gisele shudders at the request, her slick fingers moving toward her friend. Jen's tongue extends, teasing the tips before dragging slowly over them, making Gisele moan. She aches to touch herself, to chase the pleasure pooling deep inside her, but she holds back, savoring the heat thrumming between them.

That restraint snaps the moment Jen's lips wrap around two fingers, sucking them deep to the knuckle. The wet pull of her mouth sends a sharp jolt straight to Gisele's core. Lips glide back, releasing them with a soft, obscene pop, followed by a slow, deliberate kiss to the fingertips.

Gisele trembles, every nerve lit and screaming for more. *Goddamn, I want to fuck that woman.*

Her hand falls to her side, chest rising and falling as she waits, pulse-pounding, for the answer.

Jen takes the time to run her tongue over her lips with a lude gaze and starts, "Now, to answer your question. Miss Ames firmly divulged that there would be no intercourse in these sessions. That was a very intimate decision that should be made by two individuals discreetly, me being a virgin! And that subject never came to light again." Chuckling a little, she adds, "Never mentioned if Thomas was, but we now both know why!"

Not wanting Jen to have the satisfaction of pursuing this little game of hers, Gisele reaches for her friend's glistening hand. Bringing it to her lips, she slides the tongue out and licks it clean. Noises from the other room prompt Gisele to let go of her friend and both head to the couch to sit.

Dan comes back with a fresh bottle of champagne. Bill in toe finds the girls seated, chatting away. He interrupts them. "Well, you now know our dirty little secrets. We know Bills'. How about you, Gisele? What's yours?"

Gisele catches a breath, sensing all eyes on her. *I don't know how I am going to reveal my secret in a way as titillating as Jen's! But dam it, I will not be outdone!*

CHAPTER 38

Gisele lingers for a moment, allowing the other three to get comfortable. Reaching for the champagne on the table, she exposes her breast just enough to tease her hosts. She pours a generous amount of wine into her glass. Sitting back on the couch with her legs tucked under her, she senses she has all their attention. Smiling smugly, she glances at her husband and begins. "Now, I never told you about this, Bill, as it is extremely embarrassing! In fact, you three will be the only ones to hear this!" She pauses long enough to emphasize the sensitivity of what is going to be revealed. Finishing sipping from the glass, she carries on. "Somethings people outside the family don't need to be aware of. Not even my mother knows what happened!" She whispers, "I think! This all happened when I was in senior high. My father traveled a lot as a top salesman in his company. So, Mom and her best friend hung around together a lot. Going to movies, lunch dates with friends and out to dinner with one another. I never thought much of this or Sara hanging around so much. I even started calling her Aunt Sara.

"Now, I didn't know when I became conscious of how often Sara started staying overnight when Dad was away and not just on weekends, but during the week as well. It appeared a little strange to me. But Mom never liked being alone, so I never complained. Being the only child it was just us girls, so we were more liberal with our appearance. Sara, more so! Like when her robe fell open, she didn't bother to wrap it back up. Coming out of the shower with a towel wrapped around her head and nothing else as she headed to her room, or when Mom and she watched movies on the couch—wearing those pajamas that you'd swear are practically see-through—both moments linger in my mind, impossible to ignore. This started to make an impression on me. I was satisfying my sexual urges back then. You can well imagine Sara started to be the main focus of my desire! Why not!? With that striking figure, long legs going up to that luscious heart shape ass. Flat belly. Oh, and the swooping breast! They were firm, making the dark areola and pointy nipples look suspended skyward. The more I fantasized about her, the closer I wanted to get! Didn't know why I wanted to touch Sara, just knew at the time it got me aroused thinking about it.

"Now, Mom volunteered some nights. When she did, I would follow Sara around. Sit close to her. Engage in conversation about boys. On those nights, Sara wore tight-fitting shorts to show off those long bare legs and heart-shaped ass. With this, which drove me insane, was a loose crop top with no bra that displayed the hard nipples and flat belly. Now, on those occasions when we were together, whenever Sara got up to get something, I gawked at the swaying ass. And on the way back, the nipples pushed the shirt straight out. The full lips between her legs made a perfect camel toe. Some nights, I couldn't take it anymore! Thinking of my hand sliding under her shirt to pinch those hard nipples, I had to be excused to go to the bathroom to masturbate. Which didn't take long." Chuckling, Gisele takes a sip of wine and then continues. "Whether Sara noticed my attention toward her or not, she never let on." She sighs a little to take in the room and gathers up all her courage to reveal the rest.

"One night, when Sara was over, I woke up to get a glass of water. Walking down the hall, I became aware of the light coming from

Mom's bedroom door, which was ajar. Why I looked in, I don't know but I just did! There was Sara kneeling at the bottom of the bed, head buried between mom's legs, which were thrown over Sara's shoulders. I really wasn't that shocked as much as aroused! Eyeing Sara's bare ass and pussy oscillating a little every time she moved her head upwards to lick sent a light shiver through me! Standing there gazing, my hand started to go under my panties down into my pubic hair. And that broke the trance. Not wanting to get caught, I ran to my room to relieve myself!" Gisele hesitates, more to catch the reaction of her listeners than to take a drink. She tries to picture what each of them is thinking. *Ah, Jen, what are you thinking? Imagine me playing with myself while you watch.* Her eyes shift toward the men. *And you two?* she wonders, glancing at them briefly. Satisfied that all three are intrigued, she carries on.

"After that night, I tried to catch them at it again without success. The door was always tightly closed. Then it happened! Walking down the hall thinking if I am unsuccessful this time, I will give up and be happy with the images I have. But low and behold, there it was! The door was open a little wider than before. I couldn't believe my luck! Darting to the door, peering in, there was Sara straddled over Mom's face. Her head once again in between mom's legs with tongue going deep into her! This time, I couldn't help myself. Pushing my panties to my knees, I brought my hand to my crotch and parted my lips to let two fingers slide in. Pumping them to the movement of Sara's head, my eyes must have closed as my head shot backward at the peak of my orgasm! Opening them, there Sara was staring right at me! Panicking, I froze! What a sight I must have been, with panties around my knees and fingers deep inside me! Coming to my senses, pulling up my underwear, I ran to my room, lying there awake most of the night, frightened at what might happen tomorrow.

"Well, the next morning, Sara was already gone. Mom was in a good mood. So, relieved, I skipped breakfast and went to school. Sara didn't make it over the following nights. It gave me time to gather my thoughts. Then Saturday came, and Sara phoned and asked Mom out. That gave me the evening of being home. I alone loved those nights—naked, eating popcorn, watching horror flicks. I wondered what Sara would do if she knew she was sitting where my bare skin had been. That thought alone sent a thrill through me. Spreading my legs, I started rubbing my clit, and eyes half-closed as I watched the young couple on screen, fucking just moments before their brutal murder. That did it—I climaxed. As the movie ended, I noticed how late it had gotten and decided I wouldn't wait up for them.

"Slowly, I started to clean up, but by the time I was done, those two still weren't home, so I headed to bed." Pausing, Gisele feels pleased with herself for making the retelling of the memory so enticing. She pours a generous glass of champagne and takes a slow sip, letting her gaze sweep across the room. The boys sit back, relaxed, clearly enjoying the story. But Jen—Jen stares right at Gisele, not even hiding the raw desire in her eyes. *Well, hon, if I could, I would gladly come over there so you could relieve the ache between my legs, but alas, I love the high! The more you get to know me, the more pleasure you will find in that.* Grinning, not breaking eye contact, Gisele proceeds.

"Later that night, I was pulled from sleep by a hand slowly gliding over my hip as I lay on my side. It moved ever so gently across my stomach, stopping at the waistband of my underwear. I could feel hard nipples pressing against my bare back. I stayed as still as possible, pretending to be asleep. Then, a crotch pressed against my ass, and I held my breath. Warm lips grazed my ear as a whisper escaped the mouth…. *You can watch anytime you like. I will make sure the door is always open.* The hand slid under the elastic of my panties, gliding over my pubic hair. My juices flowed in anticipation of what was coming next. Bit by bit, I twisted my body, shifting to lie flat on my back as I spread my legs. Suddenly, Sara's head dipped forward, her tongue flicking over my erect nipple. A shudder ran through me as her hair brushed against my other one. She pressed closer, her lips wrapping around my nipple, then opening wider to devour my entire breast. Then, I felt her fingers spreading the lips between my legs, rubbing the hood to expose my clitoris before giving it a gentle squeeze. I arched up, pressing against her touch, losing all control. My breath came in short gasps as the orgasm peaked, overwhelming me. Slowly, Sara's hand inched farther down, her fingers slipping inside me.

"My body quivered at the movement! My ass rose and pressed against the palm as it massaged the clit, when two fingers curled, slipping into me. My juices flowed as I climaxed. The fingering went on slowly for a little longer. I felt Sara's crotch frantically rubbing, pressing against my hip. Her hand started furiously pounding harder, finger fucking me faster! Sara's body thrust firmly against me as she shivered. Her hand was motionless, fingers still buried deep. As we both relaxed, Sara slid her fingers out, kissed my forehead, and left. There I lay stock-still, not daring to move. Then, when the shock subsided, I went to the bathroom and cleaned up." Gisele stops, takes a sip of wine, and then continues.

"I never saw much of Sara after that night. Dad's company promoted him, so he got to be home every night. To Mom's dismay and mine as well. Sara still called, and they went out. But for me, I was left to my own device. Days turned to weeks and then to months. I fantasized a lot about that night while masturbating, which was one of my leisure activities."

Gisele unfolds her legs to stretch and refills her glass. "Now, I told that story, so you will get the drift of what really happened to me!" Pleased to see the other three hurry to fill their glasses and sit back, patiently waiting for her to continue, she obliges.

CHAPTER 39

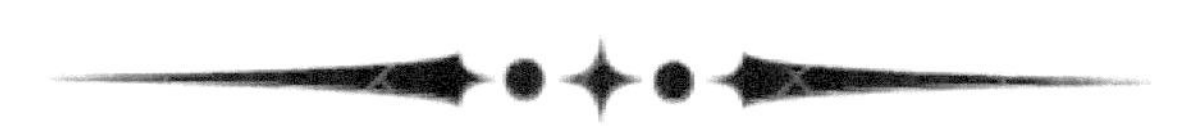

"You can sympathize with me that playing with myself was fading. Try as I might, the heightened orgasm that I had that night with Sara could not be repeated. Then it occurred to me I needed another body. But who and how would I even approach them? Turning every scenario around in my head, I couldn't come up with a plan. They say if you want something bad enough, you will always figure out a way to make it happen. That is when it hit me! I never thought much about why Sara would get the notion she could come to my bed. Then I remembered one night, a few weeks before the incident, when Sara was over, Mom was called out to help at the volunteer center. One of the other staff members didn't show up. Hearing the outside door close, I came out of my room and headed downstairs, intending to watch TV, thinking they left. Walking into the living room, I stopped suddenly. There was Sara on the couch, wrapped in a blanket, skimming through the channels, searching for a movie. Hesitating, as I was only wearing a long loose T-shirt and panties. I finally built up the courage to ask. *Can I join you, Aunt Sara?* She said, *sure, hop in. Let us see if we can find a horror movie to watch.* So thrilled, I went over, pulled the blanket aside, and sat down, covering myself.

"The warmth from Sara's body and when both of our bare legs touched sent a tingle up my spine! Wondering, is she naked? I tensed. I could barely move with that thought in my head, so I just stared at the TV. Finally, we found a movie. As the open credits started, Sara paused it, asking if I would like some popcorn and a drink. Not being able to look, contemplating on seeing a naked body emerge, I nodded ok. Well, to my delight, I wasn't far from wrong!

"Standing, strolling past me, Sara was wearing a seductive two-piece transparent pajama. I could see that smooth ass swaying in those sexy mesh pajama shorts as she continued to the kitchen, the sight stirring images of her and Mom in my mind. That memory was interrupted as I held my breath, watching Sara walk back with the snacks. The see-through crop top clung to her body, displaying her spectacular, swollen breasts, nipples jutting out against the mesh material, teasing with every step she took. Reaching me, all I could focus on was the thick patch of pubic hair covering the prize I really wanted to see and touch as she bent to hand me the popcorn dish. The sensation of her bare leg once again touching me as she hopped back under the covers brought me out of my trance.

"There we sat, eating popcorn and sipping on cold drinks as the movie unfolded before us. I was driving myself crazy, not to mention getting horny thinking of Sara sitting next to me. Finally, the snacks were done; sitting the empty bowls on the coffee table, we both snuggled under the blanket. The movie was at the part where the heroine was running from the monster in her white panties and bra. The monster reached for the girl, hooking her bra strap, which snapped with a sharp sound. Beside me, I heard a small intake of breath and tensed, staring straight ahead, not daring to look in Sara's direction. The cause of the reaction was clear—the TV now showed the girl's lush breasts, her hardened nipples fully exposed.

"As she fell, she crawled backward, trying to get away. Her legs were open, showing a very clear view of her crotch as her feet pushed her back. I sat straight back on the couch. I was so tense that all my nerves were on edge, not because of the image of the girl but more from the fact that my hand, which had been resting on my leg close to Sara, had now slipped off the side, brushing against my aunt's leg. Catching my breath, I sat motionless, so fearful that a hand would come and brush mine away. The girl in the movie had now swung the door open, running out of the house. Her ass swayed as she ran. My hand eased onto Sara's leg, resting. The girl was still running down the road. Eyes glued on the monitor, I sat stiff as a board, my hand creeping up her leg as I held my breath. The monster got closer as the girl ran, ass jiggling. Sara's rapid breathing edged me on. Inching my hand up further until my fingers were touching her inner thigh, I sensed that her legs had started to open. Then I screamed, hearing a voice behind us.

What are you girls watching!? Mom asked."

Gisele's story comes to a halt as a chuckle fills the room.

"Well, that ended that night." She continues. "But remembering it, I got a plan in motion. I would invite one of my classmates over for the weekend. I knew just the one. Connie, the whole school, talked about how she was into girls more than boys. So, one Saturday, I asked her to sleep over. After supper, we retired to my room. One thing led to another, and soon we were kneeling on the bed pillow fighting, in nothing but t-shirts and panties. Soon, it turned into wrestling. Our crotch rubbed together as we fought. Breasts pressed hard against each other as we pinned one another down. My nipples were so hard pushing against hers, more than one could endure. There I was, her leg pressed between mine as I had her pinned. Her arms were held tight above her head. I rocked back and forth so I could rub myself on her leg. Losing all self-control, I let go of her wrist, and my hand moved down between her legs. Just when I was about to touch those lush lips, she flew off the bed! *What! Are you gay? I got to call my mom to come and get me! Tell her I am sick!*

"NO! NO! It was an accident! I pleaded. But to no avail, she left. That night and all day Sunday, I was on edge. One for believing the gossip at school about Connie and two for letting my urges control me. Dam it, dam it, I should have inquired if she was gay before proceeding! Not to state the obvious I did not want to go to school the next day but couldn't get out of it. On Monday, at school, the other girls murmured and giggled as they walked by me. In the shower, they covered themselves and said *Don't let the lesbo see you naked!* This carried on for a few weeks, causing me to withdraw into my shell. Which, after a while I didn't mind. Slowly, the ridicule subsided as I got the courage to date boys, which wasn't many as I was so traumatized by the incident and so petrified of rejection that I would refuse a lot of the advances. All the while, I still visualized what it would be like to be with a girl. Then I met Bill. And as you two said, here we are."

Gazing around the room, Gisele notices Jen with a big smirk on her face. *Stop it!* she thought. She knows Jen was fantasizing about that afternoon threesome. But then, the focus went to Dan as he spoke. "Well, it is little after one. But you know the old saying. Once the cork is removed, the bottle only goes back empty! There is enough left to allow the three of us another sip." Getting up, he empties the rest in each of their glass, glancing at Bill. "I have coffee for you while we finish our drink. Don't want you getting arrested or, worse yet, an accident driving home." Returning after the task was done, he asks. "While we finish our drinks, Bill, I have to ask. What inspired you to capture people on tape? Was it the journalism that got you to push the boundaries?" Dan sits down beside his wife, patiently waiting for an answer.

"Well, if you would extend your hospitality to having my wife and I to stay over, I would exchange that coffee for another whisky," Bill inquires.

Gisele turns, peering at her husband, taken aback. *What the hell are you doing, hon? This is from a guy who will not even stay over at his parents because he lives close enough to make it home! Well, I have no idea what you are up to, but be forewarned, I am getting laid no matter where! Whether it is in the spare room with you or if I have to wander over to Dan and Jens's room to find release!* As the two scenarios form, Gisele's body shivers. Bill's voice breaks through, making Gisele sigh.

CHAPTER 40

Exchanging the coffee for the glass of whisky that was handed to him, he waits for Dan to return to his seat. Then he starts. "As for your question, Dan, you would assume that would be the case. But truth be told, I was observing people at a young age. Kind of started quite by accident. I was delivering papers and cutting lawns back then to earn money so I could buy the next new video console. So, I got to know the attractive young lady behind us. Every time I was over, mowing her yard, she would come out to offer me a Kool-Aid wearing a two-piece bathing suit, which didn't cover much. I always prayed a breast would be revealed, but that never happened. The bottoms were so tight they showed off a nice camel toe when walking towards me and nice bare ass cheeks walking away. So, she was the main fantasy of my boyhood dreams. Now comes the part of how I got into taking videos and later becoming a journalist." Bill adjusts his sitting position to get more comfortable as he raises the glass, taking a sip.

Gisele takes in her husband's movements, noticing how composed he is. *Jeez, I wonder what his thoughts are. He always weighs the pros and cons of any situation before acting! This is a little unnerving! I will just ride it out!* Gisele shivers as Bill's voice interrupts her line of thinking.

Bill, peering at his wife, winks at her as he picks up where he left off. "We lived in a two-story house with an attic, mostly used for storage. Our attic overlooked the neighbor's backyard. One day, I was up in the attic looking for an old comic. Curious, I wandered over to peer out the port hole. There, I noticed the neighbor out sunbathing. To my delight, without a top! Those beautiful breasts were out for all to see. I would visit the attic quite often after that. I caught her a few times bathing topless or on her back, showing off that nice ass. As good as the field of vision was, I wanted a closer look. This had me spending my first earned money on binoculars, which was fine for a while. Then, I wanted something I could view while masturbating when the neighbor wasn't visible. That got me to save up to get a camera. I obtained a lot of photos of her topless, on her back, that a-shape ass projecting smooth tan cheeks, and so forth. After a while, I don't know if the pictures got me aroused or observing her without her knowing got me off. The more I indulged in my activities, the more I realized it wasn't the watching that got me hard; it was the concept of getting caught that made me feel sexually excited. Fantasizing about her head turning to catch me jerking off got me cumming every time!" Bill pauses on that note. Gisele takes in the atmosphere of the room as her husband does the same, taking another sip.

Jen and Dan seem immersed in the narrative as they fondle one another. Bill, looking pleased with the outcome, goes on.

"Then, one night, coming home, I noticed lights on in her backyard. Grabbing my camera, I ran up to the attic. Setting up, I waited! Sure enough, the lady appeared dressed in a low-cut blouse and tight shorts. She walked over to the lounge chair and stretched out. I was just about to call it a night as she wasn't doing much except enjoying a glass of wine when this man came out, hair wet and nothing but a towel wrapped around him. As he got close to the chair, her hand moved up under the towel to grab his cock. As she stroked it, the towel fell. That is when she moved closer so her lips could suck on the tip. His hips thrust forward, and the shaft was in her mouth. One of his hands moved to shove apart the blouse, revealing those hard nipples. I didn't get many pictures as I put down the camera to jerk off, watching him fuck her face. As his hand moved down, she spread her legs to reveal a nice plump camel toe through those tight shorts.

"That's all it took. I came! Picking up the camera, I started taking pictures of the action! He fingered her while she gave him head. Watching that ass rise to meet his fingers got me rock hard again! Then when she stood up, took off the shorts, and bent over the chair, the camera got a close shot of that smooth ass and puffy lips. That's when I stopped taking pictures just to watch while stroking my cock slowly, trying not to cum! When he entered her from behind, it took all my willpower not to shoot my load. Watching him cum all over her back was when my knees buckled cumming the hardest I ever had! I swear I had an orgasm!"

The account of Bill's recollection is interrupted by Gisele's hand embracing her husband's cock, stroking it. With a lascivious gaze, squeezing softly, she encourages him to continue. Breathing out, Bill presses on.

"After that night, I wanted more; the pictures weren't enough! The more I thought about it, the more I knew I wanted a video of the live action to watch at my leisure. So, I worked and saved up until I could afford a camcorder. But, to my dismay, by the time I could acquire one, the lady had moved, and the people who moved in were not very exciting. That got me roaming the neighborhood looking for new subjects. All I captured on those nights were clothed people kissing. Mabe a glimpse of a couple already fucking. Nothing like the night that started all this. Still filming people when they didn't know kind of got me off. So, I extended my search to find what I was looking for. I was getting good at it. Never once did I get noticed. Then I found out there were classes I could take to get a career in the obsession I had. Who knew? That was where I met Gisele in college, and as everyone said, here we are."

Everyone sits in silence. Gisele stops fondling her husband as Dan finally speaks, getting up. "Well, that was quite captivating, Bill. Now it is late, but there is one pressing matter that has to be addressed before the night ends." Gisele looks at Jen, both thinking the same thing: *Not now, Dan! Damit! Not the dam rule!*

They both sigh in relief as he continues. "Tonight was most intriguing! If the girls will agree the highlight was the film that got us together. With that said, I would like to propose a pact. Now, my source discloses that there were a lot more tapes. But he was only instructed to take the ones I was in. Knowing there are more tapes to view is tantalizing. So, I would like to introduce a proposal that we meet, say once a month, to view other tapes in your possession." Sipping the last of the wine, Dan stops to let it sink into the group. The girls sit completely quiet, knowing they have no say. All rest on Bill's decision.

Bill finishes the whisky and puts the glass down. "Well, seeing how you three ganged up on me, and it turned out to be very interesting, I would say that is a great idea. One, enjoying my art with someone else to analyze would be fanatic. Two, with the three of you watching the videos will guarantee my secret is safe as that would make you accomplices. So yes, that is a great idea." They all raise their glass in agreement.

Gisele brings the glass back to take a sip. *Oh, so it's called art now! That's rich!* Smiling at the group, she sits back. *Well, look at them acting like they are old college buddies. That brings back the age-old question. Did they know each other when the film was shot? Was Bill asked to capture their act?* The thought gets interrupted by Dan's voice.

"Jen, would you show our guests to their room, and I will clean up. Oh, hon, one of the bedchambers upstairs."

CHAPTER 41

Gisele notices Jen whisper, "Upstairs? Are you sure?"

Dan nods. At that Jen rises and motions to Bill and Gisele to follow her. Bill stumbles, getting off the couch. *Ahaa, maybe there is nothing to my paranoia.* Gisele surmises he is just inebriated, always obliging when drunk. *We will see what he really thinks of showing off his art in the morning.* Putting her arm around Bill to steady him, she chuckles as they follow Jen.

Upon reaching the staircase, Jen turns, eyebrows raised and addresses Gisele.

"I would like to inform you that what you see in the sleeping chambers up there are for, let's say, special guests. People we have a unique bond with."

Gisele is a little inebriated and inflamed with desire. She just wants to get to a bed and finally find some relief. Throwing caution to the wind, she interrupts, "We are so honored to be included in that group. Please, lead the way."

At the top of the stairs, Gisele encounters three rooms. One on each side of her and straight ahead, down the hall, double doors face her, leading to what Gisele could only surmise was the master suite. What really catches her eye, and most intriguing, are the four-foot statues positioned against the wall beside each door. To the right of her is a statue of a woman giving a man a blowjob. The one at the double doors portrays a man on his back, a woman sitting on his face, staring at a woman who is straddling his hips facing her. *Well, that is the best way to represent a threesome. Dam, this is the right atmosphere in the state I am in!*

Gisele is diverted by Jen opening the door to her left. She only catches a glimpse of the statue at the door in all its glory of a couple imitating the doggy position as Gisele is ushered into the room with Bill under her arm. She stops in mid-stride and is just about to drop Bill. The chamber is breathtaking. The seductive glow of red lighting fills the room, drawing the eye first to a massive double king-sized bed. The pure white duvet is adorned with an embroidered image of a naked man lying on his back, a naked woman curled beside him. Beyond that, the headboard is sculpted into a shape unmistakably resembling a vagina. Gisele continues exploring the room. *This is just a bootylicious view* was her thoughts as her attention is drawn to all the eighteen by sixteen frame paintings of a man and woman in various sexual positions that encircle the wall. The last one, a man kneeling behind a woman on all fours shooting his load all over her back, is butted up against the one above the headboard that appears to be the starting point as the couple are facing each other in their underwear.

Gisele is mesmerized by the spectacular sexual undertone; she can not move! *So, I assume that each statue outside the doors sets the themes for each room. I would love to…* Bill's moan brings her back to the moment and realization of how heavy he is! She shuffles forward, plopping him down face up on the bed. Doing so causes the robe to open, exposing Bill's semi-hard erection! That, in turn, sends an electrifying jolt through Gisele, making her knees momentarily weaken—not just at the sight of it but also at the thought of Jen ogling the view. The urge to reach out and oblige Bill flickers in her mind, but Jen's voice quickly pulls her attention away.

"As you can discern, the spirit is of a sexual nature. With that said, let me assure you that everything in here is sanitized. After each utilization, everything is replaced brand new to ensure proper sterilization! That goes for the other things that are used also. The only thing I ask is that you remove the duvet before any encounters. If, for any reason, that is not possible, consider it yours. The replacement price of it is very high."

Gisele's hunch was, *Ooohhh… I will be taking that home! I am fucking Bill just as is.* She smirks as she watches Jen come over and kiss her on the cheek while eyeballing Bill's cock as it twitches.

"You have a good night. If you need any help with Bill", she winks at her friend, "let me know." Walking to the door, Jen turns, "If not, I will see you in the morning." she says and steps out of the room, closing the door behind her.

Gisele combs the room, fighting the temptation to jump on the bed and give into her sexual urge as all her senses are screaming for release. *There is something about the art on the wall. I just can't put my finger on it.* Scouring the images in the frames, she rotates slowly.

Then it hits her—if all the paintings were placed in a kineograph, they would create the motion of a couple fucking doggy style. A soft moan escapes Gisele's lips as desire takes hold, the animated sequence playing vividly in her mind.

Slipping out of her robe, she pauses, wondering who these people are. They exist on an entirely different level of sexual exploration.

With that thought lingering, she climbs onto the bed and straddles Bill.

I am but an amateur in comparison. Pressing down so the wet lips spread on each side, she welcomes the intrusion of the erection! *Oh, how I want to be the grasshopper!* Gisele chuckles at the phrase that pops into her head from an old TV series her dad watched. Sliding her hips forward, bending so her mouth is close to Bill's ears, she endures the sensation as her pussy glides smoothly along the throbbing hard-on. The head of his cock brushes her clit, sending a shiver up her spine as she slips to the end and off.

She breathes, "What's making you so hard! Let me form a titillating chimera for both of us!" She pauses to come up with a theme and wiggles her ass against the tip to make Bill's cock jerk. "Ah, you're standing in some bushes outside a couple's window watching them fuck!" Gisele is beside herself as the genre of the chambers comes to light, "when in Rome, do as the Romans do! The man is kneeling behind a woman on all fours fucking her." Gisele is breathing heavily into her husband's ear. Continuing the fantasy, she slowly pushes her hips back, causing the head to slide into her. Willing with all her might not to cum as her body spasm in response.

She hurries on as her hips push him deeper into her. "Watching like a hawk, you reach down and unzip your pants." Gisele's body vibrates, scarcely able to go on. "You spread your stance, pulling your cock out and stroking it slowly." Gisele gasps as her ass comes to a stop resting on Bill's legs. Her hips move slowly back up as she starts to rock back and forth. She stifles a moan as her body aches for release. *No! No! Let me finish!* Her whisper is shallow as the orgasm is at the peek threatening.

"You are so engrossed observing the couple in the window that you don't notice or hear a woman appear out of hedges." Gisele picks up the pace as her pussy pulsates, clenching Bill's cock matching the throbbing in her! Scrambling to finish the fantasy before climaxing, she presses on.

"You only realize her presence as she pushes your hand away so her fingers can encircle your cock. Her head moves forward as her tongue licks the tip. Her lips open wide, shoving all of you in her mouth before you can react." Gisele's back arches as the first wave of the orgasm starts. *I must end this!* Pressing closer to her husband's ear, she murmurs. "The woman's hand starts to pump your cock as she sucks! You reach behind her head to hold her in place as your hips thrust forward fucking her face!" Gisele is panting at the sensation of her ass slapping Bill's legs. She bounces faster and harder on his cock, holding that thought. The second wave flows over her as a groan is heard. That provokes her to continue. "Watching as the woman unbuttons her blouse, the other hand starts to jerk you off faster as she sucks! You are motionless as her tits are uncovered, jiggling to her bobbing head. Knees go weak at the sight. Rising your sight to the window, at the very moment, the man is pulling out and starts to jerk off all over the woman's back! At the same time, feeling the woman's mouth release you, your cock jerks, dumping your load all over her tits!"

Gisele's head rears back as the intensity of the orgasm peeks. Replaying those two images over and over, trying to hold the pleasure driving through her at bay, she straightens. Her hands rest on her husband's chest and then start to bounce hard in shorter strokes. Her eyes close in pure ecstasy as Bill's cock throbs increase and the feel of the warm sperm. Losing all control, her body finally gets the release it craved. Gisele starts to jerk as the wave overcomes her, releasing wet juices in response. As the orgasm subsides, her body goes weak. Resting her head on Bill's chest once again, she closes her eyes.

Savoring the sensation of Bill's cock softening inside her, she opens her eyes. *I have never cum that many times in a row in my life! How I held back all night is beyond me! I sure would like to repeat it. The climax was so intense it almost felt painful.* Sighing, Gisele sits up, sending a shiver up her spine as raising her leg to climb off, as her husband slips out of her. Her feet hit the floor. *Dam, I don't want to move. But Bill's old saying lingers in her head, "You better clean up. You don't want to be crusty in the morning."* Gisele grins, heading to the shower. *What does that even mean?*

Stopping at the huge smoke-glass sliding door, she pulls it open. Once again, she is spellbound by the sight before her—a luxurious two-person shower.

On the left wall, a massive gold showerhead gleams, accompanied by a matching wand. The black tile, veined with gold streaks, covers half the room, exuding elegance. To the right, an identical setup, but in silver—the showerhead and wand shimmering against black tile laced with silver streaks.

The contrast is mesmerizing, a perfect fusion of opulence and seduction.

Stepping in—it must be for that him-and-her look. She grins, seizing the gold wand, grateful she doesn't need a full shower. She adjusts the temperature and runs the water between her legs. The sensation makes her knees buckle. She angles it farther back to rinse off her ass, then brings it forward again. The warm water hitting the hood covering the hidden little button sends a jolt up her spine.

She lets out a curse, "God dam it! Stop it! Bill can not handle another pounding."

Laughing, she puts back the wand and steps out, grabbing a towel. Drying off, she heads to the table beside the bed, where a couple of folded clothes sit neatly. *Ah, they think of everything.* After tidying up, Gisele takes care of the dirty linens. She tucks her naked husband under the covers, musing *just in case I change my mind.* Then, she climbs in beside him.

Lying there, Gisele starts to ponder. *Who the hell are Jen and Dan really? With such elaborate surroundings that are so sexually driven! Are they in a cult? Or maybe some kind of high society sex club! Well, whatever it is, sign me up!* She glances at her husband. *How do I convince you is the challenge.*

Exhausted, Gisele's eyes flutter. Her mind wonders to Jen, saying, "And the other things are replaced also." It takes a moment, but the realization hits her, and a sly smile appears. *God dam it; if this was a movie, I would wake up tied spread eagle to a wall in the basement! Nothing but a full body harness to expose all my private parts. Ah, a fantasy to explore another day.* With that last thought, sleep takes over.

xxx

The door opens, squeaking a little in the darkness, followed by the faint sound of a small sliding door closing and the soft click of a latch. Whether Gisele subconsciously registers these sounds or not, she keeps her eyes closed.

TO BE CONTINUED